Wings over Per<

Wings over P

Book 7 in the British Ace Series

By

Griff Hosker

Wings over Persia

Published by Sword Books Ltd 2017
Copyright © Griff Hosker First Edition

The author has asserted their moral right under the Copyright, Designs and Patents Act, 1988, to be identified as the author of this work.

All Rights reserved. No part of this publication may be reproduced, copied, stored in a retrieval system, or transmitted, in any form or by any means, without the prior written consent of the copyright holder, nor be otherwise circulated in any form of binding or cover other than that in which it is published and without a similar condition being imposed on the subsequent purchaser.
A CIP catalogue record for this title is available from the British Library.
Cover by Design for Writers

Dedicated to Hilary. A dear friend taken far too soon.

The British Ace Series
1914
1915 Fokker Scourge
1916 Angels over the Somme
1917 Eagles Fall
1918 We will remember them
From Arctic Snow to Desert Sand
Wings over Persia

Contents

Wings over Persia 1
Prologue 5
Chapter 1 8
Chapter 2 22
Chapter 3 34
Chapter 4 51
Chapter 5 64
Chapter 6 79
Chapter 7 89
Chapter 8 102
Chapter 9 118
Chapter 10 130
Chapter 11 142
Chapter 12 155
Chapter 13 169
Chapter 14 184
Chapter 15 196
Chapter 16 205
Chapter 17 214
Epilogue 225
Glossary 228
Maps 230
Other books by Griff Hosker 231

Prologue

I had a month's leave and, instead of playing with the children and going to the pub as often as I could, we had decided to take the family off to northern France to buy a house. What was sad was that we would probably not get to holiday in it for some time as I would be deployed to Mesopotamia in less than four weeks. Mr Churchill was a hard task master. When I returned from Somaliland I had been told that I had just four weeks. It was not a long time but I had a young family and I intended to make the most of every single minute of it.

It was actually my wife Beattie who came up with the idea. We had a lovely home in Essex. We overlooked the River Crouch and it was a divine place in which to live. She had made it a wonderful home. I had been lucky. I had money. When Reginald St. John Browne had died and left me twenty thousand pounds we had decided on a home in northern France as a memorial to him and the pilots who never came back. I loved that part of the world. Many people wondered at our choice and yet, for me, it was not a sad place. I could remember the pilots and gunners who had never returned and, when I was there, it was as though they had never died. The main argument, however, was that it was somewhere to have a holiday. Beattie and I had not had a honeymoon and the children had never had a family holiday.

We packed up the car and headed across the channel. We had money to burn and a desire to live. I had seen more than four years of war and then I had been thrown into the maelstrom of the Middle East crisis. To sit behind the wheel of the car with my family inside, it was glorious! The weather was not glorious. As we left for the cross-channel ferry it rained. The children enjoyed the novelty of a ship and we made it fun. Being late spring, the weather was unpredictable. Beattie proved to be a marvel. She kept the children amused while I drove. She seemed to have an inexhaustible supply of songs and games. We based ourselves at Amiens. For me this had been the last place I had seen my youngest brother alive and it had been close to many of the airfields we had used. We found a hotel and used it as a base.

The owner, Madame Bartiaux, was a widow. Her husband and sons had died in the Great War. Discovering I was a pilot made her warm to us. The children made her adore us. Tom and Mary knew how to giggle and smile at the right times. We could not have had a more perfect hotel. More than that she told us of properties which were available. She was a practical woman. Many of the farms and horses had been left without owners. The war had been a great leveller. We found one after two weeks of searching. L'Haut Ferme was a little run down but it was perfect. The seclusion suited me. It was on the edge of a lovely little village which still had a brasserie, a boulangerie and an epicier. There had been many which satisfied me but Beattie knew what she wanted. It had to be in a village and not a town. There had to be a garden and there had to be water and electricity. The one we found was worth waiting for. We spent a week negotiating until it was finally ours. Of course, with all such matters legal negotiations and searches would mean we could not move in in the time I had left from my leave.

Beattie was ever practical, "Bill, the children do not start school for a year or two. I like it here. Instead of running back to England with you and then popping over to see to the house how about I stay with the children and we spend a few months sorting it out! You will be busy in the Middle East anyway. Madame Bartiaux has said she will give us a cheaper rate in the hotel until we can move in. She knows builders and the like. It will be exciting for me and the children."

"The language! You don't speak French!"

She looked offended, "I speak it better than when I came. And Tom has taken to it like a duck to water! Besides Madame Bartiaux can teach me." She put her hand to her mouth. "Sorry, you will need the car to get home!"

"Don't be a goose! I am a big boy. There are trains! If you are certain that you and the children want to stay here?"

"Of course, I am."

And so that was how I came to head back to England alone. I left it until the last possible minute to travel back to England and catch my flight to Baghdad. It was not a pleasant feeling as I climbed aboard a train to head to England. The weather had turned brighter and warmer. We had been told we could move into the house within a week and I was heading for another war zone. I felt quite resentful. I had served through the war with barely a leave. I had dropped everything to accommodate Mr Churchill and now I was missing out on what would be a great adventure. Life was not fair. As I sat on the train heading to Boulogne I wondered just what kind of task the irascible Winston Churchill had set for me.

Chapter 1

One of the reasons we had bought our home in Essex was because of the proximity of R.A.F. Rochford. I had asked Mr Balfour, from the Ministry, to arrange for my transport to await me there. It was not a hardship to anyone concerned and it suited me. Beattie had often said that I did not use my position as a senior officer as often as I should. As a nurse in the war she had witnessed senior officers receiving preferential treatment. That was not my way and I think that Beattie knew it.

I knew the station commander, Squadron Leader Philip Power, well. He had been a pilot in the Great War and been wounded. He would never fly again but he knew how to run a station. I rang him from home and had a car sent for me. It was a short run from my home to the airfield.

He pointed to the field with his pipe when I got out of the car, "Vickers Vimy, sir all ready for you. They are a couple of good pilots and they will be serving with you in Mesopotamia."

I nodded. I had never flown in one before but I had heard of them. "Like the one Alcock and Brown used to fly across the Atlantic."

He laughed, "Just so long as young Carruthers doesn't end up cracking it on landing as they did you should be alright." He nodded to the wings. "We have the extra tanks that Alcock and Brown had. You have enough fuel to get to Malta and a little to spare. Then off to Heliopolis. You know that place of course."

"I do." We had reached the aeroplane and I patted the lower wing. Philip said, "I think that they have ironed the kinks out. It won't have the same weight to carry as a bomber. This one is going to be an air ambulance."

I laughed, "I hope that isn't prophetic as I will be their first passenger!"

He nodded as we strolled over to the waiting aircraft. Two of his Erks carried my bags. "We sent more Vernons out for Squadron Leader Harris last week."

"And the Snipes we will be using should already be at Jaffa. It looks like this is going to be a big show."

"Rather you than me, sir. Too damned hot out there."

I nodded, "I know. I was in Somaliland. The dust gets everywhere. The poor fitters and riggers have to filter every drop of petrol and clean the engine every day."

Two young officers stepped from behind the wing. They snapped to attention and saluted. "Pilot Officer Carruthers and Pilot Officer Grundy, sir. We are your taxi drivers."

I saluted. They looked to be schoolboys and they appeared terrified. It was no wonder. They would be flying a senior officer and a British ace, no less, for four thousand miles. I smiled, "At ease. Have you many hours in these?"

Carruthers was the pilot and he beamed, "Oh yes sir. Twelve hours!"

I gave him a wry smile. "Well that will be doubled by the time we reach Malta then!" His face fell. "And you, Pilot Officer Grundy?"

"Eight hours sir." He sounded less confident.

"And as I have no hours in this bus we will all be learning, won't we?"

"You intend to fly her, sir?"

"If you think I am going to spend God knows how many hours sitting in the cabin twiddling my thumbs then you are in for a surprise. Now let's get this crate in the air."

"Yes sir." They scampered up the ladder into the cockpit.

I turned to the Squadron Leader, "Beattie will be in France for a couple of weeks. Could you have some of your chaps nip over and give the garden a bit of a tidy?"

"Of course, sir and good luck."

I climbed through the open hatch up into what would be the ambulance part when the Vimy reached the Middle East. There was a small window and a bunk. Grundy secured the hatch closed. It would not do for it to come open at ten thousand feet. It was cosy. The Erks had stowed my baggage. I was wearing my flying coat and my fur lined boots, it could get quite chilly. The cockpit was open. I had heard that there was going to be a commercial version of this type of bus with a closed cockpit for the pilots. They would have to do as we had done in France and freeze. The ground crew had, thoughtfully, supplied us with flasks of hot soup and tea. I saw, next to my bunk, on the shelf which would normally have medical supplies, tins of biscuits.

The two Lewis gun positions were not there and that meant we were a little more aerodynamic. As we were not carrying bombs we had all brought plenty of baggage. The two young officers did not know what to expect in the Middle East, I did.

I put the reports from intelligence on the shelf with the biscuits. I heard the engines start. Grundy leaned down to speak to me. "Sir, do you want to strap yourself in?"

I had no intention of taking off lying on a bed like an invalid. "No, I shall come up there with you chaps. If you don't mind." I suspected that they did mind. The last thing they wanted was for a senior officer standing over their shoulder as they took off.

Through gritted teeth I heard Pilot Officer Carruthers say, "Of course not, sir."

I crawled forward and then stood when I reached the cockpit. There was a small curtain separating the pilots from the flying sick bay. I was surprised by how effective it was at keeping the ambulance part warm. I stood behind them. There was just enough room behind their seats. The two powerful Rolls Royce engines thrummed on either side of us. Carruthers was obviously the senior of the two and we began to roll down the grass runway adjacent to the Thames. With less than a quarter of the payload she was built to carry she soon soared into the air. I was glad I was holding on to the straps of the safety harnesses. It was more powerful than I had expected. I remained silent as they climbed and then banked to head south east over France. They would take the most direct route possible. I saw that Grundy had the maps out. The flight would take twelve hours.

As soon as we were over the middle of the Channel I said, "I will do a little bit of work. I will spell one of you chaps in four hours."

"You don't need to, sir."

"Pilot Officer, it is a long journey and I will be happier if I know that you have both had a bit of rest and a cup of soup. It is not open for debate!"

I slipped back inside the cabin. It felt warmer there and I risked taking off my flying coat. I felt quite comfortable. Now that we were at our cruising altitude it was a smoother ride. I risked pouring a cup of tea. That done I propped myself up on

Wings over Persia

the bed and took out the intelligence reports. I had a pad and pencil next to me. I jotted down the key points.

It soon became clear that the removal of the Turks had merely exacerbated the problems. The Turks had been cruel rulers. However, they had also been corrupt. Bribery was rife and many of the Kurds and other ethnic groups could not come to grips with the fact that the British officials and soldiers who ran the country were not open to negotiation when it came to taxes and rules. Sheikh Mahmud had been governor of Southern Kurdistan. He had had to be dismissed when he led an armed revolt. The huge country was like a medieval state. It was filled with clans and tribes who fought with each other and often joined together against the ones they saw as oppressors. He had recently been reappointed and was Governor of the Sulaimaniya district.

Our eight squadrons of aeroplanes were replacing thirty-three battalions of infantry, six regiments of cavalry and sixteen batteries of artillery! It was a tall order. I saw that I was going to be at Baghdad where I would be in command of two squadrons of fighter bombers and one of Snipes. There would also be two squadrons of Vernons there for transport and heavy bombing. There were still ground troops but they were just there to protect major settlements. It would be our job to police the vast country that had been Persia. I saw that the key towns were Kirkuk, Ebril and Mosul.

I had also brought with me a book about the country's history. I read of Xerxes and Darius, Alexander the Great and Crassus. All had found the country difficult to control. Even the might Saracens and Seljuk Turkish rulers had found problems when the Mongols almost conquered the whole country. I was under no illusions. This would be far harder than the task I had completed in Somaliland.

I glanced out of the tiny window and saw the green of France below me. Beattie, Tom and Mary would be there. I would rather have been there than here planning to do the impossible; control a country whose size was so vast I could not even comprehend it. I returned to my reports and I drank my tea.

I managed to doze off for half an hour and woke, refreshed. I replaced the papers and my notes in my leather attaché case. Something that the Vimy had which we had not needed in the

Sopwith Camel was what my grandmother had called a gazunder. It was a pot which went under the bed; a sort of portable toilet. It saved a journey downstairs and into the yard on a cold night. I used it and then carried it to deposit it aft. The rear gun cockpit allowed me to throw it over the side. Returning to my cabin I replaced it. I slipped under the curtain and said, "Who wants a couple of hours off first?"

They looked at each other. I saw that Carruthers' hands were on the stick. I tapped him on the back, "Take over Grundy and Pilot Officer Carruthers can go and have a cuppa."

Grundy nodded, "Sir. I have the stick!"

Carruthers let go and undid his safety harness. I had to slip back into the main cabin to allow him to pass. I nodded to the bunk. "Get your head down if you can. Even if you don't sleep the rest will do you good."

"Sir."

I strapped myself in and then looked at the controls and dials. I spent fifteen minutes watching how Grundy flew. He was nervous and that was my fault. "Right Grundy. I'll try it for a while. Let me know if I am making a mess of it. I am more used to the Sopwith Camel. This is just a little bigger. It is like being in a Gunbus again."

"Sir."

I put my feet on the pedals and grasped the stick. I checked the dials and the trim and then said, "I have the stick."

It was not as heavy as I had expected but then it would not have to be as responsive as a fighter. Carrying wounded passengers, it would need to fly as steadily as possible. I saw that we were travelling at just sixty-five miles an hour. Even the old Gunbus had flown faster.

"Is this heading, right?"

"Yes sir. We used the Eiffel Tower in Paris as a marker to check and this is spot on sir."

"Good."

After a while he said, "Sir, how many Jerries did you shoot down in the Great War?"

"Over seventy I think."

"Don't you know the exact figure sit? I think I would."

"I pray that you will not have to, Pilot Officer. I lost many friends who did not even manage three or four. I know just how lucky I was. A fight in the air can last seconds. You need lighting fast reactions. This is a more noble calling. You will be saving lives and not taking them."

We flew in silence for a while. I could see that I had made him think. "This war will not be about shooting down enemy aeroplanes. We will be bombing and strafing ground troops. That is even harder than shooting down an aeroplane."

"Surely not, sir!"

"You have unforgiving terrain and anyone with a gun can bring down an aeroplane. Remember that when you fly. You have a side arm, don't you?"

"We were issued them. Mine is in my bags."

"When we land wear it. From now on you never get in an aeroplane without one. If I were you I would get yourself a Lee Enfield too."

"Really sir?"

I gestured with my thumb. "I have one in my bag as well as a German automatic pistol. If you land in hostile territory then you need to defend yourself. For most of us that means we have broken down. For you and Carruthers it will be a deliberate act to rescue someone. You will be picking up wounded men. That sort of implies the enemy will be about, doesn't it?"

"Sir." His glum voice told me he had not thought that through.

"Of course, you will have medic with you. Make sure that he is armed too!"

As we neared the Alps I had him fetch Carruthers. "Now you get your head down." Carruthers joined me a few moments later, "Did you manage any sleep?"

"Yes sir. You didn't need to do this you know, Wing Commander."

"I know but you must remember, Carruthers, that I started at the bottom of the ladder. I was an air gunner. The fact that I have achieved such an elevated rank is as much a surprise to me as anybody. We are all in this together. The day that I stop getting my hands dirty is the day I will retire." As we flew I impressed upon Carruthers the need for vigilance in the dangerous world of

Mesopotamia. He asked questions about the enemies we might be facing.

"That is the trouble, Pilot Officer, friends and enemies could be in the same room and you would not know. The smiling face could conceal a dagger. Let us just say that I will be checking my bunk each night for snakes, scorpions and spiders! I will open each door carefully and I will be watching where I put my feet."

As we passed Corsica I handed the stick over to Pilot Officer Carruthers and I went to the cabin. Grundy was asleep. I hated to wake him but I knew that I had to. "Grundy, wakey, wakey!"

He woke, almost startled, "Sorry sir I…"

"You have nothing to apologise for. I said to sleep and you obeyed orders. Well done!"

I watched the sun set to the west as we headed past Sardinia and then Sicily before we landed at the new airfield on Malta. We had been told that we would be sleeping under canvas and that was acceptable. With mechanics to check our engines we ate in the mess with the skeleton crew. Eventually this would become a vital aerodrome. On that first May night, it reminded me of the first airfields in Northern France. Tents and basic latrines were the order of the day. Surprisingly I slept better than I had for a long time.

The next leg was shorter. We would have a slightly easier time of it and this time the two young officers did not seem as worried about sharing flying duties with an old fighter pilot.

Heliopolis was no Malta. This was the front line. There was wire, machine guns and sandbagged bunkers. As we taxied along the runway a sergeant major signalled Pilot Officer Carruthers to move closer to the sandbagged guns and the huts which had been erected since last I had been here. Armed aircraftsmen ran to the side as the engines stopped.

"Sergeant Major Wilkins sir. If you would come with me. We have to move a bit sharpish like."

"Trouble, Sergeant Major?"

"It's the locals, sir! They are always complaining about something or other and the buggers, pardon my French sir, are bloody violent. They have learned that if you put petrol in a bottle and jam a rag in the end it makes a handy little bomb. It cost a few of them burned skin to get it right but now they know that our buses go up like Roman candles. That is why we keep them well away from the perimeter."

"Who is the station commander now?"

"Squadron Leader Jenkin; he only arrived last week."

Ours was a fledgling service and it was small. I had known a George Jenkin in France. He had been one of my pilots. He had survived! As we hurried in through the sandbagged doorway I saw that it was indeed, George Jenkin. He grinned as he saluted me, "Jolly glad to see you, sir. When I heard it was you who was coming I could not believe my luck."

I nodded, "Congratulations on the promotion. This is Pilot Officer Carruthers and Pilot Officer Grundy."

"Welcome to hell, gentleman! This is a lively posting. You should be glad that you are only here for one night! Sergeant Major Wilkins will show you to your quarters."

As they were led off George ushered me into his office. He took two glasses and a bottle from a cupboard. He poured two large whiskies. We had served together. We knew what the other liked.

"Cheers! Old comrades!"

I nodded, "The lads who never came back!"

We did not down it, we sipped it.

"Is it rough then, George?"

"Oh yes sir and a bit of a shock to the system. I came from a training squadron to this. I think they thought my experience with you in France might help. It doesn't. There you knew that everyone in a grey uniform was trying to kill you. Here you look sideways at the laundry boys who come in and when the boys go on raids it is even worse. Intelligence tells us where they ought to be and our lads attack. Then they bring in photographs. Women and children are with them and they have been killed too." He poured us two more. "How can they put their wives and children in such danger? We would get them far away from it if we were in the same boat."

"This is a war we can never win."

"And your war, sir, can we win that one? I am pretty certain that as soon as we are thrown out of here we will end up there."

"I fear you are right. My only hope is that we are able to do what we did in Somaliland. We managed to defeat the Mad

Wings over Persia

Mullah in four weeks. Mesopotamia is a bigger country but we can only try."

We chatted about the posting and then got on to the other war the Great War. There was a knock on the door and Sergeant Major Wilkins appeared, "Sir, will Wing Commander Harsker wish to wash and change before dinner?"

George laughed, "Which is a polite way of saying get a move on sirs! Righto Sergeant Major. Will do."

The quarters were basic but given the predicament the squadrons found themselves in it was understandable. I did not have my number ones. They were still on the Vimy and so I made do with a good wash and shave. Squadron Leader Jenkins' man removed the worst of the dust.

Dinner was pleasant. I think George had told all the stories of our squadron before I had landed and I had to fend off questions about the future of the R.A.F. in this area. I think they believed I was privy to more information than I was. I did enjoy meeting the young pilots. They were keen, talented, and hopeful. When we left the next morning, I was not as depressed as I had been.

The last hop to Baghdad was also the shortest. We landed well before dusk. I saw that the DH 9As and the Snipes were parked together on one side of the runaway while the two squadrons of huge Vernons was on the other. It was the largest assembly of aeroplanes I had ever see on one airfield and it was a daunting sight.

As the ground crew ran over to us I said to Carruthers and Grundy, "Well done you two. That can't have been easy having a senior officer watching your every move."

They were both more relaxed now, especially as their ordeal was over. "Not a problem sir. You were no trouble at all."

The Sergeant who led the ground crew saluted, "Would you be Wing Commander Harsker, sir?"

"Yes sergeant."

"Group Captain Wainwright is waiting to see you sir."

"Righto. Have my bags taken to my quarters eh?"

"Yes sir. Watson, get the officer's bags to his quarters. If you would follow me, sir." He led me towards the wooden buildings that made up the admin section. I saw the huts that were barracks, quarters and mess halls to my right. "Good flight sir? It is a long haul from Blighty."

"Yes sergeant. The Vimy is a nice bus. Slow but easy to fly."

"I remember you, sir, from France. I was an Erk then." Erk was the R.A.F slang for Aircraftsman. I looked at him to try to see if I could remember him. He smiled, "I was clean shaven in those days sir. I worked on Lieutenant Fox's bus. I am Sergeant Davis." I nodded. "You will find this a bit different, sir."

I smiled, "I was in Somaliland when the Ninaks sorted out the Mad Mullah. Not quite as different as you might think, sergeant."

Group Captain Wainwright was a throwback to the early days of the R.F.C. He had no wings on his tunic. He was not a pilot. That, in itself, was not a bad thing. Our colonel in France was not a flier. The grey hairs told me that this would the last posting for this officer. The red rimmed eyes and the shaking hand were signs that he was under stress. He was a drinker. Again, that was understandable. I had seen it in pilots who had flown one too many missions.

I smiled and held out my hand, "Wing Commander Harsker, pleased to meet you, sir."

I saw the relief on his face. I took off my flying coat and helmet. He nodded, "Too bally hot for those out here, don't ya know!"

"Quite."

He opened a drawer and took out a bottle of whisky. He poured two very large ones. I would not be flying but I decided to nurse mine.

"Awful posting Harsker!"

"It is Bill! Yes, I know. I read the reports."

"Have you met Churchill?" I nodded. "Mad as a fish. He thinks we can control this country with just eight squadrons!"

"I believe they think we can do more than ground troops alone."

"That is the trouble, Bill, the ground troops are so spread out that we just end up reacting to the problems. They radio they are under attack and we send out aeroplanes. Last week the Ninaks arrived just as the damned natives were chopping up our chaps into little bits. Damned distressing. They seem to have a Holy War against all non-Muslims."

I knew then why they had sent me. The Group Captain was out of his depth. He was an admin officer. I was the combat veteran. "Look sir, I think I can help. You know I was in Somaliland?"

"Damned fine show. You should have had a medal."

I shrugged, "Medals mean nothing."

He laughed, "A man with a V.C. and M.C. can afford to say that."

"Anyway, why don't I worry about the campaign and you can organise the airbase. It would be foolish to ignore my combat experience."

He looked relieved. I saw that he poured himself another stiff one, "If you are sure you don't mind?" He leaned forward, "Truth is I should be retired." He shook his head. "The family has a long history of service: Waterloo. Inkerman, Spion Kop. I can't let the family name down. I am the last of the Wainwrights."

"Sir, you will not let your family down. First thing in the morning I will get the other squadron leaders together and the Intelligence Officer. Who is that, by the way?"

"Major Fox, damned fine officer."

"Ralph Fox?"

"You know him?"

"We served in Egypt." Already I was more confident. Ralph Fox had been a captain. When the civil war had threatened Heliopolis he and his R.A.F. regiment had behaved impeccably.

"Good show. Another?"

"Thank you but no. I will get myself sorted out first."

As I left the office I noticed that Sergeant Davis was in the outer office, "Sarn't Davis, what is your role here?"

He smiled, "Officially, sir, I am in charge of the clerks."

"And unofficially?"

"Well sir, Sergeant Major Jennings had a funny turn last year and was returned to Blighty. We are awaiting his replacement. I sort of run the office."

"I will clear it with the Wing Commander tomorrow but you are now Sergeant Major Davis. We have a lot of work to do."

He did not seem put out. "Right sir. Where do we start?"

"I would like a meeting with the squadron leaders and the intelligence officer tomorrow at nine ack emma!"

"Roger sir! As soon as I heard you were coming I knew that you would shake things up a bit."

"Let's not get ahead of ourselves. This is not France. I want a breakdown from you of the personnel here."

"Personnel, sir?"

"Sergeant Major, don't play the innocent. It doesn't become you. Who are the chaps I can go to and who are the ones swinging the lead? This will be just between us two."

"Right sir. I just wanted to be clear. I will have that for you first thing."

My quarters were as I expected them, spartan. This was the front line. I had a bed, a table a chair, a chest of drawers and a curtain disguising a wardrobe rail. Beattie would not have been happy but I was comfortable in such functional quarters. I unpacked. I had not checked to see if they dressed in number ones for dinner. I just used the smarter of my two tunics.

There was a knock on the door. I opened it and a senior aircraftman stood there with a bowl, a jug of water and a towel. "Sarn't Davis send me sir, Aircraftman McHale, he thought you might want a wash and a shave."

"Perfect. Put them on the table there."

"I can shave you if you like sir. I shave the Group Captain."

"No thanks, McHale. But you can give me a bit of info."

"Sir."

"Is it number ones for dinner?"

"No sir. Group Captain saves that for Saturday night sir."

As I washed and then shaved I guessed that the Group Captain might need a steady hand to help him shave.

The R.A.F., in those days, was like one big family. As I found my way to the mess hall I recognised faces from France, Egypt and Somaliland. It was gratifying to see smiles accompanying the salutes. Group Captain Wainwright was at the bar. I recognised the other Squadron Leaders, Arthur Harris, Jack Thomson and Henry Woollett. Also with them was a grinning Major Fox.

Jack was one of the best Ninak pilots I had ever met. He affected a bow, "Our leader has arrived. Welcome to the east. I am the genii of the mess. Your wish is our command."

I laughed, "I can see that you haven't changed. My command is, oh genii of the candlestick, for a large whisky!"

"It shall be so, master."

Arthur Harris was always the more serious of the squadron leaders. "What is the Vimy like, sir? And the two pilots. Technically they fly in my squadron."

"The bus is good. Slow but then you will be used to that. It has the same speed as the Vernon. The two pilots know their job."

"They will have to do. They are quite likely to be operating on their own."

I nodded, "I told them to make sure they were armed."

"They will need to be, last week…"

Group Captain Wainwright said, "No shop talk eh chaps? Let's welcome Bill here. Time enough for shop in the morning."

I caught Arthur's eyes. He rolled them. The Group Captain was not only out of his depth, he had lost the confidence of some of the squadron leaders. We changed the chat to conversation about England. We spoke of Alcock and Brown's flight across the Atlantic in the Vimy. We talked of cricket. England were going to be heading to Australia at Christmas to play the first test match since nineteen fourteen. The food was fine. R.A.F. cooks produced the same food no matter where the aerodrome was!

As I headed for my quarters Major Fox walked with me. "Sir, any chance I could have a word with you before we meet the other officers?"

I knew that Ralph was not trying to ingratiate himself. If he wished to see me privately then it was important. "Of course. I shall be having a look at my new bus first thing. Have a wander over eh? That will look natural. I assume that is what you want?"

He grinned, "Spot on sir. I will be there!"

Wings over Persia

Persia

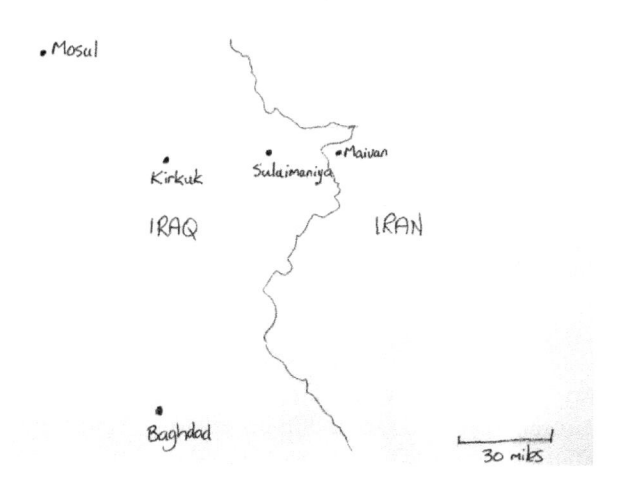

Chapter 2

I woke early. I was still on English time. In addition, I remembered that it would get unbearably hot later on. It was barely dawn when I strolled over to the Snipes. They were all in the open. I was pleased to see a pair of sentries from the R.A.F. regiment. They saluted and I recognised one, "Williams! I see you made Corporal!"

"Yes sir, and I am in with a chance of Sergeant too! Swanston is here and he made Sergeant after Egypt." Williams had been my servant and bodyguard in Egypt. He nodded to the aircraftman who continued his patrol. "This is just as hairy as Heliopolis, sir. They would steal the pennies off a corpse!"

"I think you are right. Listen, Williams, Major Fox will be coming to see me in a moment or two. Make sure we have some privacy eh?"

"You can rely on me, sir."

I recognised my aeroplane. It was the only one which had not been flown. In addition, it had the letter A before the numbers. It was a neat little aircraft. I would have to take it up before I flew with the rest of the squadron. I knew that the ground crew would have made sure she was in sound mechanical order but I had flown for enough years to know how I wanted her set up.

I heard feet pounding on the sand. I turned and saw Major Fox in shorts and vest. He grinned, "Keeps me fit and lets me get all over the place without anyone noticing."

I nodded, "I guessed that there is something you don't want the others to know."

"Not really sir. It is just that there are some of the locals who work in the offices. They are cleaners and tea makers. You know the sort of thing. The Group Captain thinks that they are trustworthy but I don't. We have had thefts and there has been minor sabotage. The Group Captain dismisses it as unimportant. There are too many occurrences for my liking. And I think that information is going from the airfield to the insurgents, sir. A couple of my lads were attacked the other day. They were the only two on leave. It was too much of a coincidence for me."

I nodded, "Do you have a solution to the problem?"

Wings over Persia

"Yes sir. It involves Corporal Williams and Swanson. As you know they are both bright lads. I was going to make them your orderlies."

"I don't need an orderly, let alone two."

"I know sir but it will give them the chance to sniff around the admin building and the officer block. They can watch the natives. In fact sir, the less you give them to do the better. They will make jobs up. They will catch the sneak thieves and find the ones who are rummaging around where they shouldn't be."

"Then go ahead with that. Anything else?"

"The other information is also for just the squadron leaders, sir. I will give you a heads up now and then more details in your briefing. This Sheikh Mahmud is stirring up the Kurds. He is supposed to be the governor. However, from what I can gather he is hiring mercenaries. He says he needs them for protection from the Turks but I think they are advising him on how to defeat us. Intelligence reports that the resistance is more organised now. Kirkuk is a hotbed of insurgents. If they rise then I can't see how the garrison will cope."

"Right. You have given me something to chew on. I might join you on the early morning runs, Ralph."

"I didn't know you were into keep fit, sir."

"I am not but it will give us the chance to examine the airfield and chat. I am not happy about the open nature of the field. If any of these buses are damaged it will be the devil's own job to get replacements."

"You are right sir. My lads can only patrol the perimeter. If the insurgents are determined they could easily find a way."

I saw Group Captain Wainwright before the meeting. "Sir, I would like to promote Davis to Sergeant Major."

He looked surprised, "Is that necessary?"

"Sir, we need a senior NCO. Sergeant Major Jennings is not returning, is he?"

"No, I believe he is in a sanitorium."

"Is there someone else we could promote?"

"Davis is the best chap for the job, I suppose but is there any need?" I sighed. I could not understand the delay. The sigh worked. "Very well, Harsker. You are a ball of fire, I can see that."

"I am a combat pilot sir. Inactivity and indecision do not sit well with me. If something needs doing then …"

He looked suddenly old, "And I am a relic who is an armchair pilot." Before I could apologize he held his hand up, "It is me saying that not you, Bill. If you see something that needs doing then do it."

I went into the briefing room to meet the squadron leaders. I had my orders from Mr Churchill via Mr Balfour, in my hand. I laid them on the table. "Here are the orders under which the five squadrons will operate. I don't propose to read them out line for line. You are all big boys and can read them yourselves." I saw them smile and light pipes and cigarettes. It was a good sign. "In a nutshell, we are to support the ground troops while ensuring that the native population does not get too restless."

Jack Thomson shook his head, "Easier said than done sir. I have been here two months and it is a nightmare identifying who is an insurgent and who is a friendly."

"I know. Major Fox has some thoughts on that." I turned to Ralph.

"The '*Griff*' we have is that the Kurds are becoming a little agitated. We think that Sheikh Mahmud is at the bottom of it along with some mercenary advisers. I know that Sheikh Mahmud is supposed to be working for us but I have seen little evidence of it. Sulaimaniya is peaceful but everywhere else has Kurds causing trouble. Sulaimaniya is the centre of Kurdistan. According to the information I have there are both Germans and White Russians there." He looked at me as he said, "I would suggest having air patrols to the north west, sir."

I nodded, "There is a problem there. The Snipes and the Vernons have a shorter range than the Ninaks. Kirkuk is as far as we can reach and still get back here."

Group Captain Wainwright had been smoking his pipe with his eyes closed. I began to wonder if he was asleep. He proved me wrong. "Well how about we have an airfield built at Kirkuk and use that to refuel. If Mr Churchill wants the land under our control then he will have to do something to help us."

I nodded. "That is an excellent idea, sir."

He nodded and rose, "Not quite ready to be put out to pasture. I will go and get this started. The sooner we get things moving the better." He left.

Squadron Leader Harris shook his head, "You have put a rocket under him sir! That is the most positive I have seen him."

"Arthur, he is not a flier like us. He is doing a damned fine job. I think it is an inspired idea. So, we use the Ninaks to patrol between here and Mosul. Jack, take your squadron out tomorrow. Henry, yours will be the day after. Alternate. Arthur, we will fly up to Kirkuk tomorrow and see if we can find a suitable site for an airfield."

"From the air?"

I nodded. "It will be quicker. I will use some of my contacts in Heliopolis to get a couple of good N.C.O.s. Kirkuk might well be like the wild west!"

I spent the rest of the day finding my way around the airbase. Corporal Williams arrived at the office in the middle of the afternoon. He had with him Leading Aircraftman Billings. "Sir, Major Fox sent me. He reckoned we might need Sergeant Swanston for other duties so it is me and my oppo here who will look after you, sir."

I gestured to the officer's quarters. "You don't need me to tell you what I need from you Williams."

"No sir. Don't you worry, sir. We will give you a service like they get at the Ritz!"

I felt happier knowing that we had two such fine fellows watching out for danger. I had enough to worry about.

The next day I met my pilots. While Arthur Harris had his Vernon loaded with bombs I briefed my eleven pilots. "We have not had much time to get to know one another. I am afraid we will have to hit the ground running. Today we fly to Kirkuk and back. We are looking for a suitable site for an aerodrome. At the same time, we are going to make our presence known. We fly low and we fly armed. If you see danger then open fire."

Flight Lieutenant Barker asked, "Sir, what if we make a mistake?"

"Don't!"

I watched him open and close his mouth. It was brutal but it was the truth. We could not afford to make mistakes.

Wings over Persia

"And another thing, make sure you have side arms with you at all times. If you have to crash land then we will get to you but you will be alone for a time. Defend yourself."

I could see that my words had had a sobering effect. I went into the office while my bus was being started. I contacted Squadron Leader Jenkins. It was time to use the old boys' network. Once I had made my request I clambered aboard the Snipe. I was going to war, again.

We flew north in three lines of four aeroplanes. Had there been any danger of enemy aircraft then I would have had them layered. However, with no enemy aeroplanes to worry about a large box looked more imposing from the ground and part of my job was to make the Kurds fearful of our air power. We needed to see as much of the ground as we could and so we flew in a large box. The Vernons of Squadron Leader Harris flew a parallel course. This ancient land of Persia was very much like Somaliland. There was a decided absence of green. The roads were made of earth. When the rains came then all movement ceased. The towns and villages were few and far between. This was not France. If we crash landed there would be no help forthcoming.

My Snipe was flying well. The DH 9A had a better top speed and a greater range but compared with the nippy little Snipe was unwieldy. If we spotted danger then my Snipes could be on the danger while the Ninak was still turning.

I spied the castle of Kirkuk. It was on high ground in the centre of the town. Nearby I saw the Union Flag which marked the British military presence. It was the Residency. The castle was just a ruin but I suppose it could be defended if it had to be. We deliberately flew low over the town. I wanted them to know that we were here. The huge Napier Lion engines would terrify the natives. I spied huge swathes of open ground to the east of the town but they looked to have too many outcrops of rock. In contrast, the land just to the west looked flat. There was not as much open land but it looked like it would do. I was tempted to try to land. Then I realised that would be a mistake. I had a squadron to lead.

We circled the town and then headed home. As we cleared Kirkuk I spied a dust cloud to the east. I signalled the rest of the squadron to return to Baghdad. I would investigate. I saw that the Vickers Vernon still lumbered south. I would be interested in what Squadron Leader Harris thought of my proposed site. The dust was slightly further away than I had expected. I was contemplating turning around when I saw that the dust was the result of horses. There were forty or fifty of them and they were circling what looked like a lorry. I recognised the solar helmets of the soldiers. They were British. I could not hear much over the sound of my engine but I knew that they were firing for I saw the flashes of their Lee Enfields.

   I had no idea why they were not moving but I cocked my twin Vickers. I had some serious firepower. I banked as I passed the lorry. I saw faces looking up. I knew they would be wondering why I had not fired. I did not want to hit friendlies. Having located where the lorry was I dropped to fifty feet and zoomed at a hundred and five miles an hour towards the horsemen. I had been an air gunner and knew how to fire in short bursts. I opened fire with both guns. I fired for four seconds with a two second break. I had no idea of the effect I was having because of the dust. I banked to the left and flew up the other side of the road. There was less dust and I saw a handful of riders. They raised their rifles to fire at me. I gave them a four second burst. Sixty cartridges sped towards the enemy every four seconds. As I banked I saw that I had destroyed the riders and their mounts. I saw the dust departing towards the east. The survivors had had enough.

   I knew I had to leave or risk running out of fuel. I banked again to fly over the road. I saw the soldiers waving at me. I saw that they had a wheel off. They had a puncture. I waggled my wings and turned south.

   My squadron had not left the runway. They were staring north, anxiously looking for me. I landed and, as I climbed out, saw the bullet holes in the wings. The rigger who ran up with the chocks looked at the holes and grinned, "Moths sir?"

"Something like. Can you repair them as soon as?"

"Yes sir."

"What happened sir? We thought you had crashed!"

"I found a British patrol under attack. It was my fault. I should not have gone alone. From now on Lieutenant Marshall, you are my wingman. You watch sir's backside for him!"

The others thought that was hilarious and from Lieutenant Marshall' face, he was less than happy about it. I went directly to the squadron office. Sergeant Major Davis was there, "You had us worried, sir."

I nodded, "I was worried too. Get on to Kirkuk and Sulaimaniya. Tell them there is broken-down lorry twenty miles east of Kirkuk."

"Sir."

I heard the Vernon as it began its approach. Ralph Fox joined me as I went out to meet Arthur. "Something up sir?"

"I just shot up forty or fifty tribesmen. I didn't expect them to be bold enough to attack British soldiers."

"That will be Sheikh Mahmud. He is based to the east of Sulaimaniya. He stirs up trouble everywhere but his town. I have no idea why Sir Percy doesn't do something about him. There was a bomb in the Baghdad bazaar today. I think they were after British soldiers. They killed twenty civilians. Things are hotting up."

I remembered Heliopolis. "Get barbed wire around the perimeter, Ralph. This could turn ugly."

"Yes sir."

Arthur Harris left his men to check his bus. "What happened, sir? I saw them repairing holes in your wings."

I told him.

He nodded. "I am having a bomb sight fitted to a couple of the Vernons and bomb racks. Is it alright with you if I fit a couple of Lewis guns?"

"Whatever you need. What did you think of Kirkuk?"

"The only place I could see was that flat ground to the west of the town."

I nodded, "I will borrow one of Jack's Ninaks. Fancy a flight up there tomorrow? We can try to land it and have a word with the local chap there."

"Suits me."

I was writing up my report when Group Captain Wainwright came in. He looked more relaxed than the first time I had seen him. "Spoke to someone in Cairo. They are going to pass the message on to England and a Squadron Leader Jenkins is sending a couple of chaps in a lorry. Two more sergeant majors I understand."

I nodded, "Good chaps both and they are more than capable of running an airfield at Kirkuk. If the Ministry send men then all well and good but we need a base there." I took a breath. "Major Fox told me that there was trouble in the bazaar today. I told him to protect the field with barbed wire."

"Good idea."

"And if I might suggest?" He took his pipe from his mouth and nodded. "I think we should have all non-British personnel banned from the base until this trouble is over."

"A bit drastic, isn't it?"

"What do we actually use them for?"

"Dhobying, making tea, serving in the mess, cleaning out the cess pits, you know the sort of thing the Erks don't like."

"I think they would rather do those jobs than wake up with a knife in their guts, sir."

"You might be right but I don't think the Arabs will like it very much."

"When the emergency is over we can re-employ those who are vetted by Major Fox. If you would like me to tell them…"

"No, of course not. My job."

When I got to my quarters I saw that Williams and Billings had tidied my room and that my uniforms were pressed. I had not seen them and I guessed they were busy watching the locals. Soon that might be redundant. Jack and his squadron landed just after I had changed. They had had two hours more flying than we had. I strolled to the office to await his arrival.

"How did it go, Jack?"

He lit his pipe and sat down. Sergeant Major Davis made some subtle move with his head and a cup of tea appeared in the hand of Aircraftman Ganner.

"Rough country up there, sir. The mountains are close and there are precious few places to land. We saw plenty of tribesmen on horses." I cocked my head to one side. "Well sir, I wondered what they were doing. We saw few animals which needed herding and they tend to use boys on foot for that job not mob handed with twenty horsemen. It struck me as wrong, that was all."

"You didn't shoot them up."

"No sir. It was tempting and I am certain they were up to no good but orders are orders."

I told him about the ambush and the attack in Baghdad. "I have recommended that the Group Captain lays off the natives until this emergency is over."

Sergeant Major Davis had been busy cross-checking lists. He coughed.

I smiled, "Yes Sergeant Major?"

"Sorry sir, couldn't help overhearing. We don't need the natives back in the aerodrome, sir."

"And why not?"

"There's been thieving going on, sir. Fuel, bullets, food." He pointed to the door, "Ganner go and fetch me four more manila files. They are in the stores."

"Sarn't Major."

As the door close Davis continued, "And there has been sabotage, or attempted sabotage at least. It was why we put the sentries on the aeroplanes, sir. The mechanics found that as well as fuel being stolen it was also being contaminated. They were clever about it, sir. You need eyes everywhere."

It confirmed what Major Fox had told me. "Thanks Sergeant Major." I turned back to Jack, "So things are going to get harder. Arthur and I found a suitable airbase. I would like to borrow one of your Ninaks to go and have another look see."

"Of course, sir. I'll go and sort one out now and then tell Henry what he can look forward to."

When he had gone Ganner returned with the files and he also had a sheet of paper, "This is from the radio room sir. They said it was for you."

He handed me the sheet. It was from Kirkuk. I read it and handed it to Sergeant Major Davis. "Better file this, Sergeant Major."

He glanced at it as he took it. "Those lads owe you their lives then sir."

"So, it would appear. At least we can expect some friendly faces when we fly there tomorrow."

It was some time since I had flown a DH 9A. Fortunately, there are a very forgiving aeroplane. I wished we had had them earlier in the war. Arthur was more than happy to be gunner. I often wondered how he ended up flying transports. He was a bomber pilot at heart. The flight north was uneventful. It was a clear morning. There was no dust. I circled the town first. I saw waves from the sentries at the British base. I was lower than I had been the previous day and I saw the armoured cars and barbed wire. I headed for the putative airfield. The area I had chosen to land would be long enough for us and the Snipe but I was not certain about the Vernons. Unlike the Snipe and the Vernon, the Ninak had a huge engine obscuring the pilot's view. I came in heavy and cursed myself. I hoped I hadn't damaged Lieutenant Foster's bus.

As the engine stopped I turned, "Sorry about the landing, Arthur."

I heard him chuckle, "These are not the easiest aeroplanes to land."

We clambered out. I waved a hand around the flat area. "There is plenty of room for buildings. There is nothing close by but how would your transports cope?"

He knelt down and patted the ground. "This is a good surface. In fact, it feels like bed rock. We might have to extend it a bit but I think we could manage."

We looked up as an armoured car pulled up and a Captain and a Sergeant climbed out. They saluted. "Captain Willoughby and Sergeant Hughes, Ox and Bucks Yeomanry."

"Wing Commander Harsker and Squadron Leader Harris."

The Captain's face lit up, "You're the chap who saved our lads yesterday sir. Good show! Lieutenant Enderby and his fellows would not have lasted long if you hadn't arrived. What brings you here? Engine trouble?"

I shook my head, "We need an airfield here where we can refuel."

Captain Willoughby's face fell, "This is dangerous country sir. There are some Russians and Germans stirring up the locals. We can't patrol the road between here and Sulaimaniya. I am not sure that they will be able to hold out. Everything comes through Baghdad and then us."

"Is that why you have to tootle around in an armoured car?"

He nodded, "They use twisted nails on the road. That is how they got the lorry yesterday. Seems they used them hundreds of years ago against cavalry. They are still effective today."

"Nonetheless we will need to build an airfield here. We will have our own chaps to protect it. I will have our aeroplanes patrol the Kirkuk to Sulaimaniya road. If you coordinate your supply columns with us I will guarantee that we can protect you."

"And Mosul sir?"

"And Mosul. It will take a week or so to get the men here to build the airfield but we will start the patrols tomorrow."

We turned the Ninak around and headed south. I had much to think about. We would not have the luxury of a day off between each patrol. Arthur must have been thinking the same for he said, as we landed. "Look, sir, it makes no sense to have a squadron of Vernons sitting on the ground doing nothing. We can patrol the road from Baghdad to Kirkuk. I have bomb sights and racks. We have a couple of Lewis guns for each Vernon."

"Are you certain, Arthur?"

"Are you joking sir? Much better than being a glorified lorry driver!"

I gathered my squadron together after lunch. "Flight Lieutenant Ritchie, you will command half of the squadron. I will take my half each morning to patrol the Kirkuk to Sulaimaniya road. You will take over in the afternoon. I intend to give an umbrella for the supplies and men on the road. We have done this before on the Cairo to Alexandria road. You have to fly low and to keep a look out for ambushes. Our buses are going to be in the air too much. Until we get the airfield at Kirkuk built I am afraid we have no choice. If we have aeroplanes there we can keep a close eye on this Sheikh and his foreign advisers."

They were keen young pilots and none of them seemed unduly worried. Suddenly there was a crack in the distance. We felt the vibration and the concussion. It was a bomb. We ran outside and saw, half a mile away, smoke rising in the air. It was beyond the gate but I could see the remains of a lorry.

Corporal Williams ran up, "Sir, the Arabs just blew up a lorry. I was at the main gate and saw it. The poor buggers inside didn't stand a chance."

I nodded. "Get the fire out and get their bodies put somewhere."

It was beginning. This was the start of a revolt. Someone was letting us know that there was no target which was safe from them.

Chapter 3

Ralph Fox had improved the security in and around the airfield. He had ordered the destruction of half a dozen mud huts which were too close to the airfield. Group Captain Wainwright had been going to object until I had a word with him. "Sir, Major Fox needs a clear field of fire. We can't risk the insurgents getting close to us. We are in a state of siege. Until we are reinforced we have to hunker down and tough it out."

"Quite."

There were sandbagged Lewis gun positions and patrols around both the inside and outside of the perimeter.

Jack's squadron was designated to the Mosul patrol while Henry took the road from Baghdad to the west. The twenty-four aeroplanes which took off seemed wholly inadequate for the task. We would overfly the convoy. Captain Willoughby had told me that the first convoy would be leaving Kirkuk at 0800 hours. That suited us for the air was slightly cooler. I had had a couple of bombs fitted under the wings of each of my flight. I was aware that we only had five hundred rounds of ammunition.

We had good visibility when we set off but there were clouds on the horizon. Group Captain Wainwright had told me that there was little rain in Mesopotamia but when it came then it would be Biblical! I saw the dust raised by the convoy. There were two lorries and the Rolls Royce Armoured car I had previously seen. We flew over the road and the convoy and waved. Climbing to a thousand feet we flew parallel to the road. Not far from Chamchamal the road began to climb and wend its way through the foothills.

I had more experience of spotting ambushes in such terrain. I had learned the hard way in Egypt and Somaliland. My experienced eyes spotted them. The insurgents were hidden from the road by rocks but not from the air. I saw that they had an ancient field piece. I was not certain how accurate it would be but they had found a good position for it. The road twisted and the gun was positioned so that it would be at almost point-blank range to the armoured car when it approached. Even as I signalled the attack I realised that they had to have some means of communicating between Kirkuk and Sulaimaniya.

The insurgents and rebels began firing at us. I dived and released both of my bombs before climbing. The rest of my flight also dropped their bombs. The concussion threw us into the air. I banked and surveyed the scene. There was a great deal of dust. Bullets were still being fired at us but mercifully few of them. I cocked my right-hand Vickers and descended. The gun had been obliterated. They must have had ammunition nearby and that had also been destroyed. The rocks had been thrown on to the road. The convoy would have to clear it before they could advance.

The survivors had fled and they had split up. There looked to be twenty or so men who were left. They had horses and camels. We had worked out a system for this. I waved my arm around my head. We would now operate as three pairs. I headed north. We really needed radios but, as yet only the Ninaks and Vernons had them. We dropped to fifty feet above the rocks and I opened fire with the Vickers. I used short bursts. At a hundred miles an hour you had a second or two to hit the target. I missed but Briggs was more accurate. I saw the horses and camels lying with their riders in my rear-view mirror as I climbed. I banked around. We were at the limit of our fuel. We headed back south. As we passed the convoy they waved. The other Snipes tucked in behind me.

We landed flying on fumes. We needed a refuelling facility. The Vernons had already landed. After I had watched the Snipes take-off I joined Arthur Harris and Ralph Fox in the office. "You had no insurgents on the road?"

Squadron Leader Harris shook his head, "There was nothing. A couple of vehicles were using the road but it was mainly men leading camels and horses."

"They knew that a convoy was coming from Kirkuk and they knew that they had an armoured car. The ambush would have taken out the Rolls Royce."

Major Fox lit a cigarette, "And you think they have spies in Kirkuk, sir?"

"It is more than that, Ralph. We know they have spies but how are they getting the information out so quickly? You said they have mercenaries from White Russia and Germany. Those two nations are more sophisticated than this Sheikh Mahmud. They are coordinating the attacks. The sooner we get to Kirkuk and the airfield the better."

Major Fox pointed towards the busy city, "Sir, I would worry more about Baghdad if I were you. That is closer to home. I have a few contacts who are locals and friendly towards us. They seem to think that the rebels want to hurt us. They believe that if they knock out the airfield then they can take our ground forces out."

Arthur tapped out his pipe, "And they would be right there. The battalions went to England and Blighty and were replaced by companies."

This would have to be my decision. "Then we will have to take on the defence of the airfield ourselves. Have the ground crews and admin staff armed. Stress that they must all carry a weapon at all times."

"Already done and I have more generators and lights. I will make night into day. Now that there are no natives working within the perimeter we are definitely safer."

The two squadrons of Ninaks landed within twenty minutes of one another. I saw that Flight Lieutenant Green's DH 9A had large holes in his wings and the others had been fired at.

I waited until Jack and his pilots made their way to us, "Trouble, Squadron Leader?"

"Yes sir. They ambushed us rather than the lorries. They had some heavy machine guns hidden in the hills. When we flew over the road and the lorries they opened fire. Green was lucky to get back. They used dynamite to blow up one of the lorries. The other three headed back to Kirkuk. We watched over them as they headed back."

Squadron Leader Harris nodded, "Your theory about some mastermind being behind this looks like it is more than just a theory, sir."

We were in a state of siege. Major Fox had extra men at the gates and every vehicle and delivery was searched. We did not need much from outside and the Vernons could bring in any extra supplies that we needed.

The next day we went up again. This time there were no convoys on the road. The residents in the three towns had decided to sit tight. I would have liked to take my Snipes to escort the Ninaks. We were a much smaller target and could react both quicker and more effectively than the faster but less agile two-seater. When all of the birds returned to the nest I was relieved. After dark, a convoy from Alexandria reached us. It was the men who would be building and running Kirkuk. Sergeant Majors Hale and Robson had served under me before. They were reliable and did not crack under pressure.

They saluted smartly and their grins told me that they were happy to be serving with me again. "Another little jaunt eh sir?"

"Yes, Sarn't Major. I have to tell you that this one will be the hardest yet. You are going to have to build and run an airfield in the middle of a revolt."

Sergeant Major hale was the organizer, "What exactly do you need, sir?"

"We need you to build an airfield so that we are able to refuel our Snipes and the Vernons. The buses won't be parked there. You are going to be a service station. The Vernons will keep you supplied. You will be self-sufficient. I know there will be a presence in Kirkuk but you will carry on as though there isn't. We will have wire for you to protect the perimeter. Major Fox will be sending up twenty men from the R.A.F. Regiment as guards. You will have Vickers and Lewis guns. Once the field is up and running, all we need from you chaps is a quick turnaround. We can stay in the air longer this way."

I did not tell them that we had put in a request for another squadron to be based there. I did not want to get their hopes up.

"Seems simple enough, sir." Sergeant Major Hale nodded. He was the sort of N.C/O. who took such problems as we had given him in his stride.

"I can see how you can transport the men and the building material but not the fuel."

"Quite right Sergeant Major Robson, we will fly you up the day after tomorrow. The fuel can follow when there is a perimeter."

Neither of them seemed overly concerned. "We'll find our billet, sir and then await your orders."

Squadron Leader Harris smiled, "The backbone of the service, chaps like that. What about an officer?"

"I am not sure they need one but," a thought struck me, "how about you? You and your chaps will be back and forth anyway. You know what you want from the field."

"It suits me. I will just keep one Vernon there and the air ambulance."

"That makes sense. We haven't needed it yet but if we do then Kirkuk is more central anyway."

The logistics would be taxing but it was a solution and, as I had found out in France, there was no such thing as a perfect answer. You compromised all the time. I was exhausted when I hit my bunk. I had not had time to drop a line to Beattie yet and I felt guilty.

I was awoken in the middle of the night by gunfire and the sound of grenades. I grabbed my service revolver and holster. I ran out into the night. It was a warm night. I saw the muzzle flashes and heard the Lewis guns. Others had run out into the night. Suddenly there was a huge explosion at the main gate. I ran towards it. Someone had driven an old truck there and used a Mills bomb to explode it. The gate no longer existed and the two machine gun crews lay dead or wounded.

Dropping to one knee I steadied my arm and began to fire at the figures I could see pouring through the gates. They had a variety of weapons. I recognised the Lee Enfield as I dropped one and then saw that the man next to him had a Mauser. I heard Major Fox shout, "Hold them! Fetch up the two spare Lewis guns."

I took my time and aimed. I should have brought my rifle. The Webley had a limited range. As soon as I was empty I reloaded. I saw a figure race towards me. He was firing a Lee Enfield from the hip. A bullet zipped over my head. I kept reloading. He fired again and this time the bullet smacked into the ground six feet from me. Raising the Webley, I fired. The range was twenty yards and I could not miss. I hit his chest and he was thrown back.

Corporal Williams appeared next to me with his Lee Enfield. "Sorry, I am a bit late sir. Charlie Billings copped one. Some bugger slit his throat." He raised his rifle and fired five shots in rapid succession. He jammed another magazine in and began to fire his measured, steady shots.

As more men emerged from the barracks they joined us in our improvised skirmish line. The insurgents were using passion to try to overcome us. Williams was an example of how to fight correctly. He was upset about his friend but he was firing calmly and methodically. The rebels ran at us shooting wildly. They seemed more concerned with screaming at us. Firing from the hip rarely resulted in a hit.

Sergeant Major Davis shouted, "Very!"

We instinctively looked down. The flare exploded in the air and then began to descend slowly. As we looked up we saw the last five insurgents. Every gun turned on them and opened fire. They fell.

I stood, "Get the wounded to the hospital. Check the enemy dead and sea if any where the chaps who worked here. Major Fox, secure the gate!"

I reloaded and turned to Corporal Williams. "How did Billings buy it?"

"He nipped to the latrines, sir, for a pee. He hadn't come back and I went to have a shufti for him. When I got there the bastard was about to take his…" he shook his head, "I shot him sir."

"Well thank God you did or this could have been worse." I wondered how the assassin had got in. It took until dawn to clear away the dead, both insurgents and ours. Sergeant Major Davis and Group Captain Wainwright were in the office. "What is the butcher's bill, Group Captain?"

"Sarn't Major?"

"Twelve dead sir, and eight wounded. They damaged one of your Snipes and two of the Ninaks."

"I thought with the Great War over I had written my last letter of condolence." Group Captain shook his head. "I think, Squadron Leader, they were hoping to stop us flying."

"Well, that won't work. I will have every aeroplane in the air today."

"Are you certain? The men will be tired."

"There is someone behind all this who plays chess sir. This is not the work of a native rebel. There is method here. If they want us grounded it is for a reason. They want to move unseen. We will have eyes on the ground!"

My pilots showed their mettle. They were all angry and wished to fly. The three pilots without aeroplanes flew as gunners on the Vernons. I briefed all of the pilots together. "Look for anything out of the ordinary. They are up to something. It might be booby traps, it might be ambushes. Whatever it is we stop them."

We had eleven Snipes and I had us spread out so that we had a gap of fifty yards between each aeroplane. I wanted to cover as much of the ground as I could. It was Simpkins on the far right who spotted them. As instructed he waggled his wings to alert the next pilot when he spied something and then banked in the direction of the threat. We all peeled off to follow him. There was a column of men moving along a wadi. Simpkins had done well to spot them. None of my men opened fire. I dived low. As soon as I did so they opened fire at me. I heard the bullets tear the fabric of the wings. I released one bomb and pulled up. I was just a hundred feet up and the bomb exploded on the top of the wadi. The rest of the squadron dived. The wadi was no more than forty feet wide and was a narrow target but the ten Snipes followed nose to tail and their bombs either hit the bottom or exploded close to the top. By the time I was in position I could see little because of the smoke. I flew down the wadi firing short bursts until my guns clicked empty. Then I rose and waited for the smoke to clear. When it did I saw that there were wounded men there but the threat to Baghdad was gone. This had been a column of insurgents come to replace those we had killed in the night attack.

The men were exuberant when we landed. We had all flown over the wadi and seen the devastation. As the other squadrons landed we heard similar reports. The insurgents had assumed that we would not be able to fly and were sending more armed men into Baghdad. The Ninaks who had been sent to Mosul had seen the least action. That meant that Kirkuk was the flash point. We had to build the airfield as fast as we could. We had stopped the advance on Baghdad. Kirkuk was a softer target. One company of the Ox and Bucks would struggle to hold a sustained attack.

Group Captain Wainwright and Major Fox had not been idle. The defences were repaired and a message had been sent to England about the threat. The Group Captain seemed relieved, "I think they are going to send another squadron of fighters for us. Mr Churchill likes the idea of an airfield at Kirkuk. There will be Bristols based there."

I sent the squadron out without me the next day, and I went up with the eight Vernons. We carried the men who would be building the field and their equipment. We had sent a message to Captain Willoughby and there were men waiting for us at the site. Sergeant Hughes came forward. He saluted, "Sorry sir but the captain is a little busy. We have had attacks all night and during the day."

"Well we can handle it from here, Sergeant. You had best get back and give the captain a hand."

I had never been afraid of hard work. I donned a sun helmet and went with Squadron Leader Harris and Sergeant Major Robson to start to clear the runway. Half of the men were busy erecting tents. Williams now had his sergeant's stripes. I had insisted. He was with the men sent by Major Fox. He would be staying at the new field until it was organized.

"Williams, take ten men and begin to start a perimeter ditch."

"Sir."

I knew that the ditch would serve two purposes. It would make it harder for an enemy to enter the field and, when the rains came, it would ensure that the field stayed dry. We did not stop for the noon day sun. If we were to leave forty men overnight they needed a perimeter with barbed wire and they needed gun emplacements. We ate sandwiches, somewhat stale by the time we finished them but we did have gallons of hot, sweet tea. It had got us through the Great War and it sustained us in the desert.

We knew we would have to take off before dark or stay the night. There were no lights for the runway. When the last gap was closed with barbed wire Sergeant Major Hale said, "You had best be off, sir. We'll be fine. We can cook a hot meal and the tents are up."

I nodded. It made sense. "We will be back in the morning and I will send the tankers off."

They were going to build one storage tank but use three of the tankers as bowsers. It was a one hundred and seventy miles journey for the tankers. I intended to use every aeroplane to ensure that they were not attacked. As well as the fuel, we would be bringing Nissen huts and more men. Food and ammunition could be brought my air.

I sat with Squadron Leader Harris as we flew south. "Are you certain you are still happy about basing your squadron here, Arthur? It is a bit primitive."

"Sir, I don't think it is going to get any easier in Baghdad if last night is anything to go by. This way all of our eggs are not in one basket."

"You may be right."

It was almost dark by the time we landed but I could see that they had repaired all of the damage. A sad reminder of the cost was the new cemetery which lay close to the chapel. I also saw a number of cars parked close to the admin block. Major Fox's men stood around with rifles and side arms.

As I walked past them I said, "Visitors?"

Sergeant Blackwood nodded, "Yes sir. The British resident. Been here a couple of hours."

I had expected this. Sergeant Major Davis and his clerks were in the corridor, "A bit crowded in there, sir. We were told to wait out here. I think the Group Captain could do with a little support."

I hated politics. Reginald St. John Browne had been an exception. He had been a British resident who was a true gentleman. Others I had met were not. I forced a smile, knocked on the door and entered. There were six men around the tables: Group Captain Wainwright, Major Fox, a white-haired gentleman, a major and two young men who looked to me to be professional diplomats.

"Sorry, sir."

The Group Captain looked relieved, "This is the Right Honourable Sir Percy Cunliffe. He is the British resident in Baghdad. Major Stevens of the Scots Guards, Mr Jenkins and Mr Crane. Wing Commander Harsker."

The Major smiled, "Heard about you, Wing Commander, British Ace eh?"

"Different times sir and I was lucky." I sat.

The Right Honourable Percy Cunliffe had a naturally quiet voice. He reminded me of a librarian, "So Wing Commander what do we do about this unrest?"

I liked his bluntness. He had come directly to the point. "If you are talking about the wider picture sir, we have begun that already. When we have an airfield ay Kirkuk we will be able to control a large part of Mesopotamia."

He shook his head, "If we lose Baghdad then that will be of no use to us. The League of Nations made us responsible for Iran. This is our first test and we are failing."

"I am sorry, sir, but we are the air force. We can't control the streets of Baghdad."

"Mr Churchill sets great store by you, Wing Commander."

I sighed, "What would you have us do?"

He smiled, "Simple. I would like you to have some of your aeroplanes flying over the city."

"When?"

"All the time! The locals are afraid of them. There are stories of your chaps dropping bombs." He gestured to the Major.

"Yes, Wing Commander. When you attacked that column the other day some of the survivors made it to Baghdad. Apparently, you killed over a hundred of their fighters. That has made them more determined than ever to destroy the airfield. So, you see your air force is a potent one."

"It is a waste of resources, sir. If we are out in the country then we can stop the enemy from moving. If you don't mind me giving you advice I would suggest that you find their leaders in Baghdad."

The Right Honourable Sir Percy Cunliffe said, "And Major Stevens is doing that along with your Major Fox but it takes time."

I looked over to Group Captain Wainwright for help. He tapped out his pipe. "How about this as a compromise? The Snipe can stay in the air for three hours and the DH 9A five and half hours. What say you send a Snipe out in the morning and a Ninak in the afternoon. You will have air cover for eight and half hours a day. That will still leave you with enough aeroplanes to stop the beast."

"We could do that but we need to take the head from the beast. This Sheikh Mahmud."

"As I am sure you know, Wing Commander, he is being advised by the ones we need to destroy. Besides which we have no evidence that the Sheikh is behind this. That is pure supposition."

It was a typically British attitude. Give the benefit of the doubt even though British servicemen were dying because of it. I turned to Major Stevens, "Then Major Stevens, you tell me where they are to be found and we will bomb them for you."

The Right Honourable Sir Percy Cunliffe smiled, "Then we have an accommodation. Excellent. We will let you know where they are hiding just as soon as possible. The Major has already arrested dozens of suspects. When he has questioned them, we should find out where they are to be found."

"It would appear that it has to be to the east of Sulaimaniya. We still have chaps in the town. There aren't many of them. The Sheikh says he prefers Kurds around him but my fellows tell me that the Sheikh often leaves Sulaimaniya to travel east. Sometimes he is away overnight."

"Thank you Major. It is even more imperative that we build the airfield. Sulaimaniya is beyond the range of all of my aircraft. You have made my task even more urgent."

When they had gone I sat with Major Fox and the Group Captain. The whisky was brought out. "It is a waste of an aeroplane you know, sir."

"Perhaps not, sir."

"Not you too, Ralph!"

"No, hear me out, sir. The locals only know aeroplanes from seeing them land and take off. Now that they have heard what they can do the myth has become a reality. Make sure your aeroplanes fly with bombs on their wings and fly as low as they can. And don't underestimate Major Stevens. He might sound posh but he knows his stuff. He has the M.C. too. I will head into the bazaar tomorrow and see what I can pick up."

"Very well. I will organize the pilots for the display and the rest will be with me tomorrow protecting the convoy. Until we get the fuel there we are vulnerable."

Wings over Persia

I prepared my weapons before I retired. The insurgents would know what we were doing at the airfield. I suspected attacks on the men building it and I expected ambushes to prevent us bringing more equipment to the site. I had designated the pilots to fly the Baghdad umbrella. With three aeroplanes still being repaired and rebuilt, I could ill afford to have two performing such a futile act. France had been simpler. There we had been free from politics and politicians.

The aerodrome was a hive of activity before dawn. The faster Ninaks would fly north first while I would have the Snipes weaving above the convoy. The Vernons had fuel on board for we would need refuelling at Kirkuk. It would take the convoy six hours to reach Kirkuk. We only had three hours endurance. The Ninaks would cover the last two hours of the convoy's journey.

After the lorries and tankers left the compound the Vernons lumbered down the runway first closely followed by the Ninaks. My ten Snipes looked forlorn on the runway. As we took off I saw the last two birds sitting and awaiting daylight. They were the Baghdad patrol. The sun burst from the east half an hour out of Baghdad. We could see the Vernons ahead of us and the convoy below. I slowed us down so that we zig zagged over the road and the convoy. We were just slightly ahead of the lorries.

The Vernons had just disappeared north when I saw sunlight glint off something. It was to the north and west. The sun in the south and east had flashed off metal. You ignored such things at your peril. I led Barker down to investigate. The rest of the squadron would remain alert and in position. Our enemy was clever. This might be a distraction to draw us away from our task. Whatever we found would have to be dealt with by two aeroplanes. I climbed to three hundred feet.

I saw that the road took a loop around a large area of rock. Had the British or the Romans built the road then it would have been straight. I found the enemy. They were in the cleft of the cliffs over the road. I dived towards them and their faces turned. We were too close to the road to risk bombs. I did not want the road blocking. I cocked my right-hand Vickers and, as I zoomed closer, gave a short burst and then another. The rock wall loomed up and I pulled up. I heard Barker's gun behind me. Climbing, I banked to come around. The enemy were firing at me. The convoy would have heard the noise and be alerted. Each of the vehicles had a Lewis gun mounted on the cab. Those in the petrol tankers would be nervous.

As I banked I saw that there were some bodies lying around the cleft. Bullets struck my tail. I swung around for another pass. I used a slightly different angle for my approach. I fired one burst and, suddenly, a wall of flame erupted before me. Rocks and debris flew through the air. I pulled up my nose and hoped that Barker had the same reactions. The insurgents had had explosives. I looked to my left and saw that there were rocks on the road. The convoy would have to clear it before they could continue. Every minute on the road represented danger to the convoy.

I led my wingman to complete a loop and make sure there were no rebels or assassins left. By the time we reached the rockfall the rest of my squadron was circling and the rocks were being removed. It took half an hour to do so and I was acutely aware that fuel was burning. When I saw Jack leading his Ninaks south to relieve us I breathed a sigh of relief. We descended towards Kirkuk.

Squadron Leader Harris was a very organized man. The Vernons were lined up on one side of what would become the runway. At we landed, it was just a landing strip. Sergeant Major Hale had erected a pole and from it blew a windsock. That was vital for safe landings. I saw that they had machine guns covering the road from Kirkuk. The airfield was a hive of activity. I had previously landed here and knew more than the rest of my squadron. I landed first, I taxied and lined up on the opposite side of the runway to the Vernons. Everything had been unpacked from the transports and their crews were beavering away with the others.

I climbed down and Sergeant Major Hale scurried over. "Everything in order, Sarn't Major?"

"The little buggers came in the night sir but we were ready. We sent up a flare and the machine guns took care of them. We buried them downwind, sir. In this heat…"

"Quite." I had a thought, "Where are their clothes?"

"Clothes sir?"

"Yes, these chaps normally wear a bisht, a flowing cloak."

He pointed, "We found four of them over there, sir. I was going to have them torn up and made into rags. The mechanics are always in need of them."

"Don't. Have them put somewhere safe. I might have a use for them." I had an idea in the back of my mind. Scouting from the air was all well and good but sometimes we might need to get into one of their strongholds. A disguise might help. Of course, I would need Major Fox but it was an idea for the future.

"The convoy might be a little late. We foiled an ambush but the road was blocked."

"Right sir. I'll get back to it."

I saw that Sergeant Major Robson had the men rolling the cans of fuel towards the Snipes. We were not on empty yet but we would be refuelled and then leave to relieve Jack's buses before they were flying on fumes.

I was startled by a crack from the north. I saw a column of smoke rising. That was where Henry and his Ninaks were. I listened and heard the sound of guns. Squadron Leader Harris, stripped to the waist, strolled over. He was grinning, "I don't think I shall be bored here eh, sir?"

"No indeed. I had Major Fox get some Mills bombs for you. They are a handy weapon against rebels in the night. The convoy will be arriving an hour later than we thought."

"That is not a problem. We are still improving the runway and deepening the ditch. One of my chaps had the idea of putting pointed sticks in the bottom. A lot of these natives are barefoot."

"Good idea. When we are refuelled we will take off and escort the convoy the last few miles." I looked at my watch. "They should be here by eleven." I nodded towards the smoke in the sky. "The insurgents are becoming more active."

Harris took out his pipe, "They are definitely organised. These are not random attacks. They are probing for weaknesses. Whoever this enemy's leader is, he knows about aeroplanes." He took out a small bag. "The Sergeant Major found these on some of the chaps they killed last night. It is sugar. I am guessing they planned on putting the stuff in the fuel."

"You are right. They must have thought we had fuel here already."

"We will put a tight guard on it when it does arrive."

I looked at my watch. "It is ten, we had better get aloft and escort them the last part of the journey. We will stay up as long as we can."

"At least we have a radio now. We can call in the cavalry any time."

"We can be here in just over an hour flying at top speed. You just need to hold whatever the threat is for that length of time."

Just then Henry's Ninaks came overhead and waggled their wings. They were all there but I saw bullet holes in the wings of a couple of them. I would have to wait until Baghdad for that story.

I whistled and circled my hand. My pilots came running. The lengthened runway was for the Vernons but it was a good surface and we got into the air really quickly. We saw the insect like Ninaks in the distance and they headed south before we reached the convoy. They would be keen to get refuelled. We performed lazy circles above the convoy and, when it was within sight of the compound, I led my Snipes south. As we neared Baghdad I spied a column of smoke rising.

We had all spent six hours in the cockpit as well as labouring under a Persian sun. We were exhausted. As we headed to the office I shouted, "First round in the mess tonight is on me!"

They all gave a weary cheer. I went directly to the office, "Problems, Sergeant Major?"

He nodded, "A riot in the bazaar, sir. They barely controlled it. Luckily the Ninak flew over and the rear gunner fired his Lewis into the air. They scattered but by then the fire had been started."

"Any news of those radios for the aeroplanes? We really are blind without them."

"They are on their way to Alexandria sir. The Engineer chaps who are to fit them are with them. Ten days?"

"That is nine days too long but so long as we get them. And how are the repairs to the three damaged buses coming along?"

"Five days, sir. They are working flat out."

"I know, I know."

"Hibbert get the Wing Commander a cup of tea. He needs it. I dare say he will have something a little stronger later."

"You are right there, Sergeant Major."

Jack and Henry came in looking as dirty and weary as I was. "What happened Henry?"

"We came upon them setting up a gun. It wasn't a little one. It looked like an old French 75. We bombed it and one hit the caisson. It went up like a Roman candle. You would think they would learn to travel at night."

"Don't give them ideas like that! I wondered if the new airfield would make them decide to take some affirmative action. The trouble is there are a lot of places they can hide guns."

Henry nodded. Hibbert brought in my tea. The Squadron Leader said, "A couple more for us eh, old son."

"Righto sir."

"The thing is sir, Mosul is in an even worse predicament. The *'hairies'* are safe over the border in Turkey. The Kurds have their own kingdom, or so it seems. They give the Turks a hard time and the French in Syria. The area to the north of Mosul is rough ground with few roads. I have flown over it and you could hide an army there."

"You seem remarkably well-informed Henry."

"I was talking to Ralph the other day. Clever chap that. He was reading History at Cambridge before he joined up. Classics."

"Then we might have to build an airfield up there too."

Sergeant Major Davis said, "Stretching things a bit thin aren't you, sir?"

"We are a lot cheaper than thirty battalions and look at the effect one aeroplane had over Baghdad today."

"What do we do tomorrow sir? The buses are in need of maintenance." Jack knew his aeroplanes and crews better than anyone. He was worried.

"Have half your squadron on the ground with the mechanics. The other half does the same as today. Jack, you escort the lorries. You have the range to stay over them the whole way and then refuel. I will take half of my flight and we will fly to the east of Kirkuk. Use the new field to refuel. When we get ammo facilities there then you can re-arm too. We have good mechanics and riggers there now. I would like to put a lid on this unrest. The resident is right in one respect, our edge is our aeroplanes. Until they get aeroplanes to use against us we should have the upper hand."

Chapter 4

We partied in the mess. The men needed to let off steam. None drank to excess. They knew they would be flying in the morning but they had a good drink. We rotated the pilots who would fly the Baghdad umbrella and increased it to three aeroplanes. We used just five aeroplanes from each squadron to patrol. What Jack had said was right. We did need to rest men and buses. The exception, of course, would be the squadron leaders. We would not rest or stand down.

I spoke with Flight Lieutenant Ritchie before I left. "I want you and the other chaps to go over the maps of the area. I will be up with you tomorrow and I want to find the route they are sending men over from the east. You are a clever lad, talk to Major Fox and put yourself in the enemy's shoes. Where is the hardest place for us to find them?"

I felt better having set someone else the task with which I been wrestling. At the moment, we were just reacting to the enemy. I wanted us to be in the driving seat and asking them the hard questions. We landed at Kirkuk. The Vernons weren't there; just the Vimy ambulance. The airfield looked bigger. Already two huts had been erected and I saw that work on the storage tank had begun.

Sergeant Major Hale saluted, "Sir. We had no bother last night. The garrison did in the town though. I think the soldiers are a bit worried. They reckon the rainy season is almost upon us. This place gets cut off. The roads become impassable."

"We have aeroplanes."

"That is what Squadron Leader Harris said. He went back to Baghdad for more supplies. He said he was going to split his buses and patrol on the way back. That is why you didn't see them sir."

"I wondered. Well get us filled up and we will head towards the east. The Ninaks will get topped up too. If we are up here then we might as well use as much daylight as we can. The lads who fly today will have a rest tomorrow. When do you reckon this will be finished?"

"We need more huts. We will have to send lorries back for them."

"Then have them go back and Squadron Leader Thomson can escort them." I knew that Jack would hate the task but it had to be done.

"Sir. In that case I reckon ten more days and we will be as secure as anywhere in this God forsaken country!"

"Sergeant Major there are academics who believe that this is where the Garden of Eden was."

"Then thank God I am uneducated sir! Garden of Eden my…"

"We took off after being refuelled and headed towards Sulaimaniya. This was Sheikh Mahmud's power base. I had only seen it in the distance. Now we had enough fuel to fly beyond it. We flew low over the town. I spied the Union Flag and the British troops there waved. As we passed over I saw that the commander had more guns facing east than west. He had the same opinion as I had. That was where the real danger lay. We flew for thirty minutes and I had just decided to turn around when I saw a smudge of smoke. I risked another five minutes flying east. Five minutes would bring us at least ten miles closer. There was another town there. It was an ancient town and looked to have a wall around it. Even as I turned I took in the armed men. I did not know the name of the place. I would have to look at the map when I returned. It looked to me to be worth investigating.

We refuelled quickly back at Kirkuk and headed south along, what was now, an empty road. I saw the Vernons as they lumbered north. Camp Harris was coming on! When we landed in Baghdad I went directly to the office and sought the maps. Major Fox came in while I was doing so. I waved him over. "I found somewhere here." I jabbed a finger at the spot. The map had no name. I estimated the position from the distance we had travelled.

"That is in Iran, old Persia. I think the place you are looking at is called Maivan."

"But, according to the map, there is nothing there!"

"The Turks were not the most efficient map makers. The only reason I know the name is because one of the men who tried to assault us the other day lived for half a day before he died. He was rambling but he said something about a little brother in a place called Maivan. The doc asked him where it was so that we could help his brother. Your description matches his."

"Then that is where the insurgents are being organized."

"And that makes sense. It is far enough from Tehran for them to be able to act with impunity and we can't bomb it because their Shah would not be happy about interference."

I took out my pipe. "So, we have a rat hole in the skirting board but as it is in a neighbour's house we can't plug it up?"

He laughed, "An interesting analogy sir but, yes, that is about it."

I looked at the map again. We had had to climb to reach Maivan and I remembered the mountains. The Turks had built a road. As I looked at it on the map I saw that, as it crossed the border it twisted and turned to make its way through the mountains. "I can see a way. The rat can enjoy its freedom for a little while longer but I will stop up its hole!"

The next day I led the other half of the flight directly to Sulaimaniya. I wish to scout out the mountain pass. Before we left I explained to Ritchie what I intended. "I want to see if we could bomb the pass and create an avalanche. They could still come across but it would slow them up."

"Sir."

"I shall take a camera. That way we can study at leisure." The Ninaks escorted the lorries with the supplies Squadron Leader Harris and the two Sergeant Majors needed as well as escorting other convoys to Sulaimaniya. I was indulging myself with this free patrol.

We were getting used to the country now. I had identified markers in the terrain and I used them to save me from constantly looking at the map. We saw the Ninaks to the north of us as they escorted the latest convoy from Kirkuk. The messages from the resident there were not good. The natives were definitely being stirred up. When we found the road, I estimated that we had travelled a hundred and ninety miles. Circling the road, I saw that there were a few travellers on the roads but they looked to be legitimate. Two or three men heading east and the same number heading west were not a band of insurgents intent upon causing mayhem. The road had been carved from the rock. It was not huge but it would accommodate a vehicle. Above the road, however, I saw rocks which looked like they were just waiting to be knocked down. This would involve some thought. I took half a dozen photographs and then headed to Kirkuk.

As we passed over the town I could hear firing. Sergeant Major Hale came over as I landed, "Trouble Sarn't Major?"

He nodded, "We had a message from the garrison sir. There was a bombing in the town. When they went to investigate the troops were attacked by rebels." He waved a hand, "Squadron Leader Harris took the Vernons back to Baghdad. Captain Willoughby requested some help, sir. The troops have been trapped in the bazaar area. He reckons it was coordinated. The bomb drew us in and then they unleashed hell."

"Then let us give them some. Have my pilots refuel their aeroplanes. Get me a lorry and Sergeant Williams. I need twenty of your men, Sergeant Major."

"Sir. I can come too if…"

"No Sarn't Major, you keep on building this airfield but I want two of those bisht we took from the dead Kurds."

There was one Nissen hut which was being used as an office. It also accommodated the radio and the armoury. I took off my flying helmet and flying coat as I went in. I threw them on a chair.

Sergeant Williams came in. "Sir?"

"We are going into to Kirkuk to give the army a hand. Lee Enfields and a Lewis gun mounted on the back of a lorry should do."

"Right sir." He disappeared into the back and came back out with a Lee Enfield for me and some ammunition. "The lads all have a rifle with them. I just get the Lewis. Sergeant Major Hale has the rest of the men with the lorry sir."

I got outside and saw the eighteen men and driver being spoken to by the Sergeant Major. "Right, lads, I want to surprise the rebels. We keep hidden and drive in as though we are locals. Sergeant Major Hale fetch me three of those bisht we took."

He disappeared as Sergeant Williams appeared, "Put the Lewis in the back of the lorry and have it facing over the tailgate." As they did so the Sergeant Major appeared with the three bisht. I chose the best two and handed one to Williams. "Right Sergeant Williams put this on. You drive." I donned mine. "You chaps in the back keep hidden. When I give the nod throw open the flap and do exactly as I say."

Once inside I checked my Webley was loaded and that I had a grenade ready. "Williams drive to the bazaar. We are locals so just try to blend in. Drive slowly. Let them think we have stolen this lorry eh?"

"Yes sir."

"Leave the talking to me." I had enough Arabic to get by.

We headed towards the town which was just half a mile away. I kept my pistol by my side and I leaned out of the window. Williams had an unlit cigarette dangling from his lip. With the hood of his bisht over his head and his suntanned skin he could pass for a native. Thanks to the time I spent in the open cockpit I, too, was swarthy. I saw shops being looted as we passed them. The British troops had been dragged into the centre. The Residency would be under siege and the rest of the troops would be trapped in the bazaar area. The closer we came the harder it was to move. I leaned out of the cab and shouted, "Out of the way, we bring help to our brothers against the British. Allah is great!"

Gradually we drew closer. Williams leaned over and said, beneath his breath, "We are almost there, sir. Around the next corner."

I banged on the back and said, "Get ready."

There were four heavily armed men at the corner. Beyond them I heard the crack of bullets. Both sides were using whatever cover they could.

"Who are you? What are you doing with a British lorry?"

I waved him over and said, confidentially, "We were sent from Maivan. We have men in the rear. Let us reverse the lorry and we can overcome them."

He nodded. I stepped up to the cab and made a circling motion with my hand. I stepped off the step and moved back to the wall. The four men were grinning. The big man said, "That Russian may have the manners of a pig but he knows the mind of the Englishmen!"

I nodded, "That he does."

It took some time for the lorry to reverse. I made sure that I was behind the four men. As soon as it stopped I shouted, "Now!"

I pulled out my gun and held it to the head of the large warrior. As the Lewis gun chattered and cleared away the insurgents closest to it one of the other Arabs turned his gun on me. Even as I brought my gun up to shoot him the big warrior stabbed at me with his knife. Williams' rifle barked twice and two Arabs fell dead. I tried to knock the knife away but he was a strong man and it scored a line down my leg. I pulled the trigger of my Webley which was pressed against the Arab's side. It tore a hole in him and the man behind. Williams finished him off.

The bazaar was empty of insurgents now. There were fifteen dead and dying next to the rear of the smoking lorry. I saw Captain Willoughby and Sergeant Hughes. They were making their way towards the lorry.

"You are a sight for sore eyes, sir."

"Yes, sorry we cut it fine."

"It worked. If you will loan us your men we will enforce a curfew." He looked down at my leg. "And you had better get to the residency. There is a doctor there." He nodded to Williams, "Off load the Lewis gun and drive him there, Sergeant."

"Sir." We both took off our bisht and jammed them under the seat of the lorry. Who knew when they might come in handy again?

"When everything is back to normal we will send your chaps back, sir."

"Before dark, if possible, Captain. We need them to guard the airfield. If things get hairy then that may well be your only way out of here."

"I know sir."

The fleeing crowds had taken away those besieging the residency. There was fire damage and bullet damage. As we approached it I said, "We learned one thing from that, Sergeant."

"What's that sir?"

"It is a Russian behind all of this. That narrows the field a little."

"We still have to catch him though sir."

"That will come Sergeant. We are narrowing down our search."

The men at the gate opened it for us when they saw our uniforms. Williams leaned out of the cab. "Where is your doctor? My officer is wounded."

The corporal said, "They are using the dining room as a makeshift hospital, Sarge. We were lucky. Just cuts and bruises from falling masonry."

I was feeling a little weak. The blood had been flowing all the time. Williams had to help me. As soon as the doctor saw my condition he shouted, "Clear a space there!"

He cut open my trousers. Even as he did so I wondered where I would get a replacement pair. He took one look at it and shook his head, "This will need stitching and I am out of morphine."

I nodded although I was feeling light headed and the action was not the cleverest one I had ever taken. "Just stitch it, doctor. I have to get back to Baghdad."

"You are going nowhere, Wing Commander."

Mercifully I passed out.

I dreamed. I was in France with Beattie and the kids and I was drinking wine. We were in the gardens of Versailles and the fountains were sending their plumes of water into the air in time to a four-piece baroque ensemble. Suddenly I heard the thunder of hooves and Cossack cavalry charged across the manicured lawns. I awoke with a start.

There was a grey-haired woman standing there. "You are quite safe, Wing Commander. Doctor Bainbridge hoped you would sleep a little longer."

I tried to struggle to my feet but I felt as weak as a kitten and the woman easily restrained me.

"You are going nowhere. It is after dark and so you cannot possible fly home but as a lady such as myself can hold you down I don't think that you are capable of flying one of those aeroplanes."

I lay back and said, with eyes closed, "But they need me!"

"Poppycock! That sounds like every soldier I have ever known. If you aren't there to do it then there will be someone else who will be! Now lie still. I am having a bed made up for you. I can't promise a decent dinner but we shall do our best."

I opened my eyes, "I am sorry to be so ungrateful and such a nuisance."

She smiled, "From what Captain Willoughby told us, Wing Commander, you are anything but a nuisance. I am Lady Isabel Palmer. My brother is the resident here. I shall enjoy speaking with you at dinner. You sound a trifle more interesting than most military types."

I did not know if I had been praised or insulted. I must have dozed off and I only woke when I felt someone dressing me. I opened my eyes with a start. There was a white-haired man fastening my trousers, "I am sorry sir. I hoped to dress you while you were asleep. I am Geoffrey, Lord Randolph's man's man."

He fiddled on with my boots.

"I tried to get your boots as clean as I could sir but they are a mess."

I smiled. He reminded me of John who had been my servant in the war. He too had always been vaguely critical of my appearance.

"Sorry, Geoffrey. I will try to do better next time."

He nodded, "I hope the trousers fit. They belonged to Lieutenant O'Rourke. He was killed earlier today, in the bazaar. A nice chap. Now then, Wing Commander, if I help you will you be able to walk to the dining room or shall I fetch a bath chair? They are all awaiting your arrival."

"I think I can manage. If you just let me put my weight on your shoulder."

It was not so much painful as uncomfortable when I put my weight on my wounded leg. The stitches felt tight. Luckily, we only had thirty or so paces to go to reach the dining room. I recognised the doctor and Lady Isabel. The others I did not. However, when a distinguished looking man strode towards me with his hand held out I knew he must be the resident.

"Well done, Wing Commander, I am pleased you could join us."

I gave a baleful look to the doctor. "It seems I had little choice in the matter."

The doctor took a healthy swig from his wine, "I am afraid that I outrank everyone when it comes to medical matters. The wound was not that deep, Wing Commander, although you needed twenty stitches, but you lost a lot of blood. Get a good night's sleep and I may consider letting you return to your squadron."

I smiled, "In the Great War I was captured by Von Richthofen. If he couldn't keep me locked up then I don't think much of your chances, doctor."

The resident, Lord Randolph Palmer shook his head, "But I wager he did not have the services of my sister!"

There was a great deal of banter around the table. I discovered that Lady Isabel's husband had been killed in the Great War and, having no children of her own had taken it upon herself to run her brother's home for him. Inevitably the conversation got around to the situation in Persia.

"There are so few soldiers these days Wing Commander, I fear for our safety."

I nodded towards the west, "And that is one reason why we built the airfield. We have a squadron of transports aeroplanes who are more than capable of air lifting the whole of the residency and the garrison to safety."

Lady Isabel lit a cigarette in her cigarette holder, "Air lift, Wing Commander?"

"Sorry, Lady Isabel, it is jargon. It means taking you all from one place to another. I first used it in Egypt. There was an outpost trapped by insurgents. We landed under fire and extracted them."

"Remarkable. I remember when I was a young woman and we saw the first aeroplane. It seemed to be held together by string."

I laughed, "I remember flying in one of those. It was called a Gunbus but they were more reliable than you might think."

Lord Randolph lit a cigar as did the doctor. I declined, preferring my pipe, "And you say there is a Russian behind this?"

"Let us say that the rebels have someone with experience in modern warfare. This is too organised to be just fermented by unhappy people. We had unhappy people in Egypt. This is not the same. And the chap who knifed me confirmed it. If we could have interrogated him we might have learned more."

The doctor said, as he blew out a lazy smoke ring, "One of the natives I was called on to tend after the last unpleasantness mentioned a Russian. He was delirious with the pain of course and I took it to be rambling. I think he used the word, Count."

Shivers ran down my neck. "This man, can I speak with him?"

"Sorry Wing Commander but he died. Do you think what he said was important?"

"I was in White Russia in nineteen. I met a really unpleasant White Russian, Count Yuri Fydorervich. He fled the country when his misdemeanours were discovered. He tried to have me killed. A thoroughly disreputable man but very clever for all that. If he is involved then everything makes sense."

Lord Randolph said, "A bit of a tenuous link, what? There must be many Counts who fled Russia and are seeking employment as military advisers."

"The difference is that most of them were not very good. Count Yuri Fydorervich was!" I placed my dead pipe on the ashtray, "It still does not help me save to make me realise that we are I even more danger than I thought."

That night as I lay in an amazingly comfortable bed, having been fortified with wine, port and finally whisky, I went to sleep realising that I did know more than I thought. The Count was a clever man but he was no hero. He surrounded himself with thugs and killers. He would not trust the locals. These would be hired men. I guessed that they would be Russians themselves. They would be ruthless. He would also surround himself with the trappings of the nobility. What I needed was eyes on Maivan!

Sergeant Williams arrived just after dawn in the lorry. I was up early and I dressed. The replacement trousers were a good fit. Apparently, as I had discovered at dinner, the Lieutenant was not a young man. Lady Isabel was also up and I saw her frowning, "Sneaking away Wing Commander? I thought better of you."

I liked Lady Isabel. She was a formidable lady. She was like an older version of Beattie- indomitable.

"Of course not, but my driver is here and I did not wish to waken the house. I have three squadrons to run. I know you believe that others could do what I do but I am not certain that is true." I took her hand and kissed it. "I shall be sure to return here and visit with you and your brother as often as I am in Kirkuk."

She laughed, "And I am certain that will not be very often. Good luck Wing Commander. I have high hopes for this air force of yours if you are a measure of the officers."

Once in the lorry I said, "Did all of our men get back?"

"Yes sir, and your Snipes went back with Mr Ritchie. Squadron Leader Harris returned last night too. He made sure that the airfield was locked up tight. Baghdad is getting worse, sir. The Group Captain has suspended transport by road. We can only bring supplies in by air from now on."

"Any more good news?"

He smiled, "That is about it, sir. Oh, Sergeant Major Robson's men did a service on your bus sir. They reckoned it was well overdue!"

Everyone viewed me as though I was an invalid when I climbed from the cab. I forced myself to smile and not to grimace at the ache in my leg. It was only the stiffness from the wound and the stitches which were causing me a problem. That would pass. Arthur Harris was grinning, "I go to Baghdad once and you end up having all the fun! Shot yourself some insurgents I hear?"

"While the cat's away and all that. Is my flight heading up here?"

He shook his head, "Group Captain Wainwright decided to keep all the squadrons close to home. Baghdad is a tinderbox. He is using the pilots and gunners to defend the airfield. I barely managed to bring my Vernons north."

"This plays directly into the Russian Count's hands."

"Russian Count?"

I nodded and told him my news. "The rebels will see their attack yesterday as a victory rather than the defeat I hoped it would be. He will be telling them that one more push will see them over the line. I will bring Ninaks and Snipes back tomorrow. I intend to put a spanner in the Count's spokes. I am going to bomb the road he uses."

The Snipe did fly better as I headed south. The mechanics had done a good job. I think they had managed to coax another two or three knots from her. I saw smoke and flames in the city as I landed. I saw that every aeroplane was neatly parked and the perimeter manned by almost the whole of three squadrons and ground crews. I climbed gingerly from the cockpit. My leg had stiffened up on the flight south. I made my way to the office. There were just two of them in there: Group Captain Wainwright and Sergeant Major Davis.

"How are you sir?"

"Fine Sergeant Major. Could you be a fine fellow and go and put the chocks under my wheels for me?" I glanced at the Group Captain.

Sergeant Major Davis nodded and said, "Will do sir and I'll put on the kettle too eh sir? Nice cuppa!"

When he had gone I said, "Sir, what are you doing?"

"What? I am trying to save three squadrons!"

"Well you are going about it the wrong way sir. This will just get men killed."

"Look Harsker I will defer to you on matters of aerial combat. You are the ace but I think I know about military strategy. There are times when you have to hunker down and ride out the storm."

"True sir but this is not one of those times." I went over to the map. "Sir, I have discovered who is behind all of this. He is a White Russian and he is based in Maivan. They are sending men from over the border in Iran. They are stirring up the Shia there. The Kurds are gaining in confidence too. I propose bombing the road from Maivan and the road to Mosul. It will buy our soldiers the time to strengthen our defences and those new aeroplanes might well arrive here. It is a waste of resources to have airmen defending streets."

He looked very old and had reverted to the Group Captain who had been there when I first arrived. "What if they come here?"

"Major Fox can handle them don't you worry. Look, I'll get the men back now and we can prepare for our air raids in the morning. I am certain that the resident would prefer our aeroplanes to be flying overhead eh?"

Sergeant Major Davis returned with three mugs of tea.

"Ah Sergeant Major. Could you go and recall our chaps? We have done enough for the time being."

He grinned, "Yes sir!"

I now had to work out a plan which would do just what I had told the Group Captain we would do.

Chapter 5

We had all our aeroplanes ready to fly but we had a problem. Three men had been wounded in the defence of the city. I was just grateful that none had died. We were air gunners short. I decided to use this as an opportunity to see how effective the Ninaks were. "Flight Lieutenant Ritchie can command the Snipes. He will patrol the city and the airfield. I will fly as air gunner on one of the Ninaks whose gunner is wounded."

Jack said, "But sir, you are a Wing Commander!"

"And I began life as a gunner. Are you saying I am not qualified Squadron Leader Thomson?"

He grinned, "No sir. I would never dream of doing that. Peter Foster is going to be delighted to have you as his gunner!"

I would be flying on the mission to Maivan but Henry knew Mosul better than I did. "What we need is for you to block the road on the Iraq side of the border. I intend to ask Squadron Leader Harris to take his birds up the following day to increase the damage. I don't think we need to refuel but we have that option now anyway. Squadron Leader Harris will take his Vernons up and patrol the roads. I have a feeling that the rebels will think they have us beat. And the day after that I want Kirkuk supplying. If we lose Kirkuk then Mosul and Sulaimaniya will both fall."

"What time do we leave, sir?"

"Before dawn. It will be cooler and we might even catch some of the rebels on the road."

We did have some good news. We had three radios. I had them issued to Flight Lieutenant Ritchie, Squadron Leader Thomson and Squadron Leader Woollett. I spoke to Arthur before I went into dinner. I wanted him under no illusions about the enormity of the task which faced us.

Pilot Officer Foster was nervous. I saw him smoking as I approached the Ninak. The cigarette ends around his feet showed that he had been there for some time. He put on a false smile, "Good morning sir!"

I smiled, "It's Peter, isn't it?" He nodded. "Listen Peter I am just flying today because I want to see the effect of the bombs.

Pretend I am your regular gunner and I will try not to let you down."

"You couldn't let me down sir. Besides Rooney hasn't had to fire the guns in anger yet. No enemy aeroplanes."

I frowned, "The Lewis has a Scarff ring. You can fire at the ground." His face showed me that they had not thought of that. This was my fault. I should have flown with the Ninaks before now to see how they performed. Jack and Henry led the two squadrons. They wouldn't be able to see what their gunners were doing. Perhaps this was a good thing.

Getting in was harder than in the Snipe. It was higher. However, once I was in the gun cockpit, it was quite comfortable. I had had the cooks make me up a flask of soup. I had also brought two Mills bombs. Old habits die hard. I checked that the gun moved freely on the scarff ring and that I had spare magazines. The problem with the Lewis gun was that you had to change your magazines too frequently. We were back to back and quite close. We would not need microphones.

"All set sir?"

"Ready when you are, Pilot Officer."

For me the most unusual part of all this was taking off without being able to see the front of the aeroplane. I saw the airfield and Baghdad below me as we climbed. When we reached ten thousand feet I said, "I will test my guns."

"Right you are sir."

I made sure that the sky behind and below me was clear. I stood up and fired a three second burst. The Lewis worked well. I settled down again. We had exactly one hundred and seventy-six miles ahead of us. We would be there in under two hours. There would be no need to refuel. I was soon aware that we were beginning to climb. We were in the second flight of four and just behind the Squadron Leader. Jack would be making these decisions. I looked over the side and saw the road snaking. There were people on it but we were too high to identify them. Jack would bring us back at a much lower altitude.

It was peaceful in the Ninak. When I had been a gunner in a Gunbus I could not afford to let my concentration drop for an instant. I was constantly scanning the skies for enemy aeroplanes. Here we knew that there were no enemy aeroplanes and our altitude ensured that we were safe from ground fire. I had time to have a cup of soup and to examine the terrain. I knew, from France, that you could never have too much information about the ground. You never knew when you were going to crash land.

"Sir! Approaching the pass!"

"Thanks!"

I stood and cocked the Lewis. I pulled my goggles over my eyes. I had not needed them yet but soon I would. The road was on our port side and so I swung the Lewis over that side. We began to descend. As I glanced ahead I saw that Jack and his first three pilots were a hundred yards ahead of us. In combat that was too far but when you were bombing it was perfect. We would be able to see the effect of the first bombs and adjust accordingly. We were using a steep dive. I was a better fighter pilot than a dive bomber. When we had developed the photographs, we had seen a huge chunk of rock which jutted out over the road. Its outline was a little bit like that of Prince Albert. As I glanced down again I saw that we were now just five hundred feet above the road. The rocky figure rose above us.

"First flight making their bombing run, sir!"

I saw the flash from the ground. We were being fired at. Now we were within the range of small arms. Then I saw the arc of bullets as they stitched holes in the nearest Ninak to us. They had a machine gun and I saw them arc. This was definitely bad news for it showed that they were coming equipped to fight and down aeroplanes. I swung the Lewis around and fired five shots. The advantage I had over the gunners on the ground was that I could see where my bullets hit. If they were not using tracer a direct hit was the only way they would know if they were on target.

I could not identify individuals but their muzzle flashes showed me that they were hiding in rocks. I fired at the rocks and gave a sustained burst. Flying chips could be just as deadly as bullets.

"Sir, they have hit Hargreaves and Hill. Their Ninak is on fire."

"Concentrate on the bomb run. Squadron Leader Thomson can call up the Vimy." I didn't add, if it was needed. Unless they managed to make an emergency landing the odds on them surviving a crash up here were slim. I changed my magazine. I heard the sound of the twenty-five-pound bombs as they exploded. The concussion made us rise and then fall.

"Our turn, sir!"

One advantage of our bomb run was that I had a better angle to hit the rebels. The disadvantage was that they would be firing at us. I could see them more clearly now. There appeared to be about twenty of them. They had two machine guns and the rest had rifles. I guessed they were Lee Enfields. I emptied my second magazine and then, as we were just four hundred above them, I took out a Mills bomb and, pulling the pin, dropped it over the side. My pilot banked and I did not see the effect. I knew that it would explode in the air. The question was how far above them?

The huge rock was almost directly in front of us. The Snipe would have easily turned but I wondered about the huge Ninak. We seemed to leap in the air as the four bombs were dropped and then Foster used full power to bank away and follow the other pilots. The angle we banked prevented me from seeing the effect of the explosions but I heard them and I felt them. As we banked around I saw that another Ninak was smoking. Standing orders meant that he would head to Kirkuk which was the closest field. I saw the huge rock begin to shiver. Large boulders fell and then more. Annoyingly, when the dust had settled I saw that half of the tower remained but the road was almost completely blocked for a distance of some three hundred yards. The men who had ambushed us were also covered in rocks. They were entombed. I was able to watch the last four Ninaks as they dropped their bombs. Without the groundfire and having seen the other bombs fall they made a much better job of it. The whole of the rock crashed to the ground. You could no longer see where the road had been.

"Well done, Peter."

"Sir." He pointed down. I could see that the first aeroplane which had been hit was now a fireball on the ground. There were two blackened shapes. The crew had been on fire and, mercifully, thrown to the ground in the crash. They were dead. We would not need the air ambulance.

I saw that the damaged Ninak was heading for Kirkuk. "Foster, follow the damaged Ninak. They may need help and he is on his own."

"Sir." I saw that Jack Thomson was organizing his Ninaks to head home. I stood and made the sign for we will follow. He waved back and they peeled off south and west. He dropped to strafing height. He had lost one his aeroplanes. There would be no pity for any enemy he spied.

We soon caught up with the ailing bomber. I could see smoke coming from the engine. He had been shot up badly. The gunner's head was slumped forward. I tried to recall his name. The pilot was Pilot Officer Cole. The gunner had to be Flight Sergeant Matthew Hugff. His head lolled about. That was worrying. I took out the map. I estimated that we had seventy-five miles to go. It would take us just under an hour, if the other Ninak held together.

I could see that the DH 9A was labouring but I was more concerned with the gunner whose limp arm showed that he was unconscious. We had lost our first aeroplane and almost lost a second. Had this been a deliberate ambush or had we just been unlucky? They could not have known that we were going to hit the road. Only the pilots knew the target. Perhaps our patrols over the road had shown our hand. If this was Count Yuri Fydorervich then he would think nothing of sacrificing twenty or thirty men to bring down one aeroplane. He had plenty of men who were fanatical enough to sacrifice their own lives for the good of their God and to kill what they saw as the invader.

Turning, I saw Kirkuk in the distance but I was aware that we had lost altitude. We would be needing Doctor Bainbridge again. As we descended to make a landing I saw that the two sergeant majors had not been idle. There were more buildings and I saw that the fuel tank was finished and that they had surrounded it with sandbags. The two sergeant majors had shown initiative. It would be harder for an enemy to sabotage it. The Vernons were not there and the Vimy was missing.

Peter allowed Pilot Officer Cole to land first and then we turned to make our own landing. The smoking Ninak had warned the men on the ground what was happening and mechanics swarmed over it as it landed. The sooner they began to repair it the more chance we would have of saving it. "You did well there Pilot Officer. That was good flying and good bombing."

"I'll pop over sir and see if Malcolm needs a hand."

Sergeant Williams, with a Lee Enfield slung over his shoulder, came towards me, "This is a surprise sir."

I nodded, "How are things here, Sergeant?"

"Hairy sir! We have had more trouble in the town. Captain Willoughby lost three men. I took a lorry load of the lads down and we helped them clear the danger."

I pointed to the gunner, "Better get the lorry and take him to the doctor. He looks badly shot up."

"Sir." He turned to go.

"Where is the air ambulance?"

"Squadron Leader Woollett has a bird down sir. They have an injured man."

He hurried off to see to Cole. My suspicions appeared to be justified. Three aeroplanes hit on one day was too much of a coincidence.

I went to the office. There was just the duty clerk there. The rest were beavering away. "Crank up the radio, Benson. I need to talk with Baghdad. And then get the kettle on. We need a brew."

"Sir."

Sergeant Major Hale came in. "The gunner is dead, sir. He must have bled out on the way back."

I nodded, "Get on to Baghdad tell them that I will be staying here overnight as will Cole and Foster."

I went back to the runway. They were laying out Flight Sergeant Matthew Hugff on a stretcher. A pilot and his gunner had a special bond. I knew exactly how Malcolm Cole was feeling. I had lost gunners myself. "Sorry about Hugff, Cole. Peter, take your friend to the office. There should be some hot tea. We will talk about this later. We are going to spend the night here."

He nodded dully, "Sir." He was about to go and then he said, "Thank you sir, for today I mean, not just the fact that you let me get on with it and didn't offer advice I appreciated all that. The grenade, that took me by surprise sir!"

I smiled, "In the early days we did not have the luxury of bombs. We learned to improvise. We will talk later."

Wings over Persia

I knew that the two of them would have to go over every detail of the raid. In Cole's case, it would be to see if he could have done anything different. Could he have prevented his gunner's death? I heard the sound of Rolls Royce engines. It was the Vimy. Carruthers and Grundy were coming back. As I waited I began to think about what else we needed at this emergency airfield. We needed a vehicle which could be used as an ambulance and we needed a fire engine. Or a lorry equipped with gear to put out a fire. Having a mob of Erks running towards a smoking aeroplane was not the answer.

The mechanics had pushed the two Ninaks under the canvas awning which served as a hangar. The Vimy had plenty of room to land. Rodney taxied it close to us. I realised, as two Erks opened the hatch, that we had no medical staff at all here. We needed first aiders. Pilot Officer Grundy was first out. "Watch out for his leg. I have applied a bandage."

I saw that there were two in the ambulance but one was not moving. Grundy looked up and threw me a salute, "The pilot's dead sir. Killed on impact. His gunner took a bullet in the leg. I applied a dressing." He nodded to the cabin. We brought back the Lewis gun sir and blew up the Ninak before we left. There were natives heading for it." He pointed to the fuselage. There were bullet holes. "They got a bit close, sir."

I put my arm around his shoulders, "You did well Pilot Officer Grundy." I turned to the men with the stretcher. "Get this man in a lorry and take him to the residency."

"Sir."

We had had a phony war up until now. We had dropped bombs, we had strafed but we had been safe and had no losses. Now with four deaths and two wounds it was becoming very real.

I was having a cup of tea when Squadron Leader Harris and his Vernons landed. We had reported to Baghdad but as Jack and Henry had not landed we did not know if we had had more losses. Benson handed Arthur a mug of tea when he landed. I told him of the raid. "We did what we set out to do but it cost us, Arthur."

"And we found the enemy too. The bombsights work but the Vernon needs a proper gunner. We found rebels on the three roads in and out of Kirkuk. They are trying to seal it off." He pointed to the sky. "The rains are due to start. We won't be able to use the roads. Captain Willoughby told me that in Kirkuk they are having to ration."

"Then tomorrow you had better take your Vernons and bring up supplies. I will come back with you and bring up the Snipes. We have to hold on until the Bristols get here."

"Bristols?"

"They are sending a squadron of Bristols to be based here."

"Thank God for that. They are a handy little bus."

"And one more thing, Arthur, we had better be prepared to airlift the residency to Baghdad. If I am correct this Russian Count would not baulk at using the women as hostages. I will go and see Lord Palmer tonight and warn him."

Sergeant Williams drove me. The air gunner was ready to be returned to the airfield. I asked for a private audience with the resident. "You look serious, Wing Commander."

"The enemy are tightening the noose around you sir. Squadron Leader Harris reports them cutting the three roads into Kirkuk. When the rains come we might not be able to keep you supplied."

He smiled, "I am not going to abandon my post not when there are two other residents north of here and they are in as much danger as I am. Would you have us all abandon our posts? It would take huge numbers to retake this land. No, Wing Commander, I am afraid that it is up to you and your aeroplanes to hold on to what we have."

I admired the resident but he was ignoring the very real danger that Count Yuri Fydorervich represented. He was ruthless. "Very well sir. We have a squadron of fighters which will be based here. I know that you may not be happy to hear this but one solution might be to bomb those parts of Kirkuk which we suspect of housing insurgents."

"That seems somewhat drastic, Wing Commander. There would be non-combatants, women, children, the old; are you sure?"

"It is a last resort but if I might suggest notices around the town warning of the consequences of further unrest."

"Quite. That would seem to be the best solution and certainly preferable to bombing them. I will have a word with the elders of the town."

I nodded but I knew that there would agents of Count Yuri Fydorervich already in Kirkuk. He had used them in the Baltic and they would be stirring up anti-British sentiments in the young who would see this as a chance to get away with murder, quite literally!

As I headed back across the hall Lady Isabel came out of the dining room. "How is the leg Wing Commander?"

"Healing. Lady Isabel I just made an offer to your brother. I can fly the women and children out of Kirkuk and take you to Baghdad."

She shook her head, "That is most kind of you but firstly our place is here with the men and secondly, from what I hear, Baghdad is just as dangerous."

I was surrounded by madmen!

The gunner, Flight Sergeant Winspear, was in the back of the lorry smoking a cigarette. "How are you Winspear?"

"Better than Mr Clarke sir. He did his best to save the bus but…"

"You both did well. And how is the leg?"

"Not so good sir. They have given me something for the pain but the doc reckons it will hurt like blazes when it wears off."

"We will have you back in Baghdad first thing tomorrow."

I sat in the cab with Sergeant Williams. "It hit him hard, sir. They had been together for over a year."

"I know Sergeant. It is almost like a marriage. I think I will put him with Pilot Officer Cole. He lost his gunner. They might be good for one another."

Once again, I spent the night at Kirkuk. There was a sombre feeling about the place. The little cemetery was growing.

Cole flew back with Foster. The Air Ambulance took Winspear and I sat in the rear of Squadron Leader Harris' Vernon. The only aeroplanes we would be able to get up the next day would be the Snipes. Flight Lieutenant Ritchie was heading north to patrol the road, as we headed south. I hoped that our two attacks had slowed down the incursions from the north and the

Wings over Persia

east. We now needed a strategy to defeat the ones who were already here.

"Any suggestions, Arthur?"

"There is one. It is simple but it is a little drastic. Have your aeroplanes fly as low as you can and shoot any man with a gun. It will drive them underground. The ones who attack in the towns can be dealt with by the army. Just keep patrolling the roads, sir, bombing the hell out of any village which looks like it might cause trouble and make them places the rebels avoid." He shrugged, "It is the best that I can come up with, sir."

"And it is more than I had. We will try that."

Once again, we were greeted by palls of smoke from Baghdad. Arthur was right. We had to cut off the supply of men and weapons to the towns. If we cut off their supplies then eventually the cells would wither and die. It still did not address the real problem: Count Yuri Fydorervich. The only solution to that would be to fly across the border and bomb his headquarters. That seemed like a tall order. As I climbed down from the cockpit an idea was forming in my mind. It was not an instant solution but, with planning and the advice of Major Fox, I believed that we had a chance.

When we landed I left Squadron Leader Harris to see to the Vernons and the Vimy. I went to the office. Sergeant Major Davis was alone. "No clerk, Sarn't Major?"

"All hands to the pump today sir. Major Fox had to use every one we could spare for sentry duties. Some Arabs tried to cut a hole in the fence last night. A couple of our lads were wounded. It is like the Alamo here, sir."

"I take it the Major is being busy?"

He grinned, "Yes sir."

"And the Group Captain?"

He frowned and lowered his voice, "The Group Captain is in his quarters, sir, unwell... if you know what I mean. I daresay he will snap out of it but I have his man looking after him. We are managing."

There was a great deal which was unsaid. My plans would have to be delayed until the ship was steadied. "Thank you, Sergeant Major. I am certain that the Group Captain appreciates your discretion."

73

"He is a good bloke, sir. This job would tax a much younger man."

"Orders for tomorrow, Sergeant Major. I will lead the Snipes. The Vernons will take whatever supplies can be spared to Kirkuk. I want the remaining Ninaks making airworthy. The day after tomorrow we make the roads around Kirkuk, Mosul and Sulaimaniya empty of any who might be insurgents. I will see the squadron leaders before dinner."

He had been writing everything down. When I finished he looked up, "And you sir, how is the leg?"

"Stiff Sarn't Major."

"Well you look out for yourself sir. The last thing we need is for you to be… unwell."

"Don't worry, Sergeant Major. I won't."

"And when you have a minute sir there is a pile of paperwork that the Group Captain has not read. We had a mail delivery from Heliopolis. It went on from here towards India. They have another airfield at Basra now. They are using a Vimy like Mr Carruthers' air ambulance." He pointed to a sack. "There was mail for the squadrons. It will cheer them up eh sir?" He picked up a pile of brown envelopes. "This is the mail for the commanding officer sir."

"I'll sort through it. I will get changed first."

I went to my quarters and changed. I knew what was going through the Sergeant Major's mind. He had served in the Great War. He had seen officers crack under the pressure. Air warfare was a new kind of war. We were learning how to fight in the air but there was also a battle of the mind. I looked at the photographs of Beattie and Tom and Beattie and Mary which lay on the bedside table. I had to be strong for them. Perhaps I would leave the service. When I had been in the mess in Heliopolis I had heard of some pilots who had left the service to begin commercial flying. From what they had told me it was well paid and would certainly be safer than doing what I did. More importantly, I could be with my family. Beattie had often spoken of bringing the children to my posting. This was a war zone. I could not bring them here. I thought of Lady Isabel and the ladies of the garrison at Kirkuk. I would not put Beattie and the children in their situation.

Wings over Persia

As I walked back in a fresh uniform and feeling cleaner the rain started. As my dad might have said, it belted down! It was just a few yards I had to run but my fresh uniform was soaked. Sergeant Major Davis looked up, "The locals warned us about this sir. We will have rain for a couple of days. The roads will turn to mud and the rivers will overflow their banks."

"Will it affect us here, Sergeant Major?"

"Will we be flooded, sir?" I nodded. "We are far enough west of the Tigris and high enough to avoid the worst of it but it is a good job we have aeroplanes. I don't think vehicles will be travelling far for a while."

"Then it is imperative that we get whatever supplies we can up to Kirkuk. I will go through that paperwork now."

I sat behind the Group Captain's desk and took out my pipe. "I'll get you a brew sir. I could do with one myself. At home, sir, when we get a shower it makes everything greener, brighter, if you know what I mean. Out here there is no green. It will just get browner. Doesn't seem right."

I nodded. The rain made me miss England more than anything. I wondered if there would be a letter for me in the sack of mail. Then I realised there wouldn't be. My family would still be in France. I would have to make do with the photographs. I opened the envelopes first with a paper knife and then took the tea from Davis. I was delaying reading the missives. The hot sweet tea was comforting and I began to read. The first four contained information about the new mail flights, promotions due to time served, lists of spares which were being sent. The fifth was good news. The Bristol Fighters would be here within a week and, even better news, there was a squadron of Ninaks. They were on their way across the Med and the ministry had decided that they were going to build an airfield at Mosul. With the one at Basra and our emergency field at Kirkuk, we now had more choices of places to land. The Ministry of War was also sending men to replace the soldiers who had been wounded and killed.

The last letter, the sixth one had good news and bad news. Group Captain Wainwright had applied for retirement and it had been granted. I was to take over temporary command until a new station commander could be appointed. The bad news was that

Squadron Leader Harris had been promoted. He was to go to India and run a squadron on the North-West Frontier. He was ordered to go there on the next mail flight. Sergeant Major Davis had told me that they were going to be every six days. I would miss Arthur.

By the time I had dealt with the paperwork it was time for my meeting. Major Fox arrived in time for the meeting. The three squadron leaders looked drawn. I used the office for the briefing.

"First of all, I have to tell you that I am in temporary command here. Group Captain Wainwright will be heading back to Blighty. Retirement."

Jack nodded, "Good, the old boy has served his country. Well done sir."

"Just temporary, there is a new station commander on his way. Arthur, congratulations to you. You have been put in command of a squadron of bombers in India. You will be leaving when the next mail flight arrives in five days' time."

"But my job here is not completed, sir!"

"We have five days and I have a feeling that the next five days will be the busiest we have had."

Henry tapped his pipe out in the ashtray, "Why sir?"

I pointed my finger to the ceiling where the rain beat down on the roof. "Rainy season. Nothing can move on the road. I know we have closed the rat holes temporarily but I am betting that there will be men in place in Mosul, Kirkuk and Sulaimaniya who will be ready to rise. "I turned to Ralph Fox. "What do you think, Major?"

"I think you have it aright sir. The Arabs used to get boisterous with the Turks in the rainy season. They knew that the Turks couldn't use the roads and places like Kirkuk became isolated. Yes, I expect an escalation. We saw the beginnings the other night when they tried to breach our fences."

"So, we have tomorrow to get the Ninaks air worthy. We take supplies to Kirkuk tomorrow and the day after all three squadrons of bombers will head out and look for any insurgents. Bomb them. I want our aeroplanes over Sulaimaniya, Mosul and Kirkuk. We now have fuel at Kirkuk. Refuel there. Squadron Leader Harris make sure that your Vernons take up plenty of ammunition, food and emergency rations. If Kirkuk becomes cut off I want them to be able to hold on until we can reach them."

We had questions, which I answered and then they went to brief their pilots. "Major Fox I would like a chat after dinner. I have a little something in mind."

"Sir."

When I entered the Group Captain's quarters I could smell the alcohol. His man, McHale looked up guiltily, "It helps him sleep, sir. He suffers terrible with his nerves."

I nodded, "I understand, McHale. You are very loyal. The Group Captain is going home." The aircraftsman gave me a sharp look, "Nothing like that. He applied for retirement and it has come through." I took the envelope and laid it on the bedside table. "When he wakes and is ready to read it you might tell him. I am certain we can get him a berth on a mail aeroplane."

He looked relieved, "Thank you sir. The climate here and all the troubles. It isn't right sir. He has done his bit."

"Of course."

Having dead air crew as well as ground crew created a sombre atmosphere in the mess. There was little point in having a sort of false bonhomie. It was better to allow everyone to make adjustments. I had learned that in France. I had given Squadron Leader Harris the letter telling him of his promotion. "I don't like to leave you with the job unfinished, sir."

"Who is your Number Two?"

"Flight Lieutenant Waite sir."

"And?"

He smiled, "And he can run the squadron." He shook his head, "Why do we think that we are all indispensable. I shall miss you sir and I have learned a great deal from you."

"And I, you. I will let you tell him yourself. It may only be temporary but if I can swing a promotion for him then I will do so."

"Thanks sir."

I went with the Major to the office. There was no-one there. I took with me a bottle of whisky. Major Fox looked at the bottle, "Serious is it sir?"

"Let us just say that I wish to pick your brains and to ask you to do something which is somewhat risky." I opened the bottle and poured two large ones.

"Cheers!"

"Cheers. What I have in mind involves you and I going into Maivan to discover the headquarters of Count Fydorervich." Major Fox almost choked on his whisky. "Don't waste it and hear me out. We both speak the language and we don't need to get close. In fact, it would be better if we didn't. All we need is the rough location and then I can bring bombers in and destroy it."

"That would mean attacking Iran. The Shah won't be very happy."

"I am prepared for the consequences." I had thought this through. If it meant the end of my career so be it. That would mean the Fates had decided I was not cut out to be in the R.A.F. It would not stop me from flying commercially.

He nodded and sipped more of the amber liquid, "How would we get in and out?"

"Two Ninaks. We get dropped our side of the border. We slip over under cover of darkness and scout it out first thing."

"I am intrigued, how will you identify it?"

"Count Yuri Fydorervich is no hero; far from it. He will have huge guards protecting him and he will be living in comfort. That is why I have to go in. When we bomb it, we will have to be precise. Maivan is in Iran and that means one of the bombers has to be sure he knows where it is."

"In that case, I am game. When?"

"We both know that unrest will begin in the next day or so. When we have quashed whatever they have in store then we will go."

He raised his glass, "Here's to another madcap adventure. Life is never dull with you around, sir. But who will command the airfield when you are gone?"

"I laughed, "I am certain that Sergeant Major Davis will make a better stab at it than either the Group Captain or myself!"

"I think you might be right, sir."

Chapter 6

It had been some days since I had been in a Snipe. I made sure that the usual walk around I did was as thorough as possible. I was acutely aware that the Snipe was the only full squadron we had until the Bristols arrived. I had briefed my men and told them exactly what we would be doing. We would fly over Baghdad first. If there was any unrest then I intended to quash it. We would head north to Kirkuk, land and refuel before checking all of the roads which led to Kirkuk. The rains had not let up but the roads had not deteriorated enough to tempt the natives into full-fledged rebellion. I had been assured by everyone from the resident in Baghdad down that this would be the case.

Once I was satisfied I mounted my Snipe and we took off. The rains had put out the fires. Blackened pockets showed where they had been. We flew in a long line. As I had told them, we were playing follow my leader. Baghdad was much bigger than Kirkuk. The resident had used the army to hold key road junctions and buildings. It was a clever strategy. I knew where they were and we flew over them. The bazaar was quiet. I saw a couple of sentries wave at us as we overflew them. We headed for the Union Flag and the British headquarters. That too was quiet.

My last call would be on the post office and telephone exchange. As we came over there was no wave from the sentries. Instead I saw them firing. I banked to get a better view. I spied the rebels. They had four vehicles of various sizes and they were using them like armoured cars. The defenders had already shot their tyres out and riddled their radiators with bullets but they were being pushed. I banked and climbed. I held my hand up three times. My squadron knew that meant three Snipes would follow me. I came in low. This would involve precision bombing and the lower I was the more chance I had. Lieutenant Vardy was a good three hundred yards behind me. That way he would see the effect of my bullets and my bombs and be able to take the appropriate action.

I had four bombs under my wings but I only intended to use one. At sixty feet, I was still in danger of hitting the roofs of some of the buildings but I took that chance. I flew up the main street, above the Post Office. I did not use my machine guns. I needed precision. Bullets zipped into the air but I was travelling at almost a hundred miles an hour. I released one bomb and then pulled on the stick to begin to rise. The bomb exploded and sent a wall of flames into the air as the petrol tanks on the vehicles exploded. As I climbed I saw Vardy come in and add a second bomb. Even as I banked I knew that we had destroyed the attack. That was confirmed when the men at the Post Office waved. The job was not finished but there were more troops in Baghdad than Kirkuk. I was needed in Kirkuk.

I led my men north and we headed to Kirkuk. I knew that there might have been innocent people who could have been hurt or even killed when I had bombed the square. That was the price they paid for being in the wrong place at the wrong time.

The rains had emptied the road north. To the west I saw that the Tigris was already beginning to overflow its banks: Samarra. Tikrit, Al Fathah, all of them had British detachments but the floods would actually help them. They might be cut off but they would be armed and those around them, not. We were twenty miles south of Kirkuk and flying at two hundred feet when I spied the insurgents. They were riding to the east of the road and all of them had guns. There was no reason for them to be there. Twenty armed men constituted a threat to the security of the Tigris valley. I waved my arm and Signalled Lieutenant Ritchie to lead his flight in to attack them.

The rain meant that the horsemen had their bisht pulled tightly about their heads and the first that they knew of the danger was when Lieutenant Ritchie's bomb exploded amongst them. The survivors scattered and the rest of the lieutenant's flight used their Vickers machine guns to destroy them. When the survivors disappeared, we headed on to Kirkuk.

Each time we arrived I noticed a difference. This time they had more sandbagged positions for the machine guns. There was an air of defiance in the camp. I was greeted with smiles and with confidence. I hoped that the loss of Squadron Leader Harris would not adversely affect the base. "Refuel and rearm the ones that need refuelling."

I strode over to the office and Sergeant Major Hale. He was smoking his pipe and sipping tea, "How is it going, sir?"

"You are doing a marvellous job here, Sarn't Major. However, I feel that the next few days will test your defences."

He nodded, "How so, sir?"

"We think that the rebels will think the rain is a perfect opportunity for them to attack Kirkuk. Be prepared to be cut off. If you think that the Residence is going to be overrun then get on the radio and we will evacuate."

"You think it might come to that, sir?"

"Possibly. We will not abandon the airfield. If we close this then we will never get it back and we will lose Mosul and the Tigris Valley. I have a squadron of Bristols coming. Once they are here we will be much stronger. I will have the Ninaks, Vernons and the Snipes using this to refuel and re-arm."

He smiled, "You want the rebels to think that we have more aeroplanes than we actually do."

"I am counting on the fact that, to them, all of our aeroplanes look the same. They won't look at the squadron identifier. When they look into the air they will just see a Ninak or a Snipe. They will think we have more aeroplanes than we do. I have ordered the squadron leaders to bomb and shoot anything which moves. Now then, what do you need?"

He smiled, "We are fine sir. I have a good set of lads here and we have made this place stronger than the residency. We will be all right!"

When we took off I led the squadron east along the road. Here the road was not even close to a valley bottom but the road surface was compacted earth and rock. The rains made it a slick and treacherous surface on which to travel. We flew for almost forty-five minutes before I banked to starboard and headed south and west to return to Baghdad. There was a small British outpost at Sherwana. Guarding a crossing of the river there were just twenty men there. Each time we had come south we had passed over the outpost. The soldiers always waved. The rains had stopped but the skies were still overcast. The Sirwan river had burst its banks. The settlement was inundated. The detachment had taken over an old semi-derelict fort which had a higher position. Bereft of buildings they used tents. As we flew over I saw that the soldiers were waving. The waves were frantic. They needed help. Waggling my wings to show that I understood I had seen their plight I looked over the side of the aeroplane and examined the ground. The village was to the north of the hill fort while to the south lay fields. I led my flight home and I flew at maximum speed.

It was early afternoon when I landed. I had the mechanics refuel my Snipe and I looked to see what else remained on the field. My pilots and their birds needed rest. The Vernon pilots were fresh. There was one Vernon. It had had engine trouble that morning and had not left with the rest of the squadron. I hurried across the field towards the mechanics. "Can this bus fly?"

Sergeant Major Maguire was wiping grease from his hands, "Yes sir. It was a blocked fuel line. We have cleared it."

"Good, get her refuelled."

I ran to the officer's mess. The crew of the Vernon were sat talking to my recently returned pilots, "Jenkins, Dinsdale. Get your flying gear."

"But sir our Vernon is being repaired."

"It has been sorted. We are going north to Sherwana to pick up the detachment there. You won't need your air gunner."

"Right sir."

I went into the office, "Sergeant Major Davis, get on to Baghdad, tell them the detachment at Sherwana is in trouble. I am going to pull them out."

"Sir." He had been scribbling down the salient points. He looked up. "Sir, how will you land? With the rain, we have had it could be a little naughty."

"We will manage." The two pilots were waiting for me when I emerged. "This could be tricky. There is an area of farmland to the south of the hill fort. I will land first. You follow my line." I smiled, "Unless, of course, I manage to make a right mess of it and crash. If I do then you will have to choose a better site."

"Sir." They both looked very serious.

"Now there are twenty men in the detachment. I know that you are only supposed to be able to carry eleven. We take them all."

"Sir."

Checking that I had my Webley I climbed into the cockpit. I had my Lee Enfield and my German pistol in the cockpit. I waved to the Vernon. I had two grenades in the pockets of my flying coat, I had a feeling that I might need them!

As we headed north, the rains began again. It made the flight unpleasant. We had to fly lower than I would have liked to keep below cloud cover. In a perfect world, we would not have flown. The detachment would not have asked for help unless things had been desperate. They were a hundred miles from Baghdad. I could not begin to imagine how isolated that must have felt.

As I neared the village I saw that the ground sloped gently up to the village and the hill fort. The fields were cleared of crops. That was a mercy. I decided to land up hill and then turn. It would mean it would be easier for the laden Vernon to take off. I had to judge the landing finely. I wanted to stop as quickly as I could. I had flown the Snipe enough times to know its stall speed. I used that knowledge now. I flew at just above stall speed. That, and the slope enabled me to stop easily. The ground was rough but mercifully free of rocks and holes. I taxied up the hill and turned at a flat area. I clambered out and stuck two stones in front of the wheels. I took out my Lee Enfield and two spare magazines as I watched the Vernon come in. I had not seen either of the pilots land before. Squadron Leader Harris had told me that they were all good pilots. This would be a real test of their skills. I saw their wings rise and fall alarmingly. They had a harder task because their wings were bigger and they were landing cross wind. I breathed a sigh of relief when their wheels bumped and then settled to roll along the rough ground towards me.

They turned and I ran towards them. "Keep your engines going. One of you get on the machine gun and I will need one of you to help me start my engine when we leave."

"Right sir. I wasn't sure we could get this big brute to land and to stop."

"You did well. Hopefully the take-off will be as successful."

I began to run the half a mile to the hillfort. I could not see its walls, just the Union Flag hanging forlornly from the flag staff. It was as I neared the walls that I heard the firing. I cocked my rifle. It was then that I realised our approach had been hidden from the hill fort by a large rock. The two aircraft were in dead ground. The rebels had not seen us. I was following what must have been the trail from the village to the fields. As I turned a corner I saw two Arabs with rifles. They were twenty feet from me and were firing at the fort, whose walls were still hidden from view. Without even thinking I raised my gun and fired five shots in their direction. They fell and I ran past them, loading another magazine as I did so.

As I turned the corner I saw that there were forty or fifty insurgents and they were making a determined attempt to take the fort. The fire from the fort was sporadic. I suspected they were running short of ammunition. I now saw that the two men I had shot had been sniping at the walls. I could see the sun helmets of the defenders but they were keeping behind the old stone walls of the fort. The attackers had not noticed my approach. They were a hundred yards from the walls and I was fifty yards from them. I contemplated returning to my aeroplane, taking off and strafing the attackers. The problem with that solution was that I did not know how close to collapse the fort was. The other alternative was a mad one. I smiled to myself. I had been a cavalryman and charged into battle against the Germans. That day I had had good fortune. I prayed I would have it again.

I took out a grenade and pulled the pin. Holding my rifle in my left hand I ran as close as I could get to the insurgents. When I was thirty feet from them I pulled my arm back and threw the grenade. None were looking in my direction. I hurled myself to the ground as the grenade went off. I stood, even as the last fragments zipped through the air. I grabbed my rifle and yelling, "Charge!" I ran towards the rebels, firing from the hip. They must have thought that I was a relief column because they began to run back towards the village. Time was now of the essence.

As I neared the gates I shouted, "I am Wing Commander Harsker. Get out of there now and follow me!" I loaded my last magazine and turned to fire at the departing rebels. I did not hit any but my bullets encouraged them to run. They would soon realise I was just one man and seek vengeance.

Wings over Persia

The old gates opened and the khaki figures came out. I saw that four were wounded and were supported by their comrades. A sergeant had an officer slung over his shoulders, "Sergeant Jones sir, this is Lieutenant Murphy. What do we do about the dead, sir? We have five lads in there."

"I am sorry, sergeant. I gave them a scare but as soon as they realise I am not leading the 21st Lancers they will be all over us. What I can do is bomb it when we leave. They won't be able to despoil the bodies. Get your men down the slope I have an aeroplane waiting."

"Sir."

I slung my rifle and took out my German automatic and the grenade. The detachment began to make its way down the slope. A bullet pinged off the rock next to me. I fired two bullets to discourage them and then ran back to the shelter of the rock where I had killed the first two men. Emboldened the insurgents left the shelter of the rocks and hurtled after me. I emptied the magazine and then hurled the grenade as far as I could before running after the soldiers. The first ones had reached the Vernon.

"Pilot Officer Jenkins, stand by the Snipe. Sergeant, get someone on the Lewis gun and discourage the others."

The Vernon would be overloaded. The transport could carry fourteen and they would have to lift off with sixteen. I saw a corporal climb up to the Lewis and begin to fire. I clambered up into the cockpit of the Snipe and put the Lee Enfield down the side. Sopwiths always started well. The engine caught and Jenkins kicked the stones from the wheels. He ran to the Vernon. I needed to get into the air and cover them. I gunned the motor and I soared into the air. The Snipe is very agile and I used that agility to good effect. I rolled and turned, zooming toward the surprised rebels. I cocked and fired the right-hand Vickers. They hurled themselves to the ground. I banked and, as I passed over the gates to the fort, at sixty feet above the ground I dropped two bombs. I needed no bombsight. The huge rock sheltered me from the blast. Stones showered down. I looked in the mirror as I climbed over the rock. The gates had disappeared along with the bodies of the dead soldiers.

The Vernon was lumbering down the slope. I knew that the two pilots would be working together. It began to rise slowly and so I banked to fly back and discourage the rebels a little more. They had taken cover and fired at me. I saw bodies littering the ground. When I flew over the fort I saw no sign of the khaki bodies. I had entombed them in the stones from the gate. When we had quelled the revolt then they would have a decent burial. They deserved that. This was now a tiny piece of England, far from home.

I took another pass over the rebels emptying my right-hand Vickers. I did not see the results of my attack but I had achieved my purpose. I had kept their head down. I soon caught up with the labouring Vernon. As she burned off fuel it would get easier. Jenkins and Dinsdale kept it as low as they could in case they had to land in a hurry. I wished we had had a radio for I could have warned the field about the casualties. My radio was coming but the delay might have cost one of the detachment his life. The Vernon made the airfield and I waited until she had landed safely before attempting my own landing.

Someone had anticipated casualties. There was Doctor McClure and his medical staff on the runway. By the time I had landed they had been whisked away. Sergeant Jones and his men were waiting. They stood to attention. "Sir!"

"Thank you, sergeant. How is your officer?"

"Head wound sir, always dodgy. We would just like to say thank you sir. That was above and beyond." He smiled, "I didn't know pilots knew how to use a Lee Enfield or a Mills bomb sir."

I nodded, "I will let you into a secret sergeant. At the start of the Great War I was a trooper in the Lancashire Yeomanry."

His face beamed, "Now is makes sense sir. You are a proper soldier!"

I don't think he realised the implied insult and I nodded my thanks at the compliment. "You will be based here until we can get vehicles up to the fort again. I am afraid I made a mess of the gates but those lads of yours have a mausoleum now."

"Thank you for that, sir. It didn't sit well leaving them there to have their bodies messed about with. Johnny Turk is a nasty bugger. I was at Gallipoli sir and I know!"

"I will get Sergeant Major Davis to sort out some quarters for you." I pointed. "There is the Erks' mess and the sergeant's mess next to it. They will have the kettle on I'll be bound."

Wings over Persia

Ralph Fox was in the office with the other two squadron leaders and Sergeant Major Davis. They looked concerned. "Problem?"

Ralph nodded, "Our predictions were accurate. It looks like Kirkuk, Baghdad and Sulaimaniya have all risen in revolt. The resident has decided to abandon Sulaimaniya. He is heading for Kirkuk."

"What about the Sheikh?"

"Apparently he is saying it is the will of the people and he will not fight against his own people. Pontius Pilate springs to mind, sir,"

"It doesn't change what we need to do by much. I will get Squadron Leader Harris to bomb Mosul, Jack, you take Kirkuk and Henry, Sulaimaniya. I will use the Snipes to buzz around Baghdad. We can use the soldiers we ferried back from the fort to bolster our defences and send more supplies up in the morning with Dinsdale and Jenkins. We knew this was coming. At least they can't send reinforcements from Iran or Turkey. The difficulty lies in the low cloud cover. If Mosul or Sulaimaniya have low cloud then my plans are scuppered. Just do you best and if we can't bomb Mosul or Sulaimaniya then concentrate on making Kirkuk safe."

"Sir."

When the officers had left I said, "Sarn't Major, see if you can get some billets for the army lads. I think they have had a rough day or two."

"As have you sir. You need to take it easy. We can't afford to have you crack, sir."

I smiled, "You were in the Great War, Sergeant Major, we both know that this is nowhere near as hard as that."

"Aye sir but then we were younger, weren't we?" he shouted, "Billings, cup of tea for the Wing Commander! I'll just go and sort out those billets."

The tea had the right effect. After I had finished two mugs and signed the daily paperwork I went to the sickbay. Lieutenant Murphy was awake. He had an enormous bandage around his head. Doctor McClure was tending to his men. The Lieutenant said, "Sir, are you Wing Commander Harsker?"

"Yes Lieutenant. Glad to see you awake. You are in good hands here. Your men are all being looked after."

"I thought it was our last stand, sir. We lost the radio two days ago. We were down to ten rounds per man when your squadron flew over. The devils had been attacking for two days and night straight. When you came over they had just retired. I knew that they would attack again."

I nodded, "We couldn't see any enemy but I assumed you needed help. What happened to your radio?"

"Sabotaged sir. We had a couple of native types. We thought we could trust them. They killed Corporal Smith, the radio operator and destroyed the radio. If I get my hands on them…"

"We removed that threat from here, Lieutenant. I know that most of the natives are trustworthy but it only takes one. Better to be safe than sorry."

"The doctor says I will be out of action for a few days."

"Then you must heed his advice. Your men will be used to defend the airfield. The populace has decided to rise all over the country. I think that what happened at Sherwana will be repeated across Mesopotamia. They are using the muddy roads to take over key crossroads and river crossings. You just get well. There will be plenty for you to do when you recover."

As I headed back to my quarters Sergeant Major Davis met me. "All the birds will be ready to fly tomorrow sir. A couple of the Erks volunteered to be air gunners in the Ninaks until the replacements are here."

"And that will be…?"

Davis pointed to the rain filled clouds above our heads, "This lot means that it will be at least a week sir. The Bristols are at Heliopolis. They can fly from there to Ramelah and then here but they have to be assembled first. The rest of the men will be coming over land and the roads…"

"Then we just have to tough it out, Sergeant Major Davis. I appreciate everything that you are doing, you know."

He looked embarrassed at the praise, "We are all doing out bit sir. It's out duty, isn't it?"

Chapter 7

As we had a nightcap in the mess I wondered about the situation in Kirkuk. Mosul had smaller numbers of civilians. Kirkuk had many officers' and diplomats' wives. Only Baghdad had more. It was the town I worried about the most. It seemed more vulnerable, somehow.

I sat with my squadron pilots. "Tomorrow we divide into two. Each half will need to do the job of one whole squadron." I turned to Paul. "Flight Lieutenant Ritchie here will take his half to attack every insurgent within the city. Major Fox has intelligence that there are more rebels flocking to join the revolt from outside the city. I intend to stop their advance and to ensure that the Baghdad road remains open for our chaps who are heading here."

Pilot Officer Franklin asked, "Sir, what if we hit civilians?"

"You will be attacking those with guns who are trying to do harm to our people. If there are civilians close by then it begs the question, why are they there? If they are close to the men with guns then they are supporting them. This is not a war I would have chosen. I prefer a war with an enemy who wears a different colour uniform. Lieutenant Murphy had men killed by Persians they thought were friends. The League of Nations have given us a job to do and by God we will do it. When you have emptied your guns and dropped all your bombs, return here to refuel and rearm. We fly so long as there is daylight. Do not waste your bombs. If the Snipe in front of you has dealt with the threat then save your bombs for the next target. If Major Fox and Sergeant Major Davis receive word of another threat then we will deal with that. I do not expect much rest over the next few days."

I saw them take that all in.

"One more thing; on no account should you damage any of their churches. Even if they fire at us from them leave them alone. I doubt that they will use them in that way but we leave them alone. Clear?"

"Sir, yes, sir!"

That night, as I wrote a little more of my letter to Beattie I thought about my words to my pilots. I sympathised with them.

They were decent chaps and did not wish to hurt anyone. The Russian Count was deliberately using civilians and the sooner I ridded the world of him the better.

It rained all night but, by the time dawn came, there was a break in the clouds. Sergeant Major Davis told me that reports had been coming in all night of rioting, buildings being attacked and insurrection everywhere. We still had radio communication with the Residence. I had told them to put the Union Flag on every building we held. I intended to attack any armed men who were not in a marked building.

Thirty-five aeroplanes make a racket when they start their engines. We left before dawn although there was a lightening of the sky to the east. The Ninaks would not be back before evening. We would have the luxury of being able to refuel and rearm whenever we chose. As we zipped over the wire I saw that there were men who were approaching the wire. They were less than half a mile from it. I waggled my wings, cocked my left-hand Vickers and dived to attack them. My flight followed in line astern. I did not use bombs as it would give others cover close to our wire. Our machine guns would alert Major Fox and once we had fired I rose and banked to starboard so that I could swing over the road from the west. Looking in my mirror I saw that there were bodies and the rebels had gone to ground, expecting us to return for a second strafing run. I had to stop more rebels from reaching the city. We had to cut off the supply of fanatical young men who were willing to die so readily.

I saw that this part of the land appeared to be peaceful. There were shepherds with their flocks and people working in the muddy fields. However, as we headed east I saw bands of men. Some were in vehicles. That had the Count's fingerprints all over it. He knew that mobility was a key factor. There were also men riding horses and camels. The muddy ground slowed up the vehicles but not the horses.

We swept down in two lines of four. I dropped two bombs. Flight Lieutenant Ashcroft did the same. I heard machine guns from behind me and, as I climbed, I looked in my mirror and saw that this particular column had been broken up but they were being rallied. The last two aeroplanes in the two columns each dropped two bombs and that was the final nail in the coffin. The survivors fled. I was under no illusions, they would rally and return but it would not be that day.

    I led the flight towards the distant road. I did not want to fly all the way to Najaf. The threat lay around Baghdad. What I wanted to was to make certain that there were no more rebels heading to reinforce the attack. I spied a bus. It was heading slowly up the road. I wondered at the folly of civilians travelling through a war zone. What was so important that they had to risk death? When the rifles popped out of the side and they began to fire I realised that I had been drawn into a trap. From the ditches bisht covered warriors rose and also began to fire rifles both ancient and modern. I saw Flight Lieutenant Ashcroft's Snipe struck by many bullets. He began to smoke. He still had time to drop his last two bombs before banking to port to head back to the airfield.

    I had passed the ambush but my wingman for the day, Pilot Officer Adams, had time to drop his bombs. By the time the two flights had passed the bus it was a burning wreck surrounded by charred and broken bodies. Three Snipes had been hit and I waved them back to the airfield. I took the last three to complete our circuit of the city. I was down to two bombs. As far as I knew one other Snipe still had a full bomb load. We hunted the enemy. On our way back, we saw more insurgents but they were in ones and twos. We used our Vickers but we could not guarantee that we had destroyed them all. It was most unsatisfactory. I headed back to the field.

    I saw mechanics and riggers swarming around the four aeroplanes which had been damaged. I taxied close to the bowsers and climbed down. They would get to my bus in time. I looked up as I heard the sound of Bentley engines. My Snipes were returning. There were just four of them. Where was the fifth?

    When I entered the office Aircraftsman Billings handed me a cup of tea. "Thanks Billings. Just what the doctor ordered. What is the score, Sergeant Major?"

    "Not certain, sir." He picked up a piece of notepaper, "The Resident says that the rebels have made no further gains and they are holding on. We have still to hear from the Ninaks, sir." He smiled, "I think it is going well."

I shook my head as I sipped the hot tea, "I have four damaged Snipes and a fifth one missing. It is not going well, Sergeant Major."

"The Resident is happy, sir and Major Fox said that your first attack saved us, sir."

"I hope they are right."

"And the mail aeroplane has left Basra. The Group Captain will be heading home."

"Is he…?"

He shook his head, "I had McHale water his drinks sir. He is fine. When he gets back to Blighty he will sort himself out. He was a good bloke sir. It is just this job and this country!"

"Right, I'll get back to it then."

He nodded, "Cookie has some corned beef sandwiches, sir. Make sure you have a couple eh?"

I smiled, "Yes Mother!"

Flight Lieutenant Ritchie looked a little drawn. He sucked deeply on a cigarette. "I lost one, sir. Pilot Officer Cook was hit just as he began to dive for a bombing run. He hit a building and …there wasn't much left sir."

That told the whole story. It would have been a violent although mercifully quick end. Alive one moment he would have been dead almost instantly. "We are hurting them as much as they are hurting us. There is nothing on the roads. This afternoon I will bring my four aeroplanes to join your five. Where is it hottest?"

"The bazaar sir. They have made it their own fortress. They have machine guns on the buildings which have a flat roof and I think they have some larger calibre weapons. I believe that was what hit Cook, sir. He just went down."

I could tell he was on the edge, "Grab a sandwich and a cup of tea. We will leave in an hour. I don't think they will expect that."

I grabbed a sandwich from the tray proffered by the cook's assistant. I could still taste cordite and fuel but I needed to eat something. Aircraftman Waring was examining my bus. "Any problems Waring?"

Wings over Persia

He pointed to the holes in the wings from the bullets and the shrapnel, "These'll need work sir but I reckon you can get up this afternoon."

"Good man. What is the mood like?"

"Oh, we will beat these buggers, sir. They are fine when it comes to sneaking up in the dark but they can't stand up to a Lee Enfield with a bayonet at the end. We'll get through this, sir. Although why anyone wants to die for this godforsaken hole I have no idea!" He waved a hand, "The Sergeant Major thinks you can get nine aeroplanes up this afternoon sir but they will need some serious work tonight."

"Thanks Waring. You chaps are doing a sterling job."

I climbed, an hour later, into the cockpit. We had lost one of our number and that had saddened the squadron. However, it had also made them keen for revenge. I had instructed the squadron to head for the bazaar. We would clear it of insurgents. I might be reprimanded but I intended to bomb every inch of it. We would then move out and machine gun anyone with a gun. They would rue the day they had threatened us.

With nine aeroplanes, we flew in three lines of three. I had told my pilots exactly what to do. The first flight would drop their bombs on the east end of the bazaar. The second flight in the middle and the last flight on the west end of the bazaar. We would then sweep the place with our Vickers before splitting up to seek out any more pockets of resistance. The twelve twenty-five-pound bombs ripped through the buildings and the defenders at the east end of the bazaar. I heard the next twelve bombs as they took out the middle and the last ones must have hit explosives for the whole bazaar seemed to light up like a barrage before an offensive. I climbed and the squadron flew over the bazaar. It would need rebuilding. No one fired at us and I took that as a sign that we had done what we intended.

This time our flight across the city brought no bullets. Instead we were greeted by khaki waves. I kept the Snipes in the air for two hours. We flew low looking for insurgents. When we began to get low on fuel we returned to the field. I saw that the Ninaks had returned too. I allowed the other eight Snipes to land before me. I saw that there had been damage to the bomber but they were all intact. I would have just one letter to write to Cook's family. I couldn't remember if he was married. Ritchie would know.

Henry and Jack were waiting for me. "I see you didn't lose any. That is good news."

"It was a tough one though, sir. They seemed to be prepared for aeroplanes. They had guns set up to fire at us on the outskirts of both towns. It was a good job we had Kirkuk to use as a refuelling and rearming field. I think we have broken their backs."

"Yes, I think I agree with you. Just to be certain take all the buses you can tomorrow and fly over both towns again. I will get Harris to do the same over Mosul."

The inevitable tea was waiting for me as I entered. "How are things here?"

"Easier now sir. We had no attacks this afternoon and we repaired some of the damage. I had radioed Kirkuk sir and informed Squadron Leader Harris that the mail transport is due here tomorrow afternoon. He is flying down tonight."

I had forgotten that I was losing one of my squadron leaders. "Get in touch with all of the residencies, Sergeant Major and ask what they need."

"Sir."

I was in the mess when Arthur Harris entered. I signalled for the mess sergeant to bring him a drink. He sat next to me. "I am sorry to be leaving you like this, sir. The job is half finished."

"But you have done more than enough, Arthur. I am grateful for what you have done. They obviously need you to repeat in India what you have done here." He nodded. "Is Mosul quiet?"

"They were waiting for us but those new bomb sights we devised worked a treat. I have asked my number two to fly over the city tomorrow but I don't anticipate much opposition. The garrison commander said it was quieter."

He took the drink and raised his glass. I raised mine, "Bottoms up!"

He smacked his lips in appreciation. "I think if we had delayed in our response it might have been different but I think the prompt action we took worked."

Ralph Fox appeared, "May I join you, sirs?"

"Of course. Did we lose any men today?"

"No sir, we were lucky. Your Snipes machine gunned the assault force and that discouraged the rest. Those were their best men." He reached into his tunic and took out a piece of paper. He handed it to me. It was Russian. I looked up and he nodded. "We found at least three others as well as two with German papers. They were not Arabs. They were dressed in turbans and wearing a bisht but they were blonde Russians and Germans. That was how we knew they were their best men. They had good weapons and explosives. They had been sent to get to the airfield. Your mysterious Count has long tentacles!"

"His time will come, Ralph."

Arthur smiled as he finished his drink and waved the steward over, "I would like to be here to see him get his come uppance. From what you have told us, sir, he is a threat which needs to be removed."

"And we will."

The next day was almost an anti-climax. I led my eight airworthy Snipes and we crisscrossed Baghdad and the roads which led to it. The main activity we saw was the recovery and burial of bodies. The bazaar would need a complete rebuild. I was both relieved and pleased to see that we had not damaged any of their mosques. That might have tipped the balance and created more rebels than we had destroyed. It would have roused those who had not participated in the general unrest.

We were about to turn and head for home when I saw the Vimy heading towards the field. That would be the mail and Arthur's ride to India. It was still on the ground when my squadron landed. I had spoken to the pilots the last time they had brought mail. On that occasion, they had spent the night. The unrest meant that they would push on to Basra and spend the night there. I walked over to speak to Arthur before he left.

"Well good luck, Squadron Leader. It is a small service and I daresay that we will meet again at some point."

He shook my hand, "And I look forward to that posting too, sir. Good luck here."

I watched him take off and then headed for the office. Sergeant Major Davis said, "There is a whole sack load of mail here sir. Most of it is for you! I will get the tea organized."

I shook my head, "First I will have a shower and get the smell of aeroplane fuel out of my nose. Then I shall fill my pipe, have a cup of tea and then begin this most arduous of tasks. If you would sort out the paperwork into urgent and can wait, that would be appreciated."

Depressingly, when I returned, the pile of urgent paperwork was higher than the other. It was not all bad news. As well as the squadron of Bristols there was another squadron of Vernons on their way. In addition, we had been promised another squadron of Ninaks. They would be based at Mosul. Engineers were being sent from Egypt to build the new airfield there. Reading between the lines the situation in Egypt had now been resolved. Squadron Leader Jenkins would have a much easier time. A new squadron leader was coming to replace Arthur and there was an Air Vice Marshall who would run, not only the airfield but all air and land operations in Mesopotamia. We now had someone to coordinate the military and that was not before time.

I wondered how Sir John Salmond would view the loss of Sulaimaniya. I was not certain that we could have done anything to prevent its abandonment. What I did know was that it brought the Count closer to me. We would not have to cross into Iran. I was clutching at straws to find any good news. The paperwork took all afternoon to dissect and organize. At least Sir John would have his own staff who would be able to deal with those issues and I could get back to my wing.

The next day I had every available aeroplane patrolling the skies over Kirkuk, Mosul and Baghdad. I knew that there were places now under rebel control but the Tigris Valley and the capital were safe and I thought that most important of my priorities. At dusk the Bristols flew in with the news that their convoy was just a little way behind them. Squadron Leader Barnes was another veteran of the Great War. I had met him before. In those days he had been a headstrong young pilot who was determined to be an ace. It had been towards the end of the war.

"Damned funny country eh sir? I mean I thought it was all desert but the bally roads were like seas of mud."

"Rainy season. You will be heading north tomorrow. I will come with you. I am glad that we have a squadron based there now. We have just been using it to refuel and rearm."

"I was not certain if there was a working airfield. It was a bit sketchy in Heliopolis."

"The chaps did a fine job of building it under difficult circumstances. There is still work which needs to be done but your fellow can do that. At least you will have barracks, a mess and a wire. Believe me you will need all three."

"And we have a new big chief I hear?"

"Yes, an Air Vice Marshall, Sir John Salmond. Do you know him?"

"Heard of him. More of an organizer than a flier but then that is what we need eh? Old warhorses like you and I can do the flying. Let someone else count the paperclips."

Having done the job, I thought he was being a little disparaging. "I think there is more to it than that. Anyway, we have barracks for you. At the moment one of the squadrons is based up at Kirkuk but we need the Vernons back here. We have a second squadron arriving soon and in two or three months another squadron of Ninaks."

There was a lively atmosphere in the mess that evening. The deaths had been forgotten as new faces and news from home filled the mess with hope rather than despair. The rains had stopped and the brighter weather lifted the spirits of everyone.

With the arrival of the new commander imminent I had everyone sprucing the place up. Sergeant Major Davis set the men to repairing all the damage from the riots and the mechanics and riggers worked on the Snipes. I took off with the Bristols and led them north. The convoy, escorted by two armoured cars, followed up the road. There had been no sign of rebels for a couple of days and I deemed it safe. Landing at Kirkuk I saw the signs of the violence all around me. The airfield itself was without damage but there were shell holes between the field and the town. The town had been damaged.

Sergeant Major Hale and Sergeant Major Robson were pleased to see me and even more delighted that they would soon be relieved. While Squadron Leader Barnes settled in I sent half of the Vernons back to Baghdad. The rest would be used to take my men back once the new squadron had settled in. A car drove up as I was watching the Vernons take off. It was Lord Randolph Palmer and his sister.

I noticed that there were two armed soldiers with them. One looked incongruous as he held a parasol over Lady Isabel to keep her from the sun. "An unexpected pleasure your ladyship, my lord."

"I just wanted to thank you in person, Wing Commander. I am not certain if we could have held out without the aeroplanes you sent to help us. We might have suffered the same fate as Sulaimaniya."

Lady Isabel shook her head, "We both know that would not have happened, Randolph!"

I saw the resident shake his head, "My sister sets great store by our soldiers as do I but I recognise that they cannot fight huge numbers. That was why poor Reginald had to flee Sulaimaniya."

"Things will change. We have a new commander, Sir John Salmond. He is in charge of everything military. I have high hopes." A thought struck me. "What will happen to the men who fled Sulaimaniya?"

"The soldiers will be absorbed into our garrison and Sir Reginald and his staff will return to Baghdad. Why do you ask?"

"We may have to bomb and attack Sulaimaniya. It would be handy to talk to a soldier. We know it from the air. I would like to know what it is like from the ground." I realised that I was not telling the whole story but I did not want to alarm Lady Isabel. If I knew which was the finest house then it would cut down the places we had to search when Ralph and I sought the Count.

"Sir Reginald has a military aide, Captain Peterson. He will be returning to Baghdad. He would be the chap to see."

"The Vernons will be leaving Kirkuk in the next two days. If Sir Percy and his staff wish a shorter journey then I suggest they get here as soon as possible."

"He can be here this afternoon."

"Good. Well I have to get back to my squadron. We have to be spick and span for our new commander."

Lady Isabel shook her head, "That should not matter, Wing Commander. It is what you do in the air that is how you will be judged and, in your case, there is nothing at all to fault. Had my son survived the war then I would have hoped he would have turned out as well as you."

I noticed that there was a smell of fresh paint when I arrived back. Sergeant Major Davis smiled when I commented on it. "Senior officers like fresh paint sir. It shows that someone is making an effort. Besides it makes everything look a bit more military sir. The last we heard the Air Vice Marshall and the Vernons will be here some time tomorrow. "

I nodded, "Then we had better get the Group Captain's quarters ready for him." I gave the Sergeant Major a meaningful look. "We painted that first sir. The only thing that Sir John will smell will be paint. I have quarters ready for his staff too, sir. There are ten of them. It will take some of the work off my shoulders anyway. Billings is all right but he is not a proper clerk!"

"You have done well, Sergeant Major. Considering none of us expected to be doing what we did we have emerged relatively unscathed."

I had spoken with Captain Peterson before he had been whisked off to Baghdad with Sir Percy. He was most helpful. "Interesting what you say about this Count. I had heard whispers of White Russians supplying arms and advice but, from what you say, he is more of a puppet master. There were rumours of someone advising the Sheikh. The Sheikh kept making trips into the desert. He said it was to speak to his tribal chiefs. It might have been but it was to stir up trouble and, from what you say, get more instructions from his advisor."

"That is what I came to think in the Baltic."

"Sheikh Mahmud is a treacherous character. Why he was appointed governor I have no idea. I knew that he was supporting the rebels. No, it was more than that, he was actively encouraging them. We could never prove it, of course and he kept his hands clean. He purports to be an ally of His Majesty's Government but the reality is that he is seeking his own kingdom! He has the largest house in Sulaimaniya. It is the former Governor's residence. That is where he lived when he was Governor. Now this Russian chap. First of all, he was not in Sulaimaniya when I was there. We may have had to abandon the place but I knew the occupants of every house. There were neither Russians nor Germans there. They were too clever for that. Now this Russian will want to have his own house and it will need to be protected. There are four such places that I can think of." He had a map with him and he circled them. "I am afraid I can't be any more specific than that."

I was slightly disappointed but it had given me a starting point. "That helps us."

"Are you going to bomb all four then?"

I shook my head. I don't want to risk innocent civilians. My plan is to go in with Major Fox under cover and scout it out on the ground."

"Risky old boy."

"We both speak the language and if the Count is using Germans and Russians then odd-looking coves will be expected. Now is the perfect time to go. The Count will be filling the town with his men. They will expect strangers. I can speak a bit of German and Russian."

"You might pull it off then. Good luck."

After he had gone I pored over the maps with Ralph. I wanted to be able to present Sir John with a fool proof plan.

I began to relax that night as I enjoyed a few drinks with Henry and Jack. I could concentrate now on commanding three squadrons. The rest was the responsibility of Air Vice Marshall Salmond.

Wings over Persia

Chapter 8

Sir John was a quiet and unassuming man but he was as sharp as a tack. As soon as he arrived and before he had even seen his quarters he took me to the office used by the Group Captain. He had a muscular looking sergeant who guarded the door.

"I thought you and I ought to have a chat before I take over completely."

"Sir."

"First of all are you happy with me taking over? I mean did you want to continue as commander of the four squadrons here?"

I grinned, "No sir. I am a flier and I prefer the air to the office. No offence sir."

He laughed too, "A plain speaking man. I like that. I want to thank you for what you did for the Group Captain. Willoughby was an old friend and I was aware of his problems. Your discretion was appreciated. Now what is your assessment of the situation here. I want this to be between us two first. I need honesty. Mr Balfour at the Ministry holds you and your opinions in high regard."

I nodded and gave him what I had learned. I ended by telling him of my plan to land close to Sulaimaniya and discover the headquarters of the Count. "I think, sir, that if we take him out then this Sheikh Mahmud will not be as much of a problem."

"Damned risky. Is there no one else you could send?"

"Sorry sir, that's not my style. I don't ask subordinates to do something I wouldn't do."

"Well you have my guarded permission but I want to talk to you before you actually go."

"Of course, sir, and we have much to do anyway."

"Quite!"

"London still hopes that the Sheikh might be brought back into the fold. From what you say I think it is a pipe dream but until we get orders to the contrary from London then Sheikh Mahmud is an ally and not to be touched. Clear?"

"Clear sir."

The next few days were busy. We had no aggressive flights but with aeroplanes arriving and personnel returned it felt like we were in a war zone. The men from Heliopolis were sent back to Squadron Leader Jenkins. I do not know what we would have done without them. Sergeant Williams returned to be my unofficial bodyguard.

My squadron was sent, along with the Ninaks, to ensure that the road to Mosul was open for the lorries which carried the men who would be building the airfield there. I was impressed by Sir John and his staff. They were calmness personified. Our appearance over the Persian countryside made the enemy flee. We did not fire our guns in anger for over a week. That, in itself, was a cause for concern. What were the enemy planning?

The third Ninak squadron arrived. We now had seven squadrons based at Kirkuk and Baghdad. As soon as the airfield at Mosul was built we would have a triangle which would secure the heartland of Iraq. Those were good days. I led my three squadrons and we learned how to fly together. Sir John was an organizer and he knew that he could leave the day to day flights to me. I learned more about the land over which we flew. They were relatively peaceful patrols. We occasionally had to fire our guns and chase horsemen back into the wilderness but for most of those six weeks we had the beating of the Kurds and the rebels. Sir John's staff were good. They knew how to organize. Sergeant Major Davis could not believe how easy his life had become. The one thorn in our side was Sulaimaniya. Sheikh Mahmud and, presumably, the Count, were using their newly acquired stronghold to build up forces that would, in time, try to make the rest of Kurdistan rise. When he was spoken to on the radio he explained that the forces were for his defence and that he had no intention of using them against the British. It was, of course, a lie but as they wore no unfirms then any rebel who attacked us could be dismissed by the Sheikh as one of his enemies.

I was desperate to fly north and to find out where the Count had made his headquarters but I was needed to run the three squadrons. Sir John had Army advisers but I was the one who was best qualified for matters aeronautical.

The Vernons were used to supply the men building the new airfield at Mosul. We had lost Sulaimaniya. The military attaché in Mosul reported that the Kurds were emboldened by the loss of Sulaimaniya as were the Turks. The defences of the town were improved. Our two squadrons of Ninaks were used to patrol the area around Mosul. It meant long days for them. They had to refuel at Kirkuk. The Bristols at Kirkuk meant that we could be used around Baghdad.

The first action Sir John took, after he had secured Baghdad and arrested all those suspected of being rebels, was to retake Sherwana. Lieutenant Murphy had recovered. Captain Shawcross arrived from India with a company of men to augment the detachment. They would have to travel by lorry as there was no airfield close by. We had landed one Vernon but that had been an emergency. We had the Vimy air ambulance standing by in case it was needed.

The actual assault would be led by my Snipes. We left at dawn. The lorries left at the same time. They had one hundred and thirty miles to cover. It would take them three or four hours. We would make one attack and then return to refuel and rearm. That way we could directly support their attack. This would be our longest day.

I saw that the rebels had not repaired the main gate. Instead they were using one of the side gates. In England, we called them posterns. They had, however, fortified it. It bristled with guns. We flew over at a thousand feet above the fort. They popped their guns at us. They were wasting their bullets. I circled the town. It was not a large one. It seemed to me that they had put all of their defences into the fort. I waggled my wings and began to sweep down to make our bomb run and attack. I approached down the river valley from the north. We flew with three of us abreast. I was slightly ahead of my two wingmen. I had decided on this formation as it would split the enemy fire and also allow us to bring six Vickers to bear. I began to fire at five hundred yards. I used short bursts. I heard bullets hit the fabric of my wings. As I neared the north wall I released two bombs and then pulled up my nose.

As I climbed I saw that Pilot Officer Franklin had been hit. There was oil coming from his engine. I circled my hand and he nodded. He headed home and his place would be taken by Pilot Officer Ashcroft. As I banked and turned I saw that our bombs had had mixed fortunes. The wall had been breached but parts of the north wall remained. When Captain Shawcross and his men

Wings over Persia

attacked I wanted them to have an easy time. I attacked the west wall for our second attack.

The defenders now knew what to expect. It was a wall of metal which greeted us. I used my second Vickers. The walls of the fort were ancient. I saw my bullets gouge holes in it and throw the defenders from it. Then I released by last two bombs. This time I did not pull up but continued firing at the men who were on the east wall. They had no embrasures to protect them. Banking to head south I saw that there were breaches in the walls of the fort. We had not destroyed it but we had weakened it. I led my eleven aeroplanes south. We spied the column of lorries snaking up the Sirwan Valley. They waved as we passed. We caught up with Pilot Officer Franklin thirty miles from Baghdad. We slowed down to match his speed. He would not be flying that afternoon. In the event we only had nine aeroplanes. Two others had been damaged.

"Flight Lieutenant Ritchie, when we attack this afternoon I want you to take your flight to attack the east west walls. I will take the others to attack the north south walls. That way we will split their fire."

"Yes sir."

"Just try to avoid mid-air collisions. We are running out of Snipes."

Rearmed and refuelled we grabbed a corned beef sandwich and a cup of tea before heading north again. We flew more economically. We needed to coordinate our attack with the infantry. We caught up with them five miles from the hill fort. Sergeant Jones and Lieutenant Murphy would be at the forefront of the attack. They knew the place better than anyone.

We circled when the lorries stopped a mile from the fort. As they disembarked I prepared our Snipes for our attack. Flight Lieutenant Ritchie led his flight to the east to begin their bombing and strafing run. My five Snipes would attack with three of us in the fore and two behind. This time Ashcroft and Adams would choose undamaged sections of the fort for their bombs.

The defenders had been busy in our absence. They had repaired parts of the wall and removed their dead. They had also managed to reinforce the walls from somewhere. The Lewis guns, rifles and muskets popped away at us as we came in at a hundred feet above the ground. Travelling at over a hundred miles an hour I hoped we would be moving too fast for their guns to be accurate. However, it meant that we needed really quick reactions.

I had time for a five second burst before it was time to release my bombs. Out of the corner of my eye I saw the four Snipes of Ritchie's section. He had timed his attack to be a minute or two after ours. There would be no chance of a collision and the defenders would not know which way to face. Pulling my nose up I banked to the east. I was able to see the effect of Flight Lieutenant Ritchie's attack. Their Vickers and the first four bombs demolished the wall. They then released their next bombs in the centre of the compound. The shrapnel scythed through tribesmen.

I continued my bank and brought all of the Snipes to assemble behind the infantry. They were advancing up the hill and were less than four hundred yards from the walls. I used my aeroplanes like mobile machine gun positions. We opened fire and kept down the heads of the defenders. I did not want to risk bombing our own men and I released my bombs as Flight Lieutenant Ritchie had done in the centre of the fort. As I climbed I saw that we had broken the defenders. They were streaming out of the fort and heading for the town. We followed them and machine gunned as many as we could. If they had escaped they would have fought us again. These men enjoyed war. They were fanatics.

By the time we returned I saw that the green flag had been lowered and the Union Flag now fluttered from the flagpole. The soldiers had their sun helmets in the air and they were waving them. They had retaken the fort without losing a single man. It had been a good day. I led my weary pilots south to the airfield.

Although we were tired I needed to debrief the squadron. We had learned valuable lessons in the attack. "You used your head, Flight Lieutenant Ritchie, we will use that technique in the future. The first bombs on the walls and the second in the centre is an effective use of bombs."

"Will we have to do this again sir?"

"I think so, Pilot Officer Franklin. When we were in Somaliland we found that they like to use these ancient forts. They were built there for a purpose. The one we attacked today might have been there since the time of Alexander the Great."

"They are not much use against aeroplanes though, sir."

"They will learn that in time. Now get some rest. Tomorrow we will make sure that our aeroplanes are air worthy and our next patrol will be the day after."

After I had showered I went to the office. It was more crowded these days. Sergeant Major Davis and Billings had been joined by four clerks and sergeants from Sir John's staff.

As Billings handed me my tea Sergeant Major Davis said, "Sir John is in Baghdad, sir. He is meeting with the resident and the commander of the garrison. He has asked for a battalion of Sikhs to be based here at the airfield."

I sipped the tea, "Interesting. Does he think we might be attacked?"

One of the sergeants from Sir John's staff said, "No sir. He likes the idea of a mobile strike force. He said that if we had had one then we could have reinforced Sulaimaniya by sending men there in the Vernons."

I could see that Sir John had a clever mind. I began to see that there was a chance we might regain some of the land we had lost.

Sergeant Major Davis said, "The new squadron of DH 9As are due here tomorrow sir."

I nodded. That meant we would have one of our two squadrons of bombers returned to us. That was good news.

Jack's Ninaks returned just before dark. "Where are Henry's Ninaks?"

"They landed at Kirkuk. We would have stayed there too but with the Bristols and Vernons it is a little crowded."

"What is it like up there?"

"They are all worried about Johnny Turk, sir. One of the Vernon pilots said he saw a build-up of troops on the border."

"You think they might invade?"

"There is a chance sir. They have armour too."

"Luckily they have no aeroplanes to speak of. I wonder if Sir John has this information."

Jack nodded, "Yes sir, he does. They sent a radio message when the Vernons landed."

Perhaps that explained the imminent arrival of the Sikhs.

Squadron Leader Williams would be landing at noon the next day. They would only be staying one night and then heading for Mosul. The airfield was not yet completed but the Ninaks could land there. Jack and I told the squadron leader all that we knew of the problems he might face. Jack summed it up succinctly, "Although you might be facing regular troops that is an advantage. You don't worry about civilians. The ones we have been fighting are quite happy to hide amongst families. At least you can shoot and bomb anything in a uniform."

"However, Squadron Leader, they will have heavier calibre guns than the tribesmen."

"Sounds like a bit of a rum do then sir."

He was north country, like me. I smiled, "As you say, Squadron Leader, a rum do."

After they had left, the next day, I sought out Major Fox. I took Jack with me. Until Henry returned and the Vernons we had plenty of space in the offices. We found an empty room and I put Sergeant Williams on the door.

"So, Jack, we need two Ninaks to take us as close as we can get to Sulaimaniya. We need to find a landing site and you need to keep the two buses under cover until we return."

He had his pipe going. Like me he used it to help him think. "It would be best if we landed as close to dusk as we could. We will need light to land but we don't want inquisitive natives poking around. How far away from the town?"

I looked at Ralph, "Four or five miles?" He nodded. "That will give us an hour to get there and a couple of hours to recce the place. Then an hour or so to return. It will mean we can take off at dawn."

Jack looked at the map and jabbed his finger at a spot to the west of the town. "There is a little valley here. It would be an easier and safer route into the town."

"Good. That makes sense."

"Sir, when you have found this Count's headquarters you intend to take a squadron up there to bomb it?"

"Yes, why?"

"Well sir, it seems to me that you are missing a trick here. We can carry seven hundred pounds of bombs. You don't need a squadron. A squadron will send them looking for cover. We will have two Ninaks there why not bomb them there and then? We are talking precision bombing anyway. If we send a squadron they will see them and hear them from a long way off. This way we can approach from Iran. They will not expect it to be the R.A.F."

I looked at Ralph. He shrugged, "Bombing is your bailiwick sir but it makes sense to me. It means we can attack early. They might even be in bed and the streets will be less crowded. It might be the best shot we have."

"Good. I will clear it with Sir John. When Henry returns along with the Vernons then we will do it."

Major Fox said, "And if I might suggest sir? Don't shave. They have a berry here which darkens the skin. I will get some."

Sir John was spending more time in the city than the airfield and seeing him was easier said than done. In fact, Squadron Leader Woollett as well as the two squadrons of Vernons had returned before I had the opportunity to speak with him.

"Sir, if I might have a word?"

"Of course. Come to my office. By the way that was a damned fine show at Sherwana. The Army were impressed that they didn't lose anyone."

"Thank you, sir. We did suffer some damage but we lost no one. We can repair our kites but men are in short supply."

He smiled and pointed to my face, "So, I take it from the fact that you have ceased shaving that you are seeking permission to go after this Russian?"

"Yes sir. If the reports from Mosul are correct then the Turks and the Kurds will take the offensive. That would strike me as the perfect opportunity for those in Sulaimaniya to advance on Kirkuk. This Sheikh is playing a clever game. He gets others to do his dirty work and we do nothing about him!"

"Classic tactics. I can see how a Russian might come up with such a strategy. Are you certain there is not someone else who could go? I would hate to lose you, Wing Commander."

"I have no intention of being captured sir. We will be going in at night and using the dark and shadows to hide us. We have decided to find the house and bomb it on the same raid. That way we ensure that we get him."

"That makes sense but don't take out the Sheikh."

"But sir, he is treacherous."

He sighed, "I know that but the politicians and diplomats think we can use him." He shrugged, "We just obey orders, Bill."

"And men will die because of this, sir."

"I know, Wing Commander, I know."

Jack asked for volunteers. Every pilot asked to come. In the end, he chose Flight Lieutenant Parr. He was a veteran and the best bomber in the squadron. We left the next morning and flew to Kirkuk where we refuelled. It felt different. There was no Hale, Williams or Robson there. Squadron Leader Barnes had made it his own. Sergeant Major Hill was, however, a career soldier and I felt confident that it would be a well-run station.

We ate and then spent the early part of the afternoon resting before the short hop to Sulaimaniya. The land to the north was empty and we intended to use that approach to arrive, hopefully, unseen. The only people we saw were shepherds. I was not even certain that they had seen an aeroplane before. We saw the shadow that was Sulaimaniya in the distance as the sun began to dip in the west. Jack was in charge. We had no time to circle. He would have to rely on his skills and those of Parr. He dropped low and found a flat piece of ground. I was facing the north as we landed. The light was so bad that I wondered how they managed it. It was a bumpy landing but we were down in one piece. The two Ninaks then taxied closer to Sulaimaniya. It was not so much to save our legs getting there but we had no idea how hot our escape might be. The closer to Sulaimaniya the better. I saw that Jack had found a fairly good landing site. There had been small rocks but nothing to damage the undercarriage.

When the engines stopped it was an eerie silence which descended. I climbed out and dropped my flying helmet into the cockpit. We were not wearing uniform. Ralph had managed to acquire the local sandals, baggy trousers and turbans. With the bisht to cover us from head to toe we would, hopefully, blend in. I had my German pistol. I still had plenty of ammunition. Lastly, we both had a wicked looking dagger. The Kurds of this region all carried such a weapon. Mine was one of a pair I had acquired in the Baltic. I remembered the dapper Mr Rees giving them to me. That had been a lifetime ago.

"Right, Jack. We should be back before dawn."

"You take care sir. We will turn the kites around so that we can have a speedy departure."

I followed Ralph and he led me down towards the gulley which would as it descended, become a verdant valley. I wanted us to get in unseen. If we had to get out fast then we would use the road. We could smell Sulaimaniya. It was the smell of animal dung and animals. It was the sweet smell of spices and charcoal. Then we began to hear the noises of the town. Once again it was animals, the squeals of children and the murmur of conversation. What was absent was the sound of motors and engines. This was a community which still used horses, donkeys and camels. In the distance, we heard the sound of the mullahs calling the people to prayer. This was a good time to be arriving in the town. The men would be heading to the mosques. It took some time to negotiate the rocky path in the dark.

The walls of buildings soon loomed above us. Ralph waved a hand and we moved up the rocky slope. We took shelter behind a mud wall. We would use hand signals. Having spoken to Captain Peterson we knew which were the most likely buildings. One was close to where we would emerge in the town. If the gods were with us then that would be where we would find the Count. If not, we would have to continue through the town to search the other three sites.

We moved down the wall keeping below the top. We could hear conversations and the sound of food being cooked over open fires. Ralph's hand came up and I stopped. He ducked his head around the side and then waved me forward. I saw that we had come to a path which led from the town to the valley. During the day, it would be busy but not in the dark and after sunset. We kept our hoods up and our eyes on the ground. We walked slowly rather than urgently. We wished to blend in.

We kept to the side. The only light came from open doors and there were mercifully few of those. An open door invited flies. As we neared the main road there was the buzz of conversation. It was men who had just returned from the prayers.

The streets were beginning to become crowded. Knots of men stood on corners talking and smoking. The first large house was to the right along the main thoroughfare. As we neared it Ralph took out a cigarette and lit it. He had taken the packet from a dead Kurd during the attacks on Baghdad. They were the type the natives used. It allowed us to stop and put our heads together. I glanced over his shoulder. The house was guarded. That, in itself, made me wonder if this was the Count's place.

We continued along the road and passed the entrance. As we did so the door opened and I saw a large, well-dressed Kurd. He spoke to the men who were guarding the entrance. Although he spoke quickly I picked up enough of what he said to realise that he was a carpet merchant. That explained the fine house and the guards. Ralph had heard too and we crossed the road to make our way to the next house. We would have to pass the residence of Sheikh Mahmud. Even had we not been told where it was we would have known for the place was ringed with armed men. We steered clear of the actual building as the men guarding were viewing all who passed with suspicion.

We turned from the main thoroughfare and headed down a narrow street. During the day, it looked to be where they had a small market. I spied the detritus of business. There were people on the streets. They took little notice of us and must have assumed that we, too, were on our way home after prayers. At the bottom of the street was a garden with lemon trees. It was the next fine house. There were no guards. We walked around the wall and saw no evidence of guards but we heard the sound of children's laughter. This was not the Count's residence.

The last two possible targets were close together and lay in a quieter part of town. That brought with it added danger. If there were fewer people then we would be more likely to be noticed. We moved through streets which did not have large numbers of people in them. We stood out. The path Major Fox led us had many turns and corners. We were not taking a direct route. He twisted and turned and stopped frequently. He was checking to see if we were being followed.

We had not even reached the house but I knew it was the one. I heard Russian. I spoke enough to understand the words. The Count's name was mentioned. I had found my old enemy. The house had a high wall. It would make it secure from prying eyes. We stopped beneath an ancient and overgrown olive tree whose gnarled branches twisted over the wall. During the day, it must have given shelter from the sun Now that we had identified the house we needed to see what lay around it. That meant crossing the road and walking past the entrance. It was a risk but we had to reconnoitre properly. There were four guards at the door and all had at least two guns. Two of them looked like Russians. There was one native and then, lurking in the corner, another. I risked glancing across as we passed the gates. They were open and there was a large American car there. I averted my gaze. The vehicle would help us to identify it from the air as easily as anything else.

Ralph headed back across the town. With luck, we would be able to reach the bombers well before dawn. Perhaps we moved faster than we intended but whatever the reason we were followed. Ralph kept to his tortuous route and it became obvious that there was someone behind us. They were wearing boots and we heard them on the stones close by the bazaar. If we turned then they would know that they had been spotted. We had to keep on the road. One advantage of a bisht was that you could slip your hand inside and have a weapon ready. I grabbed the handle of the dagger.

If this had been in the air then I might have had a better idea of what to do but we were in the streets of an enemy held town surrounded by men who would slit our throats if they discovered our identity. Ralph Fox was a thinker and he knew what to do. We had passed the bazaar and we approaching the residence of Sheikh Mahmud. If we were trapped there then the game would be up. Ralph hissed, in Arabic, "Right!"

He dived into an alley way and I followed. He ran down the alley. I heard the boots of the men behind. Their suspicions had been confirmed. One shouted, "Halt!" It was in Russian.

Ralph took a sharp turn to the left and I almost missed it but I managed to make the turn. Ralph had stopped and he had his knife out. I turned and took mine out too. The two men, I knew there were two from the footsteps, suddenly rounded the corner. I grabbed the beard of the one on the left and rammed my dagger up towards his middle. His left hand came down to stop the blade was it was too late. The dagger sliced through his palm and tore into his guts. I jerked it to the side and felt hot blood and entrails slither over my hand. I put my left hand over his mouth and held the dagger there. The scream died in his throat and I lowered him to the ground.

Ralph was in trouble. His man had managed to pull his own knife. I saw that Ralph was bleeding and the Russian was forcing his dagger towards Ralph's eye. I grabbed the man's hair and pulling back his head sliced through his neck. Ralph was showered in blood. I laid the body down. I saw that Ralph's left arm was bleeding. I tore a piece of material from the body of one of the Russians and tied a tourniquet around his upper arm.

Ralph nodded, "Thanks. We have to hide the bodies."

I looked around the alley. I could smell animals. I wandered down to where the smell seemed to be the strongest. I found a small gate and I opened it. There were four donkeys in a tiny stable. There was hay all around them. I went back to Ralph. "Found somewhere."

He tried to rise, "I'll help."

I shook my head, "No you won't. I need you to get me out of here. I will hide them." I picked up the bigger body and draped it across my shoulders. I lumbered back to the gate and went into the stable. The animals moved, obligingly, out of the way. I dropped the first body and then cleared a space at the back. I pushed the body there. I reached into the man's jacket and took out the wallet and the papers. I needed to delay discovery. I went back and lifted the second body. I was tiring and it took longer. I laid the body on top of the first one and removed his papers and wallet. Then I put hay on top of them. The donkeys did not seem concerned about the smell of blood. I closed the gate and went back to Ralph.

I helped him to his feet, "Lean on me. You direct me. I am disorientated."

"Back out and up to the bazaar. When we get there take the first road to the right and then the first road to the left. It will bring us to the main road. It is late. We will have to risk it."

As I helped him back up the alley I realised that since we had been followed we had seen fewer people. Most would be in their beds. We were not out of the woods yet. Ralph was wounded and could not move quickly. It had taken over an hour for us to make our way into the town. It would be a longer journey out. Each time we heard a noise we hid in doorways and behind walls. We looked suspicious. We had to avoid being seen. When we reached the road, I thought our troubles were over. They were not. There was a sandbagged position next to the last house. We could not get out that way. Ralph nodded to my left and I went down a twisting track which wound between houses. It headed downhill. I guessed it would bring us to the valley we had used to reach the town.

When we reached the rough ground, I did not slow up but headed along a trail which looked like it headed towards the aeroplanes. Major Fox was now leaning heavily on me and I was almost carrying him. It made our progress incredibly slow. After a hundred yards or so I stopped. I had to release some of the pressure on the tourniquet. After I had done so and blood came from the wound I reapplied the tourniquet and listed to his chest. His breathing was laboured. I opened his bisht and saw that he also had a cut in his side. That was still bleeding. I took his turban from his head and improvised it into a bandage. I tied it tightly around his waist. His breathing had improved slightly but I had to get him to the aeroplanes. He needed a field dressing.

I was aware that it was taking us far too long to make the progress I wanted. There was little choice. I could not leave him. I took the decision to put him over my shoulders. He groaned as I lifted him. The going was easier. Once I had cleared the town I began to look for the aeroplanes. It would not be long until dawn. Already the sky to the east was beginning to become greyer. I spied the aeroplanes ahead. I was less than a thousand yards from them. The valley dropped a little and I lost sight of them briefly but I felt hopeful that we would reach them and that helped me to soldier on.

It was as I was struggling up the short slope some sixty yards from the aeroplanes that I heard the sound of gunfire. It was ahead of me! I laid down Ralph and drew my German pistol. As I rose and ran towards the aeroplanes I took in that there were four tribesmen. Another two lay on the ground and I saw Parr on the ground beneath the wing of his Ninak. Jack had his Webley out and was firing at the four men. I was behind them. I had an automatic and I wanted to be as close as possible to them before I opened fire. I fired when I was twenty feet from them. I fired two bullets at each man. The last one turned around and my bullets hit him in the chest. One of those I had hit first had not been incapacitated and he raised his head. Jack shot him.

"See to Parr! I'll get the major!" I ran back to where I had left Ralph. Someone in the town had to have heard the gunfire. Would they investigate?

Ralph opened his eyes, "You should have left me sir!"

"Come on Ralph, Parr has been hit."

When we reached the Ninaks, Jack was applying a dressing to Parr's shoulder. "He can't fly, sir."

"Put him in the gunner's seat and strap him in. Give me a couple of field dressings." He threw me the first aid kit and began to help Parr towards the Ninak. In the distance, I could hear noises in Sulaimaniya. Time was running out. I quickly applied the dressings. "Sorry Ralph this is the best I can do."

"It's fine sir."

Jack arrived, "Well?"

"We found the house. You follow me in. I will drop my bombs to mark it. There should be a big American car parked outside. Let's get Ralph in the Ninak." I could now hear the hooves of horses. They were still some way away. We had time but not much. Once Ralph was in the gunner's seat I spun Jack's propeller for him. With his engine going he came to my bus and spun my propeller.

Parr said, "Sir, horsemen!"

"We will be in the air in two ticks, lieutenant."

I followed Jack who was moving along the ground. There was the hint of dawn behind us but we had little choice in the matter. I heard the Lewis gun behind me open fire. Parr said, "I can fire one handed. I am not certain I hit anything but they changed direction. I must have discouraged them."

I saw Jack's Ninak begin to climb and I followed. I banked to the north. We would keep to our plan of attacking from that direction. I turned inside Jack. The horsemen began to fire at us from the ground. Their bullets were wasted. More importantly they were four miles from Sulaimaniya. We would reach there first. It took time to loop around and approach the town from the right direction. I knew that it was on the opposite side of town from the palace. I could see that clearly for the first rays of the sun shone on its roof and the flagpole. It was the size of the house and the high wall which guided me in. The rifles which fired at me confirmed it. I came in just one hundred feet in the air. Looking in my mirror I saw that Jack had hung back so that he could spot my fall of shot. I released the bombs just one hundred feet from the wall. As I zoomed over I saw the American car. Then I pulled back on the stick to climb and banked.

Parr opened fire again as we turned. The Scarff ring meant he could fire over the side of the fuselage. As I turned I was in a perfect position to see Jack's approach. From the damage, I could see there would be no survivors but Jack's bombs would make certain. His last bomb must have hit the car for it erupted like a Roman candle when the petrol tank ignited. I spiralled up into the air and headed south. We had two airmen who needed medical help.

I talked to Parr all the way back. I wanted him awake. I made sure that he answered all of my questions. I found out that he had a girl at home and he would be marrying her on his next leave. I learned that his older brother had died at the Somme and his mother had died of a broken heart. When I saw Kirkuk in the distance I could feel pleased that a mission which had almost ended disastrously had ended well. We had survived.

Chapter 9

They now had a doctor at Kirkuk airfield and a sick bay. That would save lives. The exchange of gunfire at the take-off area and the ground fire had put a few holes in the aeroplanes. The riggers and mechanics began to work on them. Squadron Leader Barnes insisted that we stay. "Besides I can take the squadron for a look see over Sulaimaniya. I will take some photographs. We might as well assess the results properly, what?"

He was right. With the men in the gunner's cockpit both injured we had no other way of knowing if we had destroyed the nest. I sat with Jack and enjoyed a cup of tea and a bacon sandwich. Jack explained what had happened. "The poor Flight Lieutenant had just been to the relieve himself when those chaps appeared. They must have been watching us for a while and working out how many of us there were. Damian was shot without even drawing his weapon. I had to use the engine of the Ninak for cover. If you hadn't appeared then I think it would have ended badly for us."

I washed the sandwich down with the hot sweet tea. "Just bad luck. The only alternative would have been to send three bombers. Parr did a fine job with the Lewis gun. He should get a medal. I will put him in for one."

Jack leaned back and lit his pipe, "Medals? I think you should have one sir. Major Fox would be dead but for you."

I took out my own pipe and scraped the bowl clean, "Medals? I have enough. This little jaunt was my madcap idea and I risked all of your lives."

"I must confess, sir, that you did seem a little driven about this Russian fellow. Not like you at all."

"He was an evil man. There was a young idealistic Russian called Vladimir who believed in him. He died as a result of the count's machinations. There were others who died because of him. Make no mistake, Jack, he was a clever man. Sheikh Mahmud is being used. He sees himself as King of Kurdistan. Count Yuri Fydorervich saw himself as Emperor. I will lose no sleep over that Russian but I will remember the others who died because of him."

Wings over Persia

Flight Sergeant Dixon came over to us, "Sirs? Squadron Leader Barnes has had a couple of beds made up for you."

I didn't really need to go to bed but as I couldn't fly back immediately I took up the offer. My dreams were filled with a night in the Baltic and Mr Rees with his sword stick. There were flashing knives and blood. I woke in a sweat. I looked at my watch. It was noon. As I sat on the bed I saw the dagger. Perhaps I would keep that close to hand from now on. I showered and put on the battledress and trousers Flight Sergeant Dixon had laid out for me. I saw that the bisht and the other cloaks were stained with blood. The room had the stale smell of death about it. When I had dressed I realised that I only had the sandals to wear. It looked incongruous!

I went to the mess. The sergeant steward cocked an inquisitive eye at me. With the squadron still flying I was the only officer. "Can I get you a drink sir?"

"A cuppa would be nice."

"Coming right up sir."

I was on my second cup when I heard the Rolls Royce engines as the Bristols returned. I finished the tea and headed out into the sun. Squadron Leader Barnes saw me and walked towards me. "Well you did a pretty good job, sir. We saw the hole where the house had been. The trees and the wall helped to contain the blast. The buildings around it looked to be largely undamaged. There was a huge crater by the front. I am guessing that was where the car exploded?"

"I think so."

"I have my gunner developing the photographs for you to take back but this Count Yuri Fydorervich and his fellows couldn't have survived the blast. There was nothing there. I must confess you appear to have upset the old natives, sir. They were popping their guns off for all that they were worth. It is a pity we were told to lay of Sheikh Mahmud. He was talking to his men in the main square. He looked like he was working them up into a frenzy. We could have dropped half a dozen bombs and just walked into Sulaimaniya. Politicians eh?"

"They certainly make life harder for us and that is no mistake."

He looked at my apparel and shook his head. That Flight Sergeant! I told him to sort some togs out for you! Sorry about this sir."

I shook my head, "It doesn't matter."

"It does sir. Lord Palmer invited you and Squadron Leader Thomson to dinner tonight."

"How did he know that I would be here?"

"Oh, I mentioned it to him yesterday when I was in Kirkuk. We had supplies to deliver and I was at school with his Military Attaché, Captain Pendenning. I called in for a chat and your name came up. What size shoes, sir?"

"Er a nine."

"I will get some decent gear sent over."

I told Jack the news and we went to the sickbay. Both patients were sitting up. Ralph Fox still looked weak. He opened his eyes, "I am told, sir, that I owe you my life."

I shook my head, "Just gave you a bit of a hand."

He gave me a wan smile. "There is more to you than meets the eye sir. I thought I could handle myself but you managed to kill two Russians and all I could do was get myself cut up."

"It is in the past. If it hadn't been for you we wouldn't have found them. All's well that ends well." I suddenly remembered the wallets and papers I had taken. "When you are well enough I have the papers from the Russians. It might tell us more about them." He nodded, "And you Flight Lieutenant Parr, thank you for helping us to escape. If you hadn't fired the Lewis gun it might have gone badly for us."

"Aye sir well if I hadn't had to take a pee…" He shook his head. "I always had a weak bladder! Nearly cost me my life!" I had to laugh for he looked outraged that his bladder had nearly jeopardised the mission.

Squadron Leader Barnes was as good as his word. We had decent tunics and trousers as well as highly polished shoes. They were delivered by a red-faced Flight Sergeant Dixon. He had obviously been chewed out by the Squadron Leader. I had a shave and felt much cleaner. The beards had obviously helped us. I would have a haircut back in Baghdad. We were driven into Kirkuk in a lorry. We saw that the damage from the riots and unrest had all been repaired. Compared with Sulaimaniya,

Wings over Persia

Kirkuk looked almost prosperous. The residency, however, looked like a fortress. There were two sandbagged machine gun emplacements at the entrance. Barbed wire flanked them and I saw, on the roof, two riflemen. The sergeant in charge had the men stand to attention as we entered.

Lord Palmer himself appeared in the entrance. He was wearing a white dinner jacket and sporting a black tie. "Wing Commander, Squadron Leader, how good of you to accept my invitation." He waved an apologetic arm around, "Sorry about the wire and the guns but it was a little wild during the unrest. We now have a contingency plan. If it happens again then all the British will be brought here for their own safety."

The inside of the building was cool. I had been told that one of the local lords had had it built when the Turks ruled. He had done a good job. The marble hall made the rest of the residency comfortably cool.

"I have invited a few of the businessmen to dine with us tonight. When they heard you would be here they wished to come and show their appreciation. It is no secret that it was your aeroplanes which prevented the unrest from becoming a full-scale rebellion."

He opened the dining room and I saw, to my dismay, that there were twenty other guests. The dining room was full. Even worse they all applauded as we entered. I found myself blushing. I saw a wry smile on the face of Lady Isabel. Jack seemed bemused by it all. Jack was seated next to Lord Palmer and I was between the Resident and his sister. She said, quietly, as I sat, "I have never seen a man so discomfited by a compliment. You are a very modest man, Wing Commander."

"I was just doing my job, your ladyship."

"In the Great War I would that we had had men of your calibre making the decisions. Many more lives might have been saved."

Lord Palmer said, "And now I understand you have destroyed one of the men behind the attacks?"

"Hopefully yes but Count Yuri Fydorervich is a very slippery customer."

His lordship said, "I met him during the Great War." He nodded, "I agree with you. He was an incredibly unpleasant and venal man. And you say he was behind the attacks?"

"We believe so. I have some papers we took from some of his men. Perhaps that will confirm it."

"I hope so. You have done a great service to us and I am grateful."

"What I fail to understand, your lordship is why we weren't allowed to bomb Sheikh Mahmud's headquarters too. Why is he protected?"

"Do not think conspiracy, Wing Commander, it is just that he represents the only chance we have for stability. Our mandate is to make this land secure. The Cairo conference appointed King Abdullah as king but, in case you didn't know, he declined to take the crown. He prefers life in Saudi Arabia. There are moves to make his brother, Faisal, king. Sheikh Mahmud is the one who could bring the Kurds and the Shia on side. They are the ones opposed to a king. Regard Sheikh Mahmud as a rather headstrong man. He will be brought under our wing once more."

"So, we sup with the devil?"

Lady Isabel put her hand on mine, "Your world is a simpler one than the world of the diplomat, Wing Commander. Now, let us put this Sheikh Mahmud from our minds, tell me more about your family. I envy you. My son was taken from me. I wager your parents dote on their grandchildren."

"They do but we live a long way from them." Lady Isabel's words made me feel guilty. When I next had a leave, I would take them up to Burscough. It had been too long.

I enjoyed telling Lady Isabel all about my family. It brought my children and my wife closer to me. By now they would be back in England. I could expect a letter soon. The conversation lifted my spirits. As we sipped the port Lord Palmer said, "If we have a period of quiet, Wing Commander, then you might be granted a leave. You could return to your family briefly eh?"

"The R.A.F. doesn't work that way, your lordship. Besides I am not certain that peace is on the horizon. We have dampened the fire rather than extinguishing it." I said no more for I was aware that there were merchants and businessmen around the table as well as soldiers.

"You mean Turkey?" I glanced around in case anyone had heard. He smiled, "If you notice, Wing Commander, the civilians are not within earshot. I am a careful man. Turkey will risk much if it backs the Kurds. That would be a marriage of convenience which would be doomed to a very messy divorce."

Lady Isabel said, "And they have no air force. Since the airfield has been built I see how aeroplanes can change modern wars. When your aeroplanes strafed and bombed Kirkuk I was amazed at their precision. If the Kurds do try to rise I am confident that your fine fliers will quell it."

I did not like this confidence. We had been lucky and only lost a couple of men and aeroplanes. If the enemy ever realised how vulnerable an aeroplane was then things could go badly for us. As Jack and I were given our coats he said, "Nice people sir. I mean I am an ordinary chap, my dad is a clerk in a bank but Lord Randolph and Lady Isabel spoke to me without any airs and graces."

"I know. Lord Burscough was my first pilot and he was a good chap too. The trouble is that a lot of them like Lord Burscough and Lady Isabel's son died in the Great War. Where are their children? There were many who sat out the war making money. There were politicians who did nothing. That is why Sheikh Mahmud is being protected. It is self-interest and it does not sit well with me."

As I was leaving one of the businessmen came over. He had a north country accent. I placed him around Manchester. He was a portly man. I noticed that he had had plenty to drink. He pumped my hand enthusiastically, "Wing Commander, this is an honour. I am Bert Hepplewhite. You are a Lancashire lad like me. I was only in at the end of the war but I remember reading about you. When I write and tell my old dad about this he will be made up." He reached into his pocket and took out a leather pouch. "I am a tobacco exporter and I know you smoke a pipe. I had this blend made up for you when I knew we were meeting. I would be honoured if you would accept it."

"Thank you, Mr Hepplewhite, that is most kind of you."

He shook his head, "For what you did for our country in the Great War, well we can't do enough!"

We drove back to the airfield. The wine, the night without sleep and a full stomach ensured that I was asleep almost instantly. The Ninaks were repaired and Jack and I flew them back to Baghdad the next day. Major Fox and Parr were taken south in the Air Ambulance. When I went to the office it was largely empty. There was just Sergeant Major Davis and Billings there. "Sir John flew to Cairo sir. Some pow wow going on. I think they are worried about the Turks. He was pleased with the raid, sir and even more pleased that you emerged unscathed."

"Major Fox will need time to recover."

"Captain Griffiths is a good bloke sir. He ran a tight ship with the Major away. Flight Lieutenant Ritchie kept your Snipes in the air. Things were quiet around here. Mind you I think it is the quiet before the storm, sir."

"What makes you say that, Sarn't Major?"

"I know you got rid of the locals, sir but the lads who get the fresh fruit and veg from the bazaar listen to the natives and they all think that they are waiting for something." He shrugged. "Can't say what though, sir."

I went to my quarters. I needed to wear my own clothes. Borrowed ones did not sit well with me. Then I took out the wallets and papers of the two men we had killed. Most of the papers were in Russian. I could speak a few words but I couldn't understand it. I decided I would send the Russian papers to Mr Balfour. The wallets yielded a serious amount of currency. Some sterling and other east European notes. The passports, however, were British! It was the older single sheet folded into eight. There was a simple carboard cover. I had one of the brand new blue ones which had just been introduced. I knew they were forgeries when I saw the names: John Smith and Herbert Jones. The two men whom we had killed did not bear those names. I put the passports to one side. I would show them to both Sir John and Major Fox. False passports made us vulnerable. How many more were out there?

I wrote a report for Mr Balfour and took the report and the papers back to the office. I found an envelope and put the documents inside. "Any sealing wax, Sergeant Major?"

"Yes sir."

I wrote the address on the envelope and then we sealed it. "See it gets on the next mail flight to England, Sergeant Major."

"Sir. Is it important?"

"To me? No but the man I sent it to might find it useful."

I went to speak with Flight Lieutenant Ritchie. It was mainly to compliment him on keeping things going but I also warned him that we might be in action sooner rather than later. I headed to the sick bay. Major Fox looked much better. He had been shaved and looked a different man. I could tell that lying in bed did not sit well with him. "Sir! I am fine! Tell this blood sucker that I can rest just as easily in my quarters."

I smiled and held up my hands, "In this I am outranked by Doctor McClure. Besides you can do a little work for me here." I handed him the two passports. "I took this from Ivan and his mate. Everything else was in Russian. I have sent the Russian material to London. These must be forgeries eh?"

"Not necessarily sir. It could be that they have slipped someone a little bribe to buy one. These may be real passports. They don't belong to the two Russians but they could be genuine."

"What do you mean?"

"Look at the dates of birth, sir. Both are from 1870. Those chaps we fought had had a tough life but they couldn't have been above thirty years old. The men who had these could have died or some corrupt official has found their names and made a passport for them. These have to be renewed every two years, sir. They are both less than one-year old."

I smacked one hand into the palm of the other, "And now that we have the blue passports these will be of no use in two years' time."

"There may be more of them."

"I know. I shall see Sir John and then your Captain Griffiths. I will ask to have random checks on everyone who is working with the British here."

When Sir John returned, two days' later, he agreed with my assessment. "It was a good move to remove the locals from the airfield but I am afraid that there are too many people in Baghdad itself who may not be what they say they are. I will have the Military Police check the papers of everyone. I will begin with the residency. And I have to warn you that we believe war with Turkey is imminent. They will not call it war. They will say they are protecting Turkish citizens who live close to Mosul. It will be a smokescreen. I want you and Squadron Leader Thomson to base yourselves at Kirkuk. I have sent for a Sikh Battalion. They are on their way from India now and will be here within days. They are in Al Basra at the moment. I will keep the Vernons and one squadron of Ninaks here. When you get to Kirkuk I want you to be the first response. However, Wing Commander I have to caution you. We cannot risk us beginning any conflict with Turkey. The League of Nations gave us a clear mandate to protect Iraq. There are enough of our enemies who will see us as Empire building. What that means is that we have to let the Turks and Kurds attack us. You cannot cross the border. You can see why I am sending you, Bill. A great deal rests upon your shoulders."

The Air Vice Marshall looked as serious as I had ever seen him. He was worried.

"Yes sir."

He handed me a thin pink folder. "Most of the messages I will send to you will be in plain language but here is the code we will use if there is anything which is for your eyes only. You do the same but I suspect that most of your messages will be in plain language." He smiled, "It's not changed much since France eh, Bill? Not enough buses not enough pilots and no time off! What did they say? If you can't take a joke you should never have joined!" He left.

I was pleased I had not asked about leave! I went to the office and sent for Jack and Flight Lieutenant Ritchie. "Get your bags packed! We are off to Kirkuk. There may be trouble brewing."

"Sir."

Major Fox had been allowed out of sick bay so long as he was desk bound. I popped my head into his office. "It looks like trouble is coming from the north west this time, Ralph. We are being sent there. I want Sergeants Williams and Swanston and ten good lads. Send them up to Kirkuk this afternoon by lorry. Send as many spare Lewis guns and grenades as we can manage. I have a feeling that it will be a hard posting. This time we are going to be fighting regulars with armour!"

Sergeant Davis had been listening at the open door. "I will hang on to your mail, sir. The last radio message we had from Alexandria was that there was mail coming by sea. It is on a lorry now and heading here."

Sergeant Davis knew that I was waiting for a letter from my wife. "Thanks George, I appreciate that. You never know we may be back here in a day or so."

He nodded, "Aye sir and I might be the next Prima Ballerina at the Royal Ballet!"

"Any sign of the radio for my bus?"

"It is coming sir but it is with the equipment for the new squadron."

"That is alright. I will get it fitted at Kirkuk. I have a feeling that I will need it."

"Sergeant Hayes, in the radio room, said there have been problems up at Kirkuk with the radio since the new squadron went up there, sir."

"What sort of things?"

"He doesn't think they keep it manned all the time sir. When Sergeant Major Robson was there it was and the new bloke, Sergeant Major Hill, he is a proper soldier sir. It is just that we have tried to raise them and failed."

"You think it comes from higher up than the radio room?"

He gave me an innocent smile, "Not for me to say sir. That is officers' country. I just know that you wouldn't allow it would you sir?"

"No Sergeant Major." He smiled. "Anything else I ought to know before I get up there?"

"I don't think so, sir."

I realised, as I headed back to my quarters that I didn't know Squadron Leader Barnes. Everything had appeared fine when I had been at the airfield. He had seemed quite solicitous about our lack of uniform but I had been there just one night and I had been preoccupied. I would have to dig deeper before I took three squadrons into the air. Sergeant Major Davis would never have brought up the Squadron Leader if he didn't have concerns. I had been a sergeant. NCO's kept each other informed about officers. I would have to speak to this Sergeant Major Hill as soon as I arrived.

We could have left immediately but I wanted every bus checking thoroughly. If we were at the front line then we could not afford to have mechanical problems. The mechanics, riggers and fitters would have three squadrons to service, not one! It also allowed all of us the opportunity to write letters home. If we were receiving mail then Sergeant Major Davis could send letters back to Blighty. Inevitably letters crossed in the air and there might be mixed messages. Just so long as our loved ones had one letter it might be enough. I knew that the press would be reporting the few deaths we had had as something of a catastrophe. As my dad used to say, '*the best use for newspapers is to wrap chips in 'em*!' Perhaps he was right.

That night the cooks excelled themselves. One good thing about living in the Middle East was that they had excellent lamb. Sergeant Major Davis must have used his contacts and we had a lamb dinner. I had no idea where he got the carrots and potatoes. Rice and aubergines were more likely to accompany lamb in these parts. With pots of mint sauce on the tables it felt like home. It was a nice touch. Instead of talking about the likelihood of death men spoke of meals in England and whose mothers cooked the best Yorkshire puddings. Memories of first visits to pubs before Sunday lunch were recalled and the evening became a celebration of all things English.

Jack Thomson had a healthy quantity to drink. When he was like that he sang and he ended the night by leading us all in a loud and passionate rendition of Jerusalem. It seemed appropriate where we were.

And did those feet in ancient time,
Walk upon England's mountains green:
And was the holy Lamb of God,
On England's pleasant pastures seen!

And did the Countenance Divine,
Shine forth upon our clouded hills?
And was Jerusalem builded here,
Among these dark Satanic Mills?

Bring me my Bow of burning gold;
Bring me my Arrows of desire:

Wings over Persia

Bring me my Spear: O clouds unfold!
Bring me my Chariot of fire!

I will not cease from Mental Fight,
Nor shall my Sword sleep in my hand:
Till we have built Jerusalem,
In England's green and pleasant Land.

We all cheered. We were going to war and we were as one.

Chapter 10

I left my number ones in my quarters but everything else I packed and stored it inside the Snipe's fuselage. I had no idea how long we would be at Kirkuk. I did not want to run out of anything. My Snipes took off first and we flew, not directly towards Kirkuk, but up the Tigris Valley. Sir John was keen for us to show a presence. The DH 9A's, with their longer range, would fly towards Sulaimaniya. He wanted the populace to see and fear the might of the R.A.F.

Compared with the rest of Iraq the Tigris was like a long green snake. It was verdant and the people were, compared with other parts of the country, well fed. They were not normally rebellious. Empty stomachs made for rebels. The fly past was just a reminder to them that they should not join the hot heads. We landed at Kirkuk first. I saw the lorries which had brought our extra men were there already and they had tents erected. Some of the airmen would have to rough it too.

The new Sergeant Major was Sergeant Major Hill. He was known as Daddy and was something of a legend. He had been in the R.F.C. and stayed on. He ran a tight squadron and was something of a martinet. I had known pilots who had served in the same squadron and they could not speak highly enough of him. I was pleased that he was the dragon whose den we had to enter.

The Bristols were not to be seen and I guessed that they were on patrol. I went directly to the office. Sergeant Major Hill leapt to his feet and stood to attention, "Sir! Sergeant Major Hill." The hint of a smile creased his lips. "I have been looking forward to serving with you, Wing Commander. I served with Flight Sergeant Richardson and Sergeant Major Lowery. They both spoke highly of you."

"Thank you, Sergeant Major. I know you served in the Great War, I fear this posting could be as difficult as France."

"Aye sir, France with flies, sand and bucket loads of camel shit." He put his hand to his mouth, "Pardon my French sir."

"If you worked with Percy and Raymond then you know that doesn't upset me."

He nodded, "They told me sir. I have got your quarters all sorted. We will be a bit tight but you and Mr Thomson each have a room. The other pilots will have to double up."

"We'll manage. Now I brought some of the R.A.F. regiment with me. I know you have sentries but the ones we have brought have Egypt, Somaliland and Baghdad under their belts. You can rely on them."

"I know sir. We had a chat last night in the sergeant's mess. We'll be fine. I know a good soldier when I see one and those two sergeants know their stuff. Will you be taking charge of the airfield, Wing Commander?"

There was something in his tone which made me hesitate before I spoke. "I have no written orders but I suppose I am ranking officer." I closed the door to the outer office, "Out with it Sarn't Major, what was behind that question?"

He lowered his voice, "Sir, Squadron Leader Barnes is a good officer but, well sir, he can be a little bit reckless. Brave as a lion but sometimes sir, you need to be a bit more cautious like, if you know what I mean. And discipline could be a little bit tighter."

"I do Sergeant Major. I appreciate the confidence."

"Like I said, sir, you have a reputation. I can see it is well deserved."

"Tell me about the rest of the squadron then, Sergeant Major."

"The pilots are a good lot sir. Young and keen as mustard. They just need someone to give them a guiding hand sir. You will be good for them." Once again there were things unsaid. "The Non-Commissioned Officers are amongst the best I have known. Now the Erks? They are a mixed bag. The mechanics are kept in line by Sergeant Major Shaw. However, some of the others? I have only been with the squadron for a month or so. I'll sort out the slackers. You know the type sir?" I nodded. He opened the door, "McIlroy, take the Wing Commander to his quarters! Chop! Chop! Have you your luggage in the kite sir?"

"Yes."

"I'll get one of the lads to bring it sir."

As McIlroy led me across the parade ground I saw Jack's Ninaks come in to land. There was one short. Parr was still recovering. It was one thing to fire a machine gun one handed but it wouldn't do to try flying one handed. When my bags arrived, I changed from my flying gear into cooler clothes and I organized my clothes. I had learned to do that when I was in the cavalry and I had not lost the habit. Then I lit my pipe and headed for the mess. I knew that Squadron Leader Barnes and Jack would head there once they had landed. It was important for us to have a quiet chat before we began operations.

The mess was empty save for the duty steward. He was smoking a cigarette and reading a book. He looked flustered and quickly stubbed out the cigarette, "Sorry sir I wasn't expecting anyone with the squadron being in the air and…"

"What is your name?"

"Aircraftsman Ramsden sir."

"You know better than to smoke while on duty." I ran my finger down the bar. It was sticky. "Find jobs to do. This place needs cleaning. I am certain that shelves need to be filled with bottles and glasses. You have a cushy number here, Ramsden. You wouldn't want to lose it would you?" He shook his head. "Now I will have a large whisky. When you have done that make this place presentable. I am certain there are many other duties you could be given and I do not think you would find them agreeable in the least."

"Sir."

I realised that I was coming on strong but I had been a sergeant and I knew that the Ramsdens of this world would take a mile if you gave them an inch. He brought the drink over and turned. I said, "Don't you need my name for my mess bill, Ramsden?"

"Yes sir, I mean no sir, you are Wing Commander Harsker sir. I made a note of it already."

I enjoyed my smoke and sipped my whisky as Ramsden cleaned and polished the bar. He had begun to do the same with the tables when Jack walked in. He had changed from his flying gear and was in a smart uniform. He grinned when he saw me. "Ready for another one, sir?"

I stood, "I'll stand the first corner. The same again, Ramsden, for both of us and put it on my mess bill. When Squadron Leader Barnes comes in give him his usual drink and that goes on my mess bill too."

"Sir!"

I did not know this squadron. The best way to let the men know what you would and wouldn't tolerate was to find someone who had done wrong. I had done that and Ramsden would waste no time in exaggerating and telling all and sundry what a bastard I was.

When the drinks came Jack lit his pipe too. "How was Sulaimaniya?"

"We didn't fly over it, sir. They had some bigger guns. I saw them dug in along the valley you used. It seemed safer to fly low and just let them know where we were."

"If we have to take it out we will use the Vernons. Arthur's home-made sight was very accurate. He thought that they could drop from three thousand feet and the margin of error would only be ten feet. We will take Sulaimaniya but I think the Turks and the Kurds will be the next enemy we fight. When Barnes comes in we will chat about what we will do tomorrow."

We heard his Bristols as they landed and he wasted no time in coming in to the mess. Unlike Jack and myself he had not changed out of his flying gear. Ramsden had a gin and tonic ready at the bar for him.

"Good show Ramsden, you must be a bloody mind reader!"

"Compliments of the Wing Commander sir."

He came over and plopped down opposite me, "Good show sir, cheers!"

I raised my glass. "Cheers!" Gesturing outside, with my pipe I asked, "Anything happening out there?"

He shook his head, "Damned quiet. Flew to Mosul. The airfield is almost finished and then tootled up to the border and back. Nothing. No one even popped a gun at us."

"Is that unusual?"

He took a deep swallow of the drink and then nodded, "Actually, come to think about it, it is. Normally they send up a fusillade. They never manage to hit us though. I just thought they were giving up wasting bullets."

I looked at Jack, "Or it may be they are moving troops around. How high were you flying?"

"A thousand feet, why sir?"

"Tomorrow we fly at two hundred."

"Two hundred sir? If we fly at that height they might actually hit us!"

"And we will have more chance of seeing them. Don't worry Squadron Leader. I will be leading. If anyone is going to get holes shot in their buses it will be my Snipes." I could see he was confused. I smiled, "The Snipe has a wingspan of thirty-one feet and we are nineteen feet long. Your Bristols are five feet longer and have a wingspan of almost forty feet and the Ninaks are even bigger. We are a small target and we are nippy."

"Yes sir."

I saw Jack smile, "Another sir?"

"Why not?"

"What do you think; they are lying doggo eh sir?"

"I think they are up to something. All the intelligence we have is that the Kurds and the Turks are joining forces and are ready to attack us. The question is when and where? We haven't got enough ground troops and so we have to be the cavalry and the artillery. We have to find them and stop them before they even get to Mosul."

"And the airfield at Mosul, sir?"

"A squadron of Ninaks will be here tomorrow sometime. It will take time for them to orientate themselves but we will have forces close to the border. They have the harder task."

Squadron Leader Barnes said, "So are you staying here sir or moving on to Mosul? I mean you will have a shorter flight time to the front from Mosul."

I smiled, "Oh, no, we will be staying here. We can also cover Ebril, Sulaimaniya and Baghdad from here. You are stuck with us I am afraid." From the look on his face he was not happy to be sharing his base.

My pilots all began to wander into the mess. I was pleased to see that they had on smart uniforms. I saw Squadron Leader Barnes take it in. Then he looked back at us and finally he looked down at himself. He downed his drink, "Well sir, I just wanted to say hello. I will pop off and get changed eh?"

My pilots' faces showed that they were surprised at Barnes' attire. Jack's men came in next. They too were in uniform and not flying gear. I swallowed off the whisky. Jack said, quietly,

"It can happen sir. I mean when you are on your own then sometimes standards slip."

"Thin end of the wedge, Jack; you start to become slipshod in the air and that leads to deaths." I stood to go to the bar. Squadron Leader Barnes' pilots entered. Some were in flying gear. As I was standing they saluted and the room was silent. I smiled, "Thank you gentlemen, I am Wing Commander Harsker and I will be based here for a while." I allowed that to sink in. "Some of you have forgotten that you are officers and gentlemen. I will overlook it this once."

Some of the ones in flying gear looked confused but when the others in flying gear left they cottoned on and followed suit. I turned to Jack. "I will see you later. I want to check up on the other Ninaks."

As I left I saw the pilots all getting to know one another. The standards I wanted would be made clear by my pilots and Jack's. The problem lay in the Squadron Leader. He appeared to be sound but I had detected weakness already. I returned to the office. "Sergeant Major Hill who is in charge of the radio?"

"That would be Sergeant Bailey sir. He is in the radio room now." He understood the implied question. "Knows his stuff sir. A whizz with anything like that. I am an old-fashioned soldier sir but Bill is young and picks it up easily."

"Thanks, Sarn't Major. I think tomorrow afternoon, when we have come back from patrol, that you and I will have a wander around the field. We will sharpen things up."

He nodded, "You met Ramsden then sir?"

"I did and the pilots now know that flying gear is not permitted in the mess."

He looked relieved and he smiled, "It will be a pleasure sir. I will work out a tour!"

"And could you give some thought to a briefing room. It would be handy to have somewhere to talk to the squadron leaders and brief the flight commanders. We could put maps on the wall and the like."

"Leave it with me, sir."

I went into the radio room. There was a sergeant, a corporal and an Erk. They were fiddling on with some valves and wires on a table. They snapped to attention when I entered, "At ease."

They sat. I saw that they were all young. Sergeant Bailey looked to be no more than twenty-one years old. That was young for his rank and showed how good he was. "A couple of things: a radio for my Snipe will be arriving with the squadron of Ninaks who are due here in the next couple of days. Sergeant Bailey, I want you to fit it."

"Sir."

"Secondly I need to know of any important messages immediately. That means you wake me if it is the middle of the night."

"Right sir." Sergeant Bailey looked uncomfortable. "Er sir we don't keep a radio watch overnight."

"There are just three of you?"

"Four sir, Marshall is getting a brew in. The Squadron Leader doesn't think it is necessary."

"Well I do." I stroked my chin. "I will get you another Erk. Sergeant Bailey, you find one you think you can train up. When I have time, we will decide which one of your other lads becomes Corporal. I want this manned twenty-four hours a day but I want you on duty during the day, Sergeant Bailey. You are in charge and you decide the rota. While I am here then I get the messages, right Sergeant?"

"Sir."

"And the reason I want you on the radio during the day is because my Snipe, Flight Lieutenant Ritchie and Squadron Leader Thomson's DH 9A will be the only three with radios. Things could get a little hot up here soon and I will need a reliable team on the radio. What you boys do could and will save lives."

"Yes sir." Sergeant Bailey said, "Sir we have always been willing to work around the clock. I know that messages come in at night."

I smiled, "Excellent then we are all singing from the same hymn sheet... now."

That evening, at dinner, I could see that word had gotten around. The sergeant steward I had met when I had flown back from the raid greeted me when I entered. He said quietly, "Sorry about Ramsden, sir. I have put him on a fizzer."

I nodded, "Sergeant, if you had done your job and ensured that the stewards all knew the standards that were expected then you would not have needed to do so."

He glanced behind me. I was aware that Squadron Leader Barnes had entered, "Yes sir. Quite right, sir. Won't happen again, sir."

I knew that Squadron Leader Barnes was trying to make amends for his gaffe. He went out of his way to be as formal as possible. I saw Jack trying to hide his grin. I hoped that the Squadron Leader would transfer that diligence to the air. I had walked around his Bristols before dinner. The Sergeant Major Second Class who was in command, Sergeant Major Shaw, looked uncomfortable as I examined his buses. There had been just two riggers and a mechanic with him.

"Which of these will be available in the morning, Sergeant Major?"

"All of them sir."

I had poked three of my fingers through a hole in the wing of one. "I am guessing that there will be others like this one?"

"Yes sir, but the Squadron Leader doesn't mind so long as they get in the air."

I had turned and glowered at him. "From now on no aeroplane leaves the field with damage of any kind. How many Bristols will be airworthy tomorrow?"

"Five, sir."

"That is better."

I found Sergeant Major Davis and, with clipboard in hand we began a tour. Normally such tours of inspection would be announced. We caught out many men officers and Erks alike. It was not just minor things like uniform infractions but smoking close to fuel, not having side arms, rubbish left in dangerous places, food left where rodents could be attracted. Eight men were put on charges and Sergeant Major Hill was not a happy man.

"I am sorry about this, sir."

I looked at him, "We both know this is not your fault. Hopefully we have nipped the laxity in the bud. Make a list and you can begin to tighten the ship tomorrow."

"Yes sir." He nodded, "Enjoy dinner eh sir?"

As we began to eat I was silent. I was wondering what other weakness lay in Squadron Leader Barnes. More than that what about the Ninaks which would be arriving later? What about Squadron Leader Williams? I didn't know him. I knew that I would have to spend at least two days at Mosul. I made a decision as I ate the spicy soup that I would have to make Paul Ritchie temporary squadron leader. He could handle it. It might not be permanent but the experience would be good for him and show on his service record.

Squadron Leader Barnes asked, "Everything all right sir? The soup not to your liking?"

I smiled, "No, Robert, I am just thinking about the other squadron which will be arriving. Four squadrons will take some handling."

"I am happy to help sir, if I can."

He was ambitious. "Well Jack here is my deputy but I appreciate the offer. Tomorrow will be our easiest day. We will fly close to the border. We will practise low flying in formation and then come back. By then Squadron Leader Williams should have arrived."

"Low flying in formation sir? We stay together? Isn't that a waste of aeroplanes. I mean we have over thirty aeroplanes. We could cover a wider area."

"Until we can all fly as one we stay together. When squadrons operate on their own then I need to know how they will perform. I know number 5 and number 12 squadrons. Yours is the unknown factor."

I had been blunter than I had meant to be. He looked surprised, "Mine sir? They are all good pilots. You can rely on us!"

I smiled, "That remains to be seen. That was good soup. I look forward to the rest of the meal."

I had set doubt in the Squadron Leader's mind. I had looked at his service record and discovered that he had, largely, been in squadrons that operated alone. Sometimes that was a good thing but if he had learned the wrong things from his own leaders then that was a danger.

When we had finished dessert, I lit my pipe and used the spare cutlery to demonstrate to the squadron leader how we would fly. Jack knew already. He had helped me to devise this system. I didn't know if it would be too unwieldy to fly. The only way was to try it out.

"We fly in lines of four. I want each subsequent flight to be forty feet above the one below and a hundred feet back. My squadron will be the lowest of the three. Barnes your chaps will be to our port and your lowest flight will be fifty feet above my top one. Jack will do the same to starboard. You will all keep a hundred feet between flights."

I saw him calculating. "There will be four hundred feet between our lowest aeroplane and our highest."

"Exactly; now I don't think they have aeroplanes but if they do then we increase the altitude of your flight and Jack's to two hundred feet above mine."

"You will be bait." He was a bright man.

"Sort of. I intend to skirt Mosul by flying to the west and then heading north to fly along the border before returning to the east of Mosul. We will be leaving at 0900 hours. That gives you an hour to brief your pilots."

He looked surprised, "An hour to brief them, sir?"

"I will be having one of my Snipes above everyone so that I can have an idea of how well you all fly. We need to use this time of peace to learn how to fly as one. When Squadron Leader Williams gets here we will modify our formation a little more."

He rose, "In that case, sir, I had better retire. I am guessing we have a busy day tomorrow."

"Indeed, we do."

I saw that most of his pilots followed him. Half of mine had already retired. Jack said, "I'll be off."

I waved Flight Lieutenant Ritchie over, "Paul, can I have a word?"

"Of course, sir."

He sat down and took out his pipe. I pushed my tobacco over, "Try this. I was given it by a tobacco exporter. It is quite nice. Very aromatic and not too heavy."

"Thank you, sir." After scraping out his pipe, he took some out and sniffed it before rolling it in the palm of his hand and then filled it. I waited until he had it going before I spoke.

"I have a little job for you tomorrow. I want you to take off last. I want you fifty feet above the highest aeroplane."

He nodded, "Nice smoke sir."

"I want you to see which aeroplanes are not in position. Take a pencil and notepad with you and write down the numbers of those buses that are not in formation or are slow to react."

He frowned, "Problem sir?"

"I don't know. We have never tried a three-squadron formation before. This is just an experiment. It may not work."

He looked relieved, "Righto sir."

"And I would like you to be acting squadron leader."

"Me sir?"

"You are my number two and I am aware that I may have other duties. It will only be temporary I am afraid but the pay will come in handy and it will go on your service record."

"If you think I can do it sir."

I smiled, "With your eyes closed."

Wings over Persia

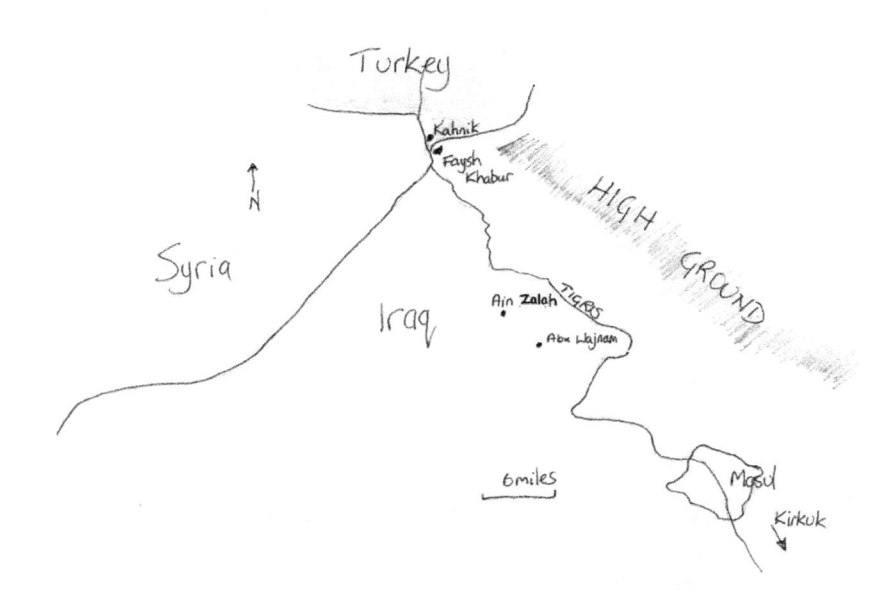

Chapter 11

Next morning, after breakfast, I went to see Sergeant Major Hill before I went to check my bus. I draped my flying coat, goggles and hat over the back of a chair. I had Sergeant Major Hill begin the paperwork for Ritchie's promotion.

Sergeant Bailey heard me and came in with a piece of paper. "This came in this morning, sir. The Ninaks are on their way up. They should be here by the middle of the afternoon. I have seen Sergeant Major Hill and I had an aircraftsman who should do. We will have round the clock radio sir."

"Good man, appreciate it."

Sergeant Major Hill smiled, "I see you have made a start sir." Just then I heard raised voices from the airfield. He gave me a wry smile, "And I think it has continued, sir." He picked up his sun helmet and swagger stick. If you don't mind sir, I think a stroll around the field is in order. Ginger the chaps up."

"Certainly, Sergeant Major."

I just had my hat on and I regretted not bringing my sun helmet. I would have to get used to that. I saw a red-faced Squadron Leader Barnes tearing a strip from Sergeant Major Shaw.

I said, mildly as I approached, "A problem, Squadron Leader?"

"Yes sir, this fool of a mechanic told me that you said he had to ground any buses with damage."

"Well done Sergeant Major, you were listening."

"But my bus has holes in the wings! You mean I can't fly either?"

"No aeroplane with damage leaves the ground. We cannot afford to lose aeroplanes and we certainly cannot afford to lose pilots."

"But."

Sergeant Major Hill said, "Sergeant Major Shaw, if I might have a word with you?" Daddy Hill would have made a fine diplomat. He was protecting his squadron leader in case he said anything untoward.

"Squadron Leader what you should have done yesterday, instead of racing to the mess for a drink was to have your air crews working on your buses to make them airworthy. You did not because that is not your way. You have been lucky hitherto. We cannot rely upon that luck continuing. I want you to have your second in command lead the squadron today. It will be good practice. Hopefully your crews will have the buses ready for tomorrow but remember, Squadron Leader, your air crews now have to service three squadrons not one."

He opened his mouth and closed it. Then as he turned to go away he said, "My family is connected, Wing Commander."

I laughed, "Excellent! Then I can expect some juicy stories in the mess. When I served with Lord Burscough I heard plenty I can tell you. If you would send your number two to see me when he is ready."

Sergeant Major Shaw came over, "We will get them all ready for tomorrow sir. Daddy had a word with me. He is right. We have been a bit lax of late. It won't happen again sir."

"And you know you have three squadrons to service?"

He nodded, "I'll give the lads a good kick up the backside. They won't want to face Daddy Hill's wrath sir!"

Flight Lieutenant Cartwright came over to me. He looked nervous. "Sir, you want to see me?"

I nodded and pointed to Paul Ritchie who was busy checking the Snipes. "That is Acting Squadron Leader Ritchie. Yesterday he was my number two and a Flight Lieutenant. He has shown me that he can lead a squadron. Today you have a chance. I want you to lead your squadron. It might be just two flights but it is your chance. If anything happened to Squadron Leader Barnes then you would have to lead."

"Sir, Squadron Leader Barnes is a legend."

We were standing next to his Bristol. I put three fingers through one of the holes, "And even legends can get shot down. I have had three crashes. I am lucky I walked away from them all. Now you know what to do today?"

"Keep fifty feet above your last flight and a hundred feet behind."

"Good. Now we should have an easy time of it today but be ready in case something unexpected happens. You command. Acting Squadron Leader Ritchie will be above you. He is my sheepdog."

He smiled, "Yes sir. I'll give it a go."

"Good man. Take-off in thirty-five minutes. Go around your chaps and ginger them up eh?"

I went to my Snipe. A good pilot always checked their own bus. I knew that my rank would afford me the closest attention but I had been a mechanic myself and I liked to check things. I checked my watch. There was ten minutes to go. I donned my flying coat and flying helmet and climbed up into the Snipe. With luck, I would soon have a radio. I knew that there would be a knock-on effect in terms of storage and weight but it would be worth it. I could always trim the aeroplane. Once my engine was running I had the chocks removed and taxied to be ready to take off. The runway was wide enough for four Snipes to take off at the same time but I did not want to risk a collision. We took off in twos and then made wide circles over Kirkuk until the rest of the squadron had joined me. Once we were all in formation I checked in my mirrors and over my shoulders. The Bristols and Ninaks were behind and above me like camouflaged ladders.

We had a hundred miles to fly to Mosul and then another twenty or so to the border. We would not be running on empty when we returned but we would not have a great deal left in our tanks. The border town was Kahnik across the river from the Iraqi town of Faysh Khabur. I was mindful of Sir John's words and I did not wish to stray over the border and spark an incident. Once I saw the town I would turn and head home. I kept the Tigris to starboard and the main road to port. The ground over which we flew undulated. It took concentration to hold altitude. A hundred feet was probably too low but I wanted to see if the Turks or the Kurds had infiltrated Iraq. That was easier said than done for the Kurds lived in both countries. I was looking for that which appeared out of the ordinary. I ignored the shepherds. I had no doubt that they would be spying for the Kurds in Turkey but they were not the threat. Horsemen, riders on camels and donkeys, these were the ones I was watching for. I was seeking gatherings of men outside of the towns. The places we passed like Ain Zalah were just tiny collections of huts. None would have large numbers. I did not see huge numbers of men nor did I see rifles. That, in itself, was worrying. These tribesmen all had a weapon. Some of them dated back to the Napoleonic war but they all prized their weapons. Where were they?

When I spied the town of Faysh Khabur I began to turn. I had binoculars and I peered at the Turkish border stronghold. I saw the Turkish flag and guns. Mercifully they did not fire. Had they done so then it would have meant that war had begun and we were not ready for that; not yet. I could see no bridge over the Tigris. That meant nothing for they had animals and they could swim it. What I didn't see was evidence of tents and an armed camp. That worried me. Either the intelligence we had was wrong or they were gathering somewhere else. I flew for a further ten miles before turning and heading south.

As I flew east I saw, to my port side high uninhabited mountains. They would be perfect cover for rebels. I noticed that the high ground mirrored the Tigris. If I was going to attack that would be the direction I would use. It meant an attacker could head for Ebril or Kirkuk if Mosul was too heavily defended. There were too many things I did not know. I had kept glancing in the mirror on the journey south and every aeroplane appeared to be in formation. That was good. As we approached the field I saw that Squadron Leader Williams' Ninaks had arrived. The fact that he had landed there rather than at Mosul spoke well. Had he gone directly to Mosul I might have thought we had another Squadron Leader Barnes.

I landed and parked my aeroplane. Sergeant Major Shaw appeared and saluted. "All the kites are ready for tomorrow, sir."

"Good. We saw no action today. Just wear and tear." I pointed to the other DH 9A's. "They will be gone tomorrow."

"I know sir. Their crews have just arrived too. I think they are going to push on and try to make Mosul before dark. Rather them than us sir. And your radio has arrived. Sergeant Bailey said you wanted him to fit it?"

"With your help, of course, Sergeant Major. You know where to put it for the weight and he knows the best place for the reception."

He nodded, "Bill is a good lad. Young for his rank but I don't hold that against him sir. He knows his stuff. All them wires!" He shook his head, "All I need is a hammer and a spanner!"

Sergeant Major Shaw was old fashioned and there was nothing wrong with that. The aeroplanes we flew were, essentially the same ones we had had at the start of the Great War. By the time I reached Sergeant Major Hill's office I had come up with a plan. I saw that would have to wait when I entered. Squadron Leader Barnes was deep in conversation with Squadron Leader Williams.

Sergeant Major Hill pointedly stood, "Good flight sir?"

I nodded, "It certainly was." I turned to the new squadron leader. "I am Wing Commander Harsker and you must be Squadron Leader Williams."

He saluted, "Yes sir. Squadron Leader Barnes was just telling me that he had to set up an airfield and he was giving me some advice."

I saw the smug look on the Squadron Leader's face. "Every airfield presents its own problems. I have just flown over yours. The airfield is a good one but you are less than thirty miles from Turkey and the Turks are keen to have Mosul."

"Yes sir, Sir John told me in Baghdad."

"Well get yourself cleaned up and we will have a spot of tea in the mess. Sergeant Major have McIlroy arrange it and invite Squadron Leader Thomson too. It will be a good chance to get to know one another."

"Sir."

"And have Williams and Swanston come to see me eh?" I turned to Squadron Leader Barnes, "Your chaps did well today. Flight Lieutenant Cartwright will have learned from the challenge."

The squadron leader seemed unimpressed and he just nodded and said, "See you in the bar then David?"

Squadron Leader Williams said, "Seems a nice chap. Very helpful sir. Do you know he is distantly related to someone in the Royal Family?"

I saw Sergeant Major Hill roll his eyes, "I'll go and sort out the tea sir and find those two chaps for you."

"Yes, Squadron Leader but it doesn't mean much out here, does it?" We were alone and I was able to speak. "Look, David, isn't it?" He nodded. "I was not joking about being out on a limb. The Kurds do not have a lot of technology but they are fierce fighters. The Turks never completely conquered them and they don't know when to give up. You and your boys will need to be able to get your buses in the air really quickly. Your ground crews will need to keep guns by them all the time. Use your radio to send for help and do not be proud. We are a thin blue line here and we are all that stand between Turkey and Baghdad."

"Don't worry about me sir. I know the dangers. Sir John put the fear of God into me."

I had more confidence in him than the brash Barnes and he left the office as Williams and Swanston appeared with Sergeant Major Hill.

"Right lads, I want you to choose four good men. Take a lorry and when the lorries head north with the Ninaks' fitters go with them. "Sergeant Major write out orders. I want you to stay the night and then tomorrow drive to the border. There is a place call Faysh Khabur. I need you to discover as much as you can about the town opposite. There will be a detachment in the town. Ask them but use your eyes."

"You want us to nip over, sir?"

"It is tempting but we daren't risk it. Just see what you can from the town. Head back when you are done. Whatever information you can gather will be vital."

Sergeant Major Hill had been busy writing and he handed them two pieces of paper. "Here is a chit for a lorry and here are your orders. If you would just sign it sir." I scribbled my signature. The two sergeants left. It was as though I had asked them to do some meaningless errand. I wanted more men like them and less like Barnes.

I went to have a shower. I was hot and I needed to change into clean clothes. When I had shaved and felt clean once more I dressed and headed for the mess. I knocked on Paul Ritchie's door. "Pop along to the mess. We are having tea and the other squadron leaders will be there."

"Are you certain, sir?"

"Of course. You know Jack. They won't bite."

"Right sir." He did not sound happy.

Mess Sergeant Robson had done a good job. It was a proper tea. He had found spicy chutney from somewhere and that was on the cheese sandwiches. It was a Muslim country and so there was no ham but he had corned beef and mustard sandwiches and he had even baked scones. Jack grinned, "Proper tea party sir! Damned civilised!"

Williams and Ritchie also seemed happy but Barnes had a scowl on his face. I had come to realise that my arrival had upset his world.

After the tea was poured and they began to eat their sandwiches I started to speak. "We need some standing orders and procedures. David, I want you to put half a flight up every morning at first light. Call it the dawn patrol if you like. You have five hours' endurance. We will arrive at noon and that will give your lads chance to stand down. At three you send the other half of your flight up. That way we have the area between Turkey and Mosul covered during daylight hours."

He nodded and continued eating.

Barnes said, "Isn't that going to be a bit predictable sir? I mean they will know where we are."

"That is right. We will be in the air and preventing them from attacking. It is not like the Great War when you were worried about a Jasta jumping you. They have, so far as we know, no aeroplanes. They never had many and their pilots, according to Intelligence were fairly poor. If I am worried about anything it is that they will attack at night." I nodded to David. "You need to keep in close touch with the army detachments. It will be in both your interests."

Ritchie asked, "Will we be bringing three squadrons over from Kirkuk every day?"

"Good question, Paul, just the first day. That will be the day after tomorrow."

"We have a day off then sir?" Squadron Leader Barnes had been listening. That was a good thing.

"You mean tomorrow?" He nodded. "No. You and the chaps who didn't fly today need to fly with us. We fly the same way on every patrol. You need to see how we did it." I turned to Flight Lieutenant Ritchie. "How were they today?"

"Couldn't fault them sir. When they were out of position it was only for a moment sir. They will be fine."

"So, Squadron Leader Williams, you leave tomorrow whenever it suits you. We will leave at 0900 again."

It was a more confident Wing which took off the next morning. Almost all of us had done this before. Acting Squadron Leader Ritchie was back in formation. Perhaps because we had done it once before I was able to identify more. As we passed Abu Wajnam, just a few miles from Mosul I noticed that there were a few more men in the village than there had been. That did not worry me. The waves did. They all waved as though we were liberators. From their dress, they were Kurds. I was suspicious. The same thing happened at Ain Zalah. By the time we reached Faysh Khabur every village which had had men had waved. The ones without men had not. I saw Williams and Swanston. They were looking at Kahnik.

I risked flying as close to the river as I could get. The Tigris carried on north but there was a smaller river which fed into the Tigris. That formed the border. It made the hill fort a stronghold. The Turkish flag fluttered and I saw field pieces. They were ancient but they would easily be able to fire at Faysh Khabur. I knew from the reports I had read that it was only defended by a company of Indian troops. There were more guns than there had been the previous day. The offensive was imminent.

When we headed south I took us further towards the high ground. I saw defiles and gullies. They criss crossed the hills. Inaccessible to vehicles, the mounted Kurds could use them to strike swiftly into the hinterland. Mosul could be cut off. That was the Turk's first objective. They had believed it was theirs by right and did not constitute part of Iraq. Of course, they would take and keep whatever they could of their former empire.

Sergeant Bailey was waiting with a message for me when we landed. I knew it was urgent. "Sir, this came from Baghdad. The Air Vice Marshall was insistent you get it immediately."

I gestured to the Snipe when he handed it to me. "The day after tomorrow you can fit the radio. I will stand down for the day."

"Right sir. It shouldn't take long."

"And I have a message for Baghdad. I will read this and come directly over."

It was not coded. Sir John had intelligence that the Turks and the Kurds would begin their attack within the next forty-eight hours. That almost made my message redundant. I was merely going to confirm it with my suspicions. I read further on and discovered more bad news. There was a suspicion that they had some aeroplanes. It could not be confirmed. I went to the radio room and began writing on the pad which was there. I handed it to Sergeant Bailey. "Let me know when the Air Vice Marshall has read it."

"Yes sir."

Once in my quarters I took off my tunic and shirt. I could not be bothered to shower and so I had, what my dad would have called, a *'good swill'*. That done I lit my pipe and took out the map. This was like a game of chess. I was trying to anticipate a move from the enemy. There was no bridge close to Faysh Khabur. That meant they had to cross further east. The more I looked at the high ground the more sense it made. If the Turks and the Kurds had made an unholy alliance then they would try to join up. Neither trusted the other. That mistrust worked in our favour.

There was a knock at the door. It was McIlroy. He had a grin on his face. "Sergeant Major Hill apologises for not being in the office sir, he was sorting out the mail. Here is one from Mrs. Harsker!"

"Thank you, McIlroy. I think this deserves a drink to accompany it. Just shut the door, will you? I want to read this and be undisturbed."

"Of course, sir."

I got myself a whisky and filled my pipe before sitting down to read the letter.

L'Haut Ferme

Bill,

This place is idyllic. Of course, you got out of all the hard work of painting and the like! Only kidding. I enjoyed it and the children were marvellous. I have found a local electrician and plumber. Actually, Madame

Bartiaux found them. That means they are reliable and reasonable.

I don't know when I will get this letter to you. It will have to wait until we get to England and then I will have to find a way to get it sent to you. Minor problems.

The children's French is coming on well. They have both taken to it like ducks to water. Mine is improving but I know when I have made a gaffe! They hide their smiles behind their hands. I decided that the children and I would clear the garden. You can do the digging when you get home. Have you any idea when that will be? We miss you. The children asked me the other day if you will always be abroad. It almost broke my heart.

Perhaps we can come out to you. They would be able to pick up another language that way. It is just a thought but if you are not home in six months then we are coming out.

I noticed that the pen had changed.

As you can probably tell we are now home. The weather was lovely in France and it has not stopped raining since we got home. Squadron Leader Power called by this afternoon and said he could send the letter, if it was finished, there is a new mail service. This is not finished, not by a long chalk, but I want you to have something. Please find enclosed a couple of photographs I had taken

of the children in France. Just so you don't forget us.
Love you
Beattie.
xxx

I shook the envelope and there were two photographs of the children at the farm. I read the letter three more times. The last thing I wanted was for them to come out. This was a dangerous world. I finished my drink and then dressed. I had four months to get a leave. That was incentive enough. If I had to I would fight the Turks and Kurds on my own!

We all had mail and there was a happy atmosphere in the mess that night. A letter from home lifted the spirits. I showed the photographs to Jack. He had no children yet. I was not certain that his wife could actually have children. It was not the sort of thing one asked. The fact that he looked so happy when I showed my children made me think that he had not given up on the hope that he might have some one day.

Inevitably we spoke of the patrol we had taken and Sir John's message. "Perhaps it is a good thing we will have three squadrons in the air tomorrow eh, sir? If they tried to come over we would be mob handed! We could catch them with their trousers down."

"Perhaps but I am still worried about those mysterious aeroplanes which have just appeared. That has all the hallmarks of the Count."

"He is dead sir, remember?"

"He could have made those plans weeks ago. It could be a trick and that is the worst, not knowing,"

"Williams and Swanston will be back today, sir."

I tapped my pipe out and began to fill it. "You are right and those two have common sense. They can sniff out danger."

As we headed north, the next day, I reflected that the formation worked. Of course, we had not used it in combat but it had the advantage of giving us aerial cover from an enemy who did possess aeroplanes whilst also allowing us to bomb in waves and see the results of our bombing. The men I had seen the previous day were missing and that was ominous. We did pass the lorry with our men returning south. They might have noticed something on the journey. When we reached the border, I flew further north and east along the river. I saw bridges. I had suspected that there must be bridges but now I had it confirmed. The British detachments at the two bridges we saw looked woefully inadequate. The only thing in their favour appeared to be that they had a lorry each with a machine gun mounted upon it. They could flee. In this kind of terrain that might be the best option.

When we reached the high ground, I risked flying lower. It looked different. I signalled to my wingmen to keep formation and I dropped to thirty feet above the ground. It was risky but I was looking for something. I saw many tracks and piles of animal dung. A large body of men on either horses or camels had passed this way recently. The question was, were they moving east or west? I could not determine that from the air but the question nagged at me all the way home.

Williams and Swanston were waiting for me. "Well?"

"That fort, sir, it's a front."

"A front, Sergeant?"

"Half of the so-called guns were just metal barrels. We watched it for a good three hours. Most of the sentries didn't move. If I was a betting man I would say that there were a handful of men inside the fort."

"I believe you. There were men in the towns you passed on the way up were they there when you came south?"

"Funny you should say that sir. What we did notice was a load of horse shit, sir. It wasn't there when we went north, at least not in the same quantities."

"Thanks, you lads have done well. Have the day off tomorrow. I think that, in the next day or so, we could find ourselves knee deep in trouble."

"Aye sir, you might be right but we can handle it."

I returned to the radio room and wrote out another message for Sir John. Sergeant Bailey had yet to go off duty. He said, "He hasn't received your first message yet, sir."

"Thanks. Have me woken any time the message comes in."

"Sir."

As I went back to my room it felt as though we were teetering on a precipice.

Chapter 12

I had a Wing briefing the next morning. Every pilot and gunner was there. I needed to lay out, quite clearly, what were the rules for this action.

"Gentlemen. Today we begin our patrols. This will be the last time we all go out together. After today we will be sending up a squadron at a time. All of the rest will be on standby. If there is daylight then every pilot will be in flying gear and ready to fly. Unless I give the order, no one will cross the border into Turkey! Is that clear?" There were many nods. "That is as much for your safety as anything. God knows what the Kurds would do to a pilot or a gunner if they got their hands on them. So far, up here in Mosul, we have not had to fire our weapons or drop our bombs. That will not last. Good luck. I will let the squadron leaders know the rota when we land."

As I headed out to the Snipe Sergeant Bailey found me, "Sir, Sir John has replied." He handed me a sheet of paper. The notes had been scribbled but the gist was that he agreed with my assessment but reiterated that we were not to cross the border.

"Thanks Sergeant. Get this one typed up and put in the log with the others. I will organise them when I get the chance."

It felt more like we were on a war footing. The land below us was empty although I noticed, as we passed Mosul to starboard, that there appeared to be many more people in that city. The Resident would have received the same messages as I had. He would know what to watch for. I wondered if we would be called upon to clear the streets there as we had in Baghdad.

I took us low over Faysh Khabur. I saw that they had sandbags and the detachment now had two artillery pieces there. They waved. From what Williams and Swanston had said it was unlikely that the attack would come from there. I flew to the two bridges. I wondered if bombing the bridges would be considered an act of war. Of course, it would! Such an act would, however, prevent a Turkish attack. It would do nothing to stop the Kurds but the Kurds would not be armed with modern weapons. They would not have armour and artillery. Flying over the high ground I saw figures on horses. There were too few to constitute a threat but their presence told me that they were readying. The patrol went without incident. I had demonstrated that we had air power and I hoped I had tempted the enemy into thinking that they could predict our movements.

As we came in to land I wondered if I should have the whole Wing in the air the following day? I dismissed the idea immediately. That was putting our entire clutch of eggs in one basket.

Sergeant Major Shaw approached my bus, "Will you be going out in the morning sir? It is just that you said you wanted the radio fitting."

"No Sergeant Major I will not be going out but every other bus is on standby. We have another patrol this afternoon and after that they are all yours. Give them a good service tonight." I looked down at his uniform. "Where is your sidearm, Sergeant Major?"

"They get in the way, sir. Me and the lads leave them in our barracks. We can always run and get them if we need them."

"Keep them close to hand. You don't need to wear them but take them from kite to kite as you work on them. That is an order."

"Sir."

On my way to the radio room I called in to the office, "Sergeant Major Hill, it seems some of the chaps were not listening the other day. Make sure they all have a side arm." He looked up at me in surprise. "Yes, I know we told them but…"

"I will check every one personally, sir!"

I opened the door to the radio room, "Any more messages, Sergeant?"

"No sir but there is radio traffic. The Resident in Kirkuk told Baghdad about increased numbers of tribesmen in the town and Baghdad reports the same."

"Does Sergeant Major Davis and Captain Griffiths know?"

"Yes sir. Everyone is pulling an extra duty."

As I climbed into my Snipe I reflected that we all wanted something to start. This waiting was hard on the nerves. I saw more men in Mosul as we passed that town. This would-be Squadron Leader Williams last opportunity to sort out the problems he had found at the airfield. There would be some. It was inevitable. The men who built the field and repaired the aeroplanes did not fly them. There would be minor annoyances that needed to be dealt with. I saw that the Ninaks were parked closely together. That was unwise if the enemy had bombers but if they were tribesmen then it made sense. They would be easier to protect.

The roads also had more traffic. Individually none posed a threat but the numbers were worrying. Once again, they waved and that did not inspire me with confidence. When we reached Faysh Khabur I headed towards the bridges. I wanted to bomb them but I daren't. I was just about to turn and head south when I caught the glint of something in the sky to my left. I held my course. We had done this a couple of times now and I knew we had fuel to spare. I saw that it was three Halberstadt fighters. I recognised it as the D. II. I knew that the Turks had used them in the war but I had never fought them. They had a top speed of just one hundred miles an hour, with a following wind and just one machine gun. They did not carry bombs. What were they doing?

I realised they posed no threat to us but I held our course just to see what they would do. The Bristols, on my port side, all had a machine gun in the rear. Twelve Lewis guns could easily deal with them. They kept flying towards us. Was this a suicide mission? If they crossed the river and engaged us then it would be. They reached the river and then turned to fly in the opposite direction. The pilots cheekily waved at us. They were across the river and war had not been declared, they were safe. I turned and we headed south.

Once again, I saw more signs of the enemy. They were coming.

When we landed Sergeant Bailey and Sergeant Major Shaw raced over to my bus. "We thought we would get a head start on this sir."

"Good. The radio room is manned though, Sergeant?"

He nodded, "Yes sir Corporal Whittaker is there and he is a solid chap."

"Good." I noticed that they both wore their side arms. Daddy Hill had had an effect.

We now had a briefing room and I went there. Sergeant Major Hill saw me enter and a few minutes later McIlroy brought me a cup of tea. He shook his head and smacked the Lee Enfield on his shoulder, "Can't be doing with this sir! It weighs a ton! I haven't fired it since basic training!"

I sipped the tea, "I wouldn't worry about that. Just so long as you fire and twenty others do at the same time one bullet might get through!"

Ritchie followed me in and nodded to McIlroy who scurried off. "What was that about, sir? I mean with the aeroplanes. What were they doing?"

"I am not too certain. My guess is that they wanted to tempt us across the river and that would have been an act of war. A little foolhardy."

Jack came through the door and he had obviously heard the end of the sentence, "Too right it would have been foolhardy, sir. One of us could have taken all three out in the blink of an eye. They were obsolete almost as soon as they were built. That is why they shipped them off to Johnny Turk. That looked too easy to me. I smelled a trap."

The door almost banged open, "So we run away from the Turks now, do we sir?" Squadron Leader Barnes looked angry.

I stood, "I would watch your tone, Squadron Leader. You are bordering on insubordination. Would you care to rephrase the question?"

I saw him take a step back, "Sorry sir. I meant nothing it is just that there were three easy birds for us to take. I was the closest to them. We could have shot them down without crossing the river! We looked like damned fools in front of our men. We might have to fight them some other time."

"And do you think they will be any harder to shoot down?"

"That's what I mean sir. They were such an easy target."

Acting Squadron Leader Ritchie said, "And that is what has the Wing Commander worried sir. There had to be a reason for the action."

McIlroy came in with three mugs of tea, "This rifle sir! I nearly dropped sir's tea!" He was trying to juggle the mugs and the rifle.

He looked so comical that Jack, Paul and I all laughed. It eased the tension. Barnes was still unhappy about the affront to his honour. He took his tea and just sat down.

We sat around the table. I took out my pipe. I was annoyed with Barnes and I needed to calm down. I could have put him on a charge but there was acrimony enough between us already. When I had the pipe going, I began.

"So tomorrow we begin our regular patrols. I intend to vary the aeroplanes and the areas we begin our patrols. They are obviously watching for us. Those three Halberstadt were waiting for us. Jack, you will leave at dawn tomorrow. Fly the reverse of our route. Up along the high ground. Down to the bridges and then back over Ain Zalah. Robert, you will take off at 1000 hours and fly the same route as we did today. My kite is having the radio fitted. You both have a radio. Start to use it now. Let the field know what you can see. Tomorrow my flight will be the back-up and we will be ready to take off in case the invasion starts. I will have the morning flight the day after and Jack the afternoon. This way every squadron gets one day off in three. We will have wear and tear but this will minimise it."

Barnes said, "And the standing orders about the river and the border still stand sir?"

"They do. If the Turks break the peace then I will make the decision. That is for your protection. If I make a mistake then I will be court martialed and not you."

I was uncertain if Barnes took in what I had said but it had been made abundantly clear and I had witnesses.

I did not drink heavily that night. I was worried about the next day. I was up early to watch the Ninaks take off. I went to the radio room and Corporal Whittaker shook his head. There was no attack. I began to doubt myself. Had I seen enough to justify saying there would be an attack by the Turks? Air Vice Marshall Salmond seemed to think so. Major Fox did. What were the Kurds and the Turks up to?

I did a little paperwork and then went to see how the radio was coming along. The two of them were beavering away. "Almost done, sir. Be ready by lunchtime. We can have a little practice if you like."

It would stop me worrying and second guessing myself. "Excellent. I will be either in the office or the radio room if you need me." I heard the Bristols start up and watched them taxi and then take off. I looked at my watch. It was 1000 hours. They would pass Jack's aeroplanes close to the Tigris. I hoped I was keeping the Turks and Kurds thinking.

Sergeant Major Hill tried to make me eat but I was not in the mood. After I had tested the radio I decided that the attack would probably start the next day. Jack had sent back three messages. All stated that the border was quiet. He also reported that the three Halberstadt had appeared again. They were up to something.

By 1300 hours I had become worried that I had not heard from Squadron Leader Barnes. He should have reported when he reached the border and when he passed the bridges. He had done neither.

Sergeant Bailey was back on duty, "Sergeant, raise Squadron Leader Barnes. Ask him for an update."

I listened as the Sergeant spoke into the microphone. After three attempts, he shook his head. "I think there is something wrong with his radio sir. I am getting nothing; not even static. I will check it when he returns."

I was about to go to watch for Jack's Ninaks when Sergeant Bailey began to speak. He scribbled something down on his pad. "Sir, that was Sergeant Dickinson at Mosul Airfield. He said that they had a message from Faysh Khabur that half of the Bristols crossed over the river. Only three of them returned. The squadron is now heading south."

I was bereft of words. Barnes had gone too far, quite literally, he had ignored my orders and, even worse he had, it appeared, lost three valuable aeroplanes. "Try to get more details and then see if you can raise Squadron Leader Barnes again. I am going to the field to wait for Squadron Leader Thomson's Ninaks."

I heard them in the distance and watched as they descended. I needed to speak to someone in Barnes' squadron but I would make do with Jack until then. Marshall came running from the radio room, "Sir, Mosul is under attack. Squadron Leader Williams is attacking the Turks and Kurds. They are coming from the high ground sir."

I nodded and yelled, "Number 5 squadron, scramble!"

It had been some years since I had issued such an order. My flying coat and helmet were in the Snipe. I was in the cockpit before any of my pilots. I fitted the ear pieces for the radio. Then

I donned my helmet. My men were getting to their Snipes as fast as they could but I was impatient. Was this Barnes' fault? If it was I would have him court martialed; friends in high places or not! As my engine had already been started I taxied. As soon as my wingmen joined me I would take off. We could be over Mosul in forty-five minutes. I hoped that would be in time.

I did not try to conserve fuel. I wanted to be there as fast as I could. I resisted the urge to speak on the radio. They would keep me informed and I had nothing to report, yet. I looked in my mirror. My squadron were all on station. I scanned the horizon for sign of fighting. Mercifully, there was none. Thirty-five minutes into the flight we passed Ebril. I saw, in the distance, horsemen. There looked to be hundreds of them. Ebril was about to be attacked. Having something useful to say I sent the message back to Sergeant Bailey who told me that one of Number 7 squadron had been brought down. Luckily it was close to Mosul and we would not need the Vimy. I cocked my guns. I told Bailey to get Number 12 squadron rearmed and refuelled and get to the aid of Ebril.

I saw the Ninaks twelve minutes later. They were heading back to Mosul. That made sense. They would need to refuel and rearm. If I could see them then they could see me and Sergeant Bailey would have given them my progress. This would be a real test of the training we had undergone together. My squadron needed to be disciplined.

I saw that, on the plain there were armoured vehicles. There were eight of them and they looked like the old German Ehrhardt. Clumsy looking and very high they were a tough vehicle to destroy. Luckily, we had bombs. Interspersed amongst the armoured cars were horsemen and men on foot. They were moving quickly and using cover well. I saw the remnants of a British detachment fleeing towards the walls of Mosul. Even as I watched the machine gun on one of the Ehrhardt armoured cars opened fire and two men fell.

We were less than a mile away and I dropped to fifty feet. We were seen by the Turks for they had the armoured cars and their machine guns opened fire. The horses and men took cover behind the imposing vehicles. I did not waste my bullets. I would save those for the horses and men. I felt bullets striking the undercarriage and the wings. I readied my two outer bombs. I dropped them and then prepared to fire my Vickers. I saw a knot of horsemen. They were firing at me. I gave them a short burst. At the same time, my bombs exploded. One destroyed an Ehrhardt. They might resist bullets but not a twenty-five-pound bomb. The second exploded in the open and the shrapnel scythed through advancing men. I prepared to drop my next two bombs at two Ehrhardts which were close together. This time I fired my right-hand Vickers as the bombs dropped.

Pulling up to begin a climb I looked in my mirror and saw that I had damaged both of them but they were still capable of firing. Acting Squadron Leader Ritchie took care of them both with his Vickers. I had damaged them and they both exploded when his bullets hit their fuel tanks. I banked to bring me back round. I was aware that I had no bombs left and I had used a fifth of my bullets. I left the remaining vehicles to those of my squadron who still had bombs and I went after the horsemen and Kurds on foot.

They were brave men. They fought recklessly. It paid off for them. I saw Pilot Officer Barker's Snipe hit. He peeled off, smoking, and I watched him head towards the airfield at Mosul. He had the chance to be repaired. I banked to port. There were more men coming from the high ground. I left the ones closer to Mosul for Ritchie and his two flights. I led my seven aircraft to sweep across the open ground and shoot up as many as we could. I did not fly in a straight line. I almost zig zagged as I sprayed as many Kurds and Turks as I could. These were experienced fighters and they took cover behind rocks. Had we had more bombs then the attack would have ended there and then. As it was my guns clicked on empty and I waved my arm to signal the others to head back to Mosul with me. I saw that Pilot Officer MacDonald was also damaged. He was ahead of us and smoke was coming from his cowling. I radioed Bailey and told him what we intended. As I turned I saw that we had stopped their armour but the men on foot were now using them as strongpoints.

When we approached Mosul Squadron Leader Williams' men were already heading back out to attack the enemy. My two damaged kites were being tended to. As soon as I had landed I leapt out of the cockpit, "Get my Snipes rearmed and refuelled!"

The mechanic saluted and shouted, "Sir!"

I looked at my watch. We still had time, before dusk, to drop our bombs, strafe the enemy and then head for Kirkuk. Mosul might soon become isolated. It was not fair to use all of their ammunition and fuel. They were now the forlorn hope! I ran to Acting Squadron Leader Ritchie. "We hit them again and then head south."

He nodded, "What about the two damaged Snipes, sir?"

"They can stay here. Go around and tell the rest of the men what I intend."

"Sir!"

I ran to Pilot Officer Barker; he was the closest. "Are you alright?"

"Yes sir. My bus is a bit damaged but other than that…."

"Get your birds repaired. Stay here tonight with MacDonald and join the first flight to attack if they can fix them. Head down to Kirkuk tomorrow if you can."

"Sir!"

I ran back to my Snipe. I had taken damage. I saw that I would need a new propeller. There were splinters missing. The Snipe would not fly as smoothly and I had holes in my wings. I had been lucky. They had missed my engine and the controls. I would live with that. The mechanics and riggers were busy working on her even as I examined the damage. I kicked the tyres. They had escaped damage too. The Corporal saluted, "All done sir. You going back up?"

I smiled, "Seems like the thing to do! Thanks chaps. Don't worry we can beat these fellows." In many ways, it was meaningless but they seemed to like and cheered. So long as a man had hope then he could survive horrendous odds. I had seen countless bodies and there looked to be more willing to die.

Acting Squadron Leader Ritchie came over, "They are all singing from the same hymn sheet sir. What are the orders?"

"Plough the field. Use the bombs to destroy any armoured cars that might become strongpoints and then use the rest of the bombs and your guns to kill as many as we can. These chaps don't know the meaning of defeat. We kill them or they kill us."

I climbed into the cockpit and the mechanic spun the propeller. I taxied slowly. I did not know this airfield. My wingmen formed up with me. Adams had replaced Barker. I saw that the squadron, all ten of us were ready and I opened the throttle to race down the runway. This would be a short and savage action. We had to stop them and allow the army the chance to bolster their defences. I hoped that Jack would have had the chance to slow down the attack on Ebril. If that fell then Mosul would be cut off from Kirkuk.

I forced my mind to return to this battle. Jack and the fate of Squadron Leader Barnes would have to wait. I saw the Ninaks diving and using three machine guns to decimate the Kurds and Turks. It was obvious that the Kurds had more heart for the fight. They stayed and fought. I saw uniforms heading north and west. Some of the Turks had had enough. They were going back to safety. It did not mean they were defeated, just that they had had enough for one day. I led my flight towards one Ehrhardt which was still firing. I dropped two bombs and had the satisfaction of watching it blow up in my rear-view mirror. I saw a derelict Ehrhardt; bullets zipped from all around it. I lifted my nose and dropped my last two bombs. Because I dropped them from a slightly higher altitude the shrapnel appeared to have more effect. There would be few survivors.

I had an easier task now. I flew along the battlefield firing at any one I saw with a weapon. Five hundred rounds later I climbed into the sky to await my squadron. I circled and, one by one, they joined me. No more birds had been damaged and I headed south to Kirkuk. I radioed ahead to tell the airfield that we were on our way. Had we averted disaster? I would need to speak with Flight Lieutenant Cartwright, assuming he too, was not a casualty. I radioed to have Flight Lieutenant Cartwright and Jack waiting to see me in the briefing room.

It was getting on to dusk when we finally landed. It was not dark enough to give us problems but I knew that my men would be tired and we had the morning patrol. This time we knew that it would not be a peaceful one. As I stepped from the aeroplane I saw that there were just eight Bristols which were parked ready to take off. Another one was being worked on by oil lamp. I counted twelve Ninaks. Jack had the only whole squadron left to us. As weary as I was I knew that, before I could eat I would have to report to Sir John and then interview the survivors from 18 squadron. If I had any time left then I would speak with Jack. I was grateful that I had at least one senior officer that I could rely upon.

As I headed for the briefing room Sergeant Major Hill met me with a cup of tea. "Here you are sir. Sergeant Major style," he winked.

As I sipped it I realised that there was a hefty tot of rum in it. "Thanks, Daddy, I needed this."

"Don't worry sir. We will come through this."

I felt better as I entered the room. The tea and Daddy's optimism did that. Flight Lieutenant Cartwright looked ashen. It was though he had died and someone had dug up his corpse. Jack was smoking his pipe and he shook his head, a warning.

I took out my pipe and my penknife. I reamed the bowl and tapped it out. I filled it with fresh tobacco and, after sipping my tea, lit the pipe. I waited until it was drawing. I saw Flight Lieutenant Cartwright's eyes. They were wide and they stared at me. I said, quietly, "What happened?"

He took a breath. "We were on patrol and we saw the three Halberstadt. Squadron Leader Barnes made the signal for the first two flights to attack."

I nodded, "You are certain?"

"Yes sir. I thought it was a mistake. I remembered your words but he was my senior officer and…"

"You followed orders and there are others who saw the signal?" I was thinking of Cartwright's career.

"Yes sir."

"Go on."

"We began to catch them almost as soon as they were across the river. They dived to less than forty feet. The Squadron Leader was leading and he had no shot. Suddenly the whole valley was lit up as they ambushed us. They had all sorts of guns: artillery pieces, machine guns and rifles. The Squadron Leader and Pilot Officer Dawkins just exploded. Harrison was damaged and I led the rest up into the air and we headed back across the river. I brought the squadron back." He shook his head. We didn't get to fire a shot or drop a bomb!"

Had that been Paul Ritchie then the guns would have been bombed and the gunners killed. Barnes had paid the price for his failure to command. "Get some sleep. You will be up again tomorrow. I don't have the luxury of spare buses. I need every one in the air tomorrow."

"I can't lead sir! You were wrong! I don't have it in me!"

"You might yet but not tomorrow. I will have Acting Squadron Leader Ritchie lead you. Don't worry. You will get your revenge."

When he had left us Jack said, "A bit of a cock up eh, sir?"

"We both knew that Barnes was a bad egg. It was my fault for not bringing charges. Ebril?"

"No armour there, sir, and we beat them back but they will try again. I spoke with Bailey. Kirkuk and Baghdad are under attack too."

"Tomorrow you go back to Ebril. I will have Ritchie lead the Bristols and cover Kirkuk. I will go to Mosul." He nodded. "Ask Paul to pop and see me eh?"

He left and I looked up at the map. If Count Yuri Fydorervich had still been alive then I would have expected an attack from a different direction the next day. The ground to the north and west of Mosul would not suit armour but I guessed we had destroyed enough of the enemy armour for them to conserve the little that remained. The ground to the east would provide cover for attacking men. There were wrecked vehicles and craters. I began to write a report for Sir John. It was going over the radio but he would be able to read between the lines.

I was half way through when the door opened and Acting Squadron Leader Paul Ritchie stood there. He looked drawn, "Tough day?"

He nodded, "I was just talking to Steve Cartwright, sir. You want me to lead the Bristols?"

"Sit down. It is a difficult job but we both know that Cartwright is in a bad way. He can't lead. If I had more pilots I would ground him but we need every bus in the air tomorrow and I need every squadron led by someone who can keep their head."

"And that is me sir?"

Wings over Persia

"It is. I want you to lead the squadron but let me know when Cartwright is ready to lead. I need you back with me."

"Sir. And what do I do with the squadron? Go back to Mosul?"

"No, Paul. I am worried about Kirkuk. Fly to Sulaimaniya and back. Look for any signs of insurgents and take action. Technically the land between here and the border is still Iraq. Any enemy is fair game. I know that Sheikh Mahmud is supporting the rebels but he is playing a clever game. I don't think there will be any visible rebels in Sulaimaniya. He will be sending them to Ebril and Kirkuk."

"What will you do about the Halberstadt sir?"

"What I won't do is fall into the trap that Squadron Leader Barnes did. I will bide my time but those three aeroplanes are doomed. Believe me."

"I do sir."

I finished off my report and I smoked my pipe. I needed Ritchie back with the squadron before my own plan to trap the Halberstadt could go into action. They were a danger. Any aeroplane was a danger but there was too great a risk to follow them over the border. I hoped that an easier flight from Kirkuk to Sulaimaniya might help Cartwright get over his nerves.

I went to the radio room and handed my report to Marshall. He handed me a typed sheet. "This came in this afternoon sir. It is in code so Sergeant Bailey typed it out."

"Thanks." I headed to the office. This was another job I would have to do before I could head to the mess. I took out the pink folder from the locked desk. This was the first time I had used the code. It took me some time to work it out. Once I had done so I began the laborious task of transcribing the message. I discovered quickly where I had made a mistake and I concentrated on every word. It meant that I didn't get the full ramifications until I had finished. I read through it.

The Turks had ten Halberstadt. That was vital information. There was Intelligence that Kirkuk would come under attack soon. I was relieved that I had given Ritchie the orders I had. However, the end of the message was the most chilling. Count Yuri Fydorervich had survived the attack. He was still at large and was still advising Sheikh Mahmud. The attack which had almost cost Fox and Parr their lives had been a failure and now I knew that there was a cunning puppet master pulling the strings.

Chapter 13

My depleted squadron, all nine aeroplanes, left at dawn. I had warned Paul of the problems he might encounter and brought Jack up to speed too. If anything happened to me there would be someone who knew what to do. I had spoken on the radio to Squadron Leader Williams at Mosul. He also had eight aeroplanes which were fit to fly. My two Snipes were still under repair. I ordered Williams to fly to the east of Mosul and I would patrol as far as Faysh Khabur.

The Squadron Leader had requested more supplies of fuel and ammunition. That meant the Vernons would have to bring them. The presence of such large inviting targets brought more danger. There was rioting in the streets of Mosul. There were enemies within and without. We would have to destroy those outside the town and hope that the small garrison could deal with the dangers within. I scribbled another note for Bailey to send. I made it clear that we had to have fuel and ammunition taken to Mosul by the end of the day.

I saw the Halberstadts in the distance as we approached Faysh Khabur. The detachment there was under attack. There were five aeroplanes strafing the mud walls. As soon as they saw us they fled across the border. I saw the flashes from the guns at Kahnik. The Count was alive or there was a Turk who had the same sort of mind as he had. I saw that there were large numbers of men trying to attack the walls. It was just a company which held the tiny town. A hundred and odd men could not expect to hold out against artillery and a ground attack. I got on to the radio and contacted Mosul to tell them of the attack. I was told that the detachment had not been in contact for twelve hours. Had they been under attack all night?

Now that the Turks had attacked I felt justified in crossing the border. I would not pursue the Halberstadt. Instead I led my squadron up to a thousand feet. I wanted an almost vertical attack. Their larger guns would not be able to fire at us and their machine guns would find it harder to hit us. We had attacked enough for me to be confident that the eight pilots who followed me knew what to do. I glanced in my mirror and saw that they were all on station and waiting for me and my two wingmen to attack first. I began my dive.

Williams and Swanston had been right. There were false guns on the walls but there were real ones too. A barrage of small arms erupted. It is harder to hit an aeroplane diving at you. When it flew horizontally then you could lead it. The Turks were not using tracer and could not see their shot. I did not fire my guns. They would be more useful later. I dropped two bombs and pulled up. My wingmen were with me. I felt the concussion from the explosions. A few seconds later there was another explosion. We had hit ammunition.

As I levelled out I saw Flight Lieutenant Jackson leading the second flight in. We had breached the walls and damaged some of the guns. Jackson and his flight were going to finish off the rest. By the time they had finished the fort was rubble. My squadron formed up on me and we headed back to Faysh Khabur.

They were no longer being shelled but I saw that they were being penned in by waves of Kurds and Turks who saw their chance to butcher British soldiers. Their artillery pieces lay wrecked. They were almost defenceless. We could not use our bombs and so I led my squadrons to fly as low as we dared and strafe the attackers. We caught them by surprise and our first pass cut a swathe of death through their ranks. The survivors took shelter in the town. As I passed over I saw that the walls of the fort had been breached. The Turkish artillery had damaged them. I saw more Kurds approaching on horses. As we circled above the town I signalled to Flight Lieutenant Simpkins to take his Snipes and deal with them. They had four bombs each. As they flew off I saw something flashing from the walls of Faysh Khabur. It was a signal. I waggled my wings to show that I had seen the signal and, circling, watched as they began it again. It was short and simple. 'Out of ammo. Going to break out in fifteen minutes. Need help.' It was repeated.

I waggled my wings when they had finished. I radioed Mosul and told them what was going to happen. We would have to blast a route through the town for them. The Kurds would wait for us to leave and then finish off what they had started. I saw, as we circled, that the detachment had seven lorries. I signalled to my two flights to take station inline astern. That way they could all emulate me. Simpkins and his flight were still busy with the Kurds who were trying to join the attack. I looked at my watch. They were coming out in six minutes. I began my bombing run.

On my first bomb run I had used my two inner bombs. I gambled that if I flew down the road then I could bomb both sides and still leave a clear escape route for the lorries. The danger lay in making a crater in the road. I dropped my bombs forty yards from the gates. I knew that my wingmen would bomb progressively down the road. We still had our machine guns and, as we cleared the town I began to climb and circle. I made the signal for two columns. Normally Squadron Leader Ritchie would have led the other. It fell to Jackson to take on that role.

Ahead I saw the gates open and we began to dive as the seven lorries raced out. The houses on both sides had been demolished for two hundred yards. That was, largely the extent of the village. I guessed that some of my squadron still had bombs left. That could come in handy on the way back to Mosul. I zoomed over the houses at less than fifty feet and I fired my left-hand Vickers. I was largely firing blind but I wanted to keep down the enemy heads. Five hundred .303 bullets a minute would discourage anyone from lifting their heads. Those that did so would lose them. I pulled up as I neared the fort and it was a good job I had. The commander had booby trapped it with explosives and, as Kurds raced into the headquarters' building, it exploded. They might have been short of ammunition but they had explosives left.

I climbed and our two columns took station on either side of the road. I cut the engines a little to conserve fuel and to help us keep pace with the lorries. They were driving flat out. Simpkins' flight came to join us. They used their guns to scatter the last of the Kurds who lay in their path. We flew elliptical loops once Simpkins joined us. We were able to fly ahead of the column and still cover the rear. I saw Williamson suddenly leave formation and dive. I watched as his last two bombs dropped behind a rock. As I passed it I saw that he had surprised Kurds setting an ambush. The machine gun and small mountain gun lay with the twenty dead and dying tribesman and their horses. It proved to be the last opposition. When I saw the airfield ahead and, aware that we were running out of fuel, we left the column and headed to the field.

As we came in to land I was aware of firing in the centre of Mosul. There were explosions and the sound of light arms. The Ninaks of Number 7 squadron had not returned yet. They had a longer range than we did. The Senior Sergeant Major came hurrying over to me. "Get them refuelled and rearmed. See if any have damage."

"Sir, but we are running short of ammo and if it goes on like this we will run out of fuel."

"Then don't rearm the bombs just one belt of ammo for each aeroplane. That will have to do." He nodded, "How are the two Snipes?"

"Their pilots are going to take them up for an engine test sir but you can have them back by this afternoon."

"Good."

Squadron Leader Williams had the luxury of an adjutant. Barnes should have had one but I guessed he thought he could do without one. I went in to the office. Flight Lieutenant Charlton was older than I was. When he stood to greet me, I saw that he favoured one leg and a stick rested against the desk. His fruit salad showed that he had been decorated. He was a veteran of the Great War. Many such pilots stayed in. He would not rise above the rank of Flight Lieutenant unless he was very lucky.

"Wing Commander, this is a pleasure. I didn't get a chance to say hello when we came through Kirkuk."

"Did we serve together?"

"No sir but John Charlton was my cousin. He told me all about you."

I remembered him. He had been a flight observer and he had not survived the war. I nodded. "He was a good man. It was a great loss." I pointed to his leg, "When did you cop the wound?"

"Two weeks before the end of the whole shebang. Ground fire. I have to walk with a stick. Still worse for some of the other lads eh sir?"

"Quite right. Now tell me what is going on here."

"Do you mind if I sit, sir."

"Of course, I am sorry, I should have realised."

He smiled and took out a map. As he spoke he pointed. "No problem sir. Now this is Mosul. The Kurds infiltrated over the past week or so. Colonel Ayre did not realise until it was too late. They have been causing mayhem. And we can't do a great deal about them from the air." He jabbed a finger. "They control here and here sir. If those two enclaves join up we are in trouble. And they have cut the telephone wires sir. We only have the radio now for contact."

"And Squadron Leader Williams?"

"He has managed to stop any reinforcements joining them in the city. That is the good news but he radioed not long ago and said he had to return as two of the Ninaks were damaged and they had run out of ammo."

"I know we have a problem. I have some Vernons arriving here, probably later today. I know that will give you a headache, watching them overnight but at least you can fight back. I take it all the men are armed?"

He patted his Webley. "Yes sir and I have a couple of Mills bombs handy too."

"Good. Well my chaps and I will grab some food and then I will see what we can do about these two rebel held areas in the town." I held my hand out, "Give me the map and I will see if there is a way to bomb them."

My pilots all ate with me. Barker and McDonald were keen to get into the fight. Their aeroplanes had passed their first test. They had taken off and landed successfully. "Tell me, do your Snipes have bombs still?"

They nodded. Pilot Officer Barker said, "We only used two each and they rearmed us this morning for the test flight."

Gowland said, "And I have two left too sir."

"Excellent." I took out the map. "These are two rebel held areas. I need you three to bomb them both. You will have to do it by releasing one bomb at a time. We cannot afford collateral damage. You need to be as accurate as you can."

Barker grinned, "That means as low as we can go then eh sir?"

"Precisely. We have all afternoon to do this. The rest of us will fly alongside each of you and keep down the opposition's heads. I want these two areas to be obliterated." I had a sudden thought. "And the rest of you, see the quartermaster. Take up two Mills bombs each. If we are going in that low then we can use them as bombs. If they explode in the air that will be just as good."

They were all excited at the prospect. They knew that I had used the grenades in that way and it appealed to them.

"One thing more. If I have enough fuel I am going to fly to the place where Barnes and the others were reported shot down."

Barker looked appalled, "It is a terrible risk sir!"

"If those pilots and gunners were still alive and waiting for help how could I live with myself? You bring back the squadron when I peel off. I will go alone. Tell the chaps."

"Sir!"

I went back to see the adjutant, "Get on the radio to this Colonel Ayre. Tell him my aeroplanes are coming in to try to clear the two enclaves. When we leave, he should be able to retake them."

"Risky sir and it demands a high level of skill."

"Flight Lieutenant, these young lads were dropping bombs from their first flights onwards. We had to learn how to use them. They will be fine. Tell him we will begin our bomb run at 1300 hours." I heard the sound of the Ninaks returning and I left the office to greet Squadron Leader Williams.

He looked tired, "How did your raid go sir?"

"I am afraid they retook Faysh Khabur but we managed to extract the detachment there. Colonel Ayre now has almost a hundred more men. We are going to try to bomb the two rebel enclaves. Are you and your lads all right to go back out?"

"There will only be six of us but yes sir. If we don't plug up this hole then Mosul will be filled with even more rats."

"Good man. I have Vernons coming this afternoon with more fuel and ammo."

"They can't bring enough sir. We will need a convoy of bowsers."

"I know. I will try to get that arranged when I get back to Kirkuk." I looked at my watch. "It is time we were off then."

We flew in three lines of three and a rear pair. The first three each had a Snipe with bombs. The last two would mop up any survivors. I led us out to the south. I wanted to come in with the sun behind us. It would make it harder for them to see us and, therefore, hit us. We did not waste fuel and time gaining altitude. Instead we kept low. To the rebels we would appear like little angry hornets who came from nowhere.

Even without the map I would have been able to see where the rebel held areas where. They had raised the Kurdish and Turkish flags and they also popped away at us. Barker dropped his first bomb at the closest enclave. I dropped a grenade as we passed over. We were so fast that, despite every gun firing at us, most missed. The next flight was three hundred feet behind us. As we banked to join the circus once more I saw the effect of the bomb. We had brought down part of a house. There was a danger that such ruins could become strongpoints. Barker's last two bombs would be reserved for those ruins. They would become dust.

I was able to watch MacDonald's strike. He hit the second enclave. I saw two Mills bombs as they were thrown. They exploded in the air and I saw men on the tops of the buildings scythed down. Gowland only had two bombs. His first one was dropped in the same place as Barker's. Then it was our turn again. I saw that the bombs had started fires and there was smoke to contend with. That made it hard for every pilot but doubly so for the bombers. This time I fired my machine gun, briefly, at the enclave before bringing my nose up and joining Barker as he banked.

We suffered our first casualty when MacDonald made his second run. Pilot Officer Briggs was hit. I saw his Snipe buck. My pilots knew better than to fly a damaged bird and he banked and headed back the few miles to the airfield. I saw Barker look over and I pointed to his bombs and held up two fingers. He nodded. He would drop two bombs on the next run. I could see that the two enclaves were now charnel houses. It had been a lucky shot which had damaged Briggs but there was no point in risking a second lucky shot. MacDonald emulated Barker. I waved to Barker and he nodded. I turned the Snipe and headed for Turkey.

Technically I was in breach of standing orders flying into Turkey but, as the Turks had invaded, I thought it a moot point. A few Turks fired at me but I was at four thousand feet and they had no chance of hitting me. Barnes had followed the Halberstadts at a low altitude. He had been an easy target. I stayed high. I saw the guns. They tried to elevate them but they had been set to fire across the valley and I was safe. I saw the aeroplanes in the distance. After flying a little further north and banking I began my descent. I saw the three Bristols. They had been burned out. It looked to have been after the crash. I risked dropping to two hundred feet. Coming in from the north I was beyond the guns. I spied the six crew. The Turks had made it easy for me. They had beheaded them and put their heads in a line close the bodies. I hoped that it been done post death. I climbed.

I had one machine gun which I had not used. I would use it now. I headed deeper into Turkey and then swung around. I dropped to a hundred feet. When I reached the eastern side of the valley I dropped to fifty feet. I flew down the line of guns and gunners. I fired a burst at each emplacement. There were six of them and the final one endured the last of the belt. I must have hit some ammunition for, as I climbed to head back to the field, I saw, in my rear-view mirror, the emplacement as it exploded. Barnes and his men were dead but I had not left them trapped behind enemy lines. I would be able to sleep at night.

My men were euphoric. I saw that as I taxied. They were gathered around in a group and their arms emulated their wings as they described to each other what they had all done. It had been a most masterful display of precision bombing. Of course, it would not have worked against an enemy who had heavy guns and more machine guns. As soon as I landed I ordered the Snipes to be refuelled. I went to the adjutant. He was beaming, "Just came off the radio with the Colonel. They have retaken the enclaves. There are fifteen prisoners too. He says he owes you a drink!"

"It is a small start. I will take my Snipes back to Kirkuk. We have more ammunition and fuel at Kirkuk. Besides this will get crowded later when six Vernons arrive."

He nodded, "You seem a little down Wing Commander."

I spoke quietly. The adjutant would tell the squadron leader my news later. It would not do to hear it from an office Erk. "I just found the crews of the Bristols which went down. They had been beheaded and their kites burned. Our enemies do not appear to play by the same rules as us."

"Good God sir! Savages! Bloody savages! At least the Bosch never did that!"

We took off and flew the ninety miles to Kirkuk. Alarmingly there were fires in the city and evidence of unrest. I saw bodies by the side of the road a mile or so from the airfield. They had come close. As we descended I saw the Vernons to the west of us heading for Mosul. It would not be much fuel that they could carry but it would augment what they had. I saw that Captain Daniels had slit trenches and sandbags everywhere. He waved at me as I climbed down from the Snipe.

Sergeant Major Shaw said, "Been a rum old day sir. A bunch of wild men attacked the main gate not long after you left. And then when Squadron Leader Thomson came back he surprised a column of men sneaking up to the east sir." He patted his Webley. "I thought I was going to have to fire this in anger, sir!"

"I am pleased that you are carrying it."

I headed for the office. Sergeant Major Hill snapped to attention, "Glad you are back sir. McIlroy, tea! The Kurds have taken over parts of Kirkuk. Captain Daniels sent Williams and the extra lads in to help out. They managed to clear a corridor from the field to the Residency but I am not certain that the lads there can hold out, sir."

I nodded, "I know. We had the same in Mosul. We can't go on bombing the centres of the towns. Eventually we will have civilian casualties and that will turn the peaceful ones against us." McIlroy brought the tea. "I will be in the briefing room writing up my report. When Squadron Leader Thomson and Acting Squadron Leader Ritchie arrive send them both in will you?"

"Sir."

Both Squadron Leaders had left reports for me. There were no damaged aeroplanes to worry about but they had both struggled to stop the two attacks. It seemed that there were large numbers coming from Sulaimaniya as well as the natural homeland of the Kurds in Turkey. What worried me was that they could come at night. So far, they had not tried that. We couldn't operate at night; not safely anyway. For that we needed ground troops. I began to write a message to send to Baghdad. I had no idea if things were as bad there but I doubted it.

Acting Squadron Leader Ritchie arrived first. He looked exhausted. "Well that was fun, sir!"

I laughed and pushed my tobacco pouch over. "Have a fill of my baccy and then tell me all about it."

He got his pipe going and I saw the relief on his face. McIlroy slipped the mug of tea on to the table. "The Snipe and the Bristol are different beasties. They fly differently, sir. It was hard to keep formation. Mind you the bomb load is handy. We found large numbers heading over to attack Kirkuk. They even had a couple of ancient lorries. I think they were Ottoman, from the war, sir. Anyway, we stopped them. We went out again this afternoon and used our guns to make them take cover. They are out there, sir but they are using the natural spaces in which to hide." He took a swig from his mug. "However, sir, tonight? I reckon they will be all over Kirkuk like fleas on a dog."

"I agree with your assessment. I will nip into Kirkuk tonight and see if the resident will consider pulling the civilians back here. The Vernons are only at Mosul. We could take the women and non-essential personnel down to Baghdad."

When Jack came he reported almost the same. I shouted, "McIlroy, fetch Captain Daniels for me, will you?"

"Sir."

I had finished my radio message and I passed it to Jack. "What do you think?"

He read it and said, "I agree sir. We need the other Ninaks, supplies and, if they have them, ground troops."

Acting Squadron Leader Ritchie said, "What if we don't get them sir?"

"Did you do history at school, Paul?"

"Did you study the Afghan war?"

"No sir."

In eighteen seventy-nine the Amir of Afghanistan, Sher Ali Khan signed a peace treaty with the British. It allowed us to have a presence in their cities. On September, the 3rd Sher Ali Khan incited his people to rise in the city. They massacred Sir Louis Cavagnari and every British man woman and child. The non-

Muslim men were all castrated before they were killed. That, I am afraid, is what would happen in Kirkuk, if we allowed it."

"I didn't know."

"I am afraid that the Muslims do not follow rules as we do. So, tomorrow, I want the Ninaks to return to Ebril. If that is quiet then head to Mosul. Acting Squadron Leader Ritchie, keep the road to Sulaimaniya clear of Kurds."

Jack drained his tea, "And you sir?"

"That depends upon the result of my visit to Lord Palmer this evening. If he refuses to take my advice then I will be keeping Kirkuk safe."

Captain Daniels appeared at the door. He looked tired. I think we all were. "Captain, what is your assessment of the situation in Kirkuk?"

"It is dire sir. Sergeants Williams and Swanston are holding on to a corridor to the Residency by the skin of their teeth. If the Kurds come tonight, and I think they will, then we will have to pull them back and the Residency will be cut off." He shrugged, "Sorry sir that is an honest assessment,"

"And it is my opinion too. I want a lorry and three men. I will head into Kirkuk and try to persuade the resident to bring out the women, children and civilians. We can protect them here and, if necessary, evacuate them. I have six Vernons to take them away."

"Should I come sir?"

"Thank you for the offer but I think we need you inside here. I want the defences beefing up. Make this into a fortress."

"Sir!" He saluted and left.

I went to my quarters and took out the pink folder. It took me an hour but I encoded my radio message. I handed it to the corporal. "It is in code. If I get a reply I want it no matter what time it is."

"Sir!"

I went to my quarters and changed into a fresh uniform. The other had begun to smell. I could have used a shower but I needed to get into Kirkuk. I took out my German automatic and a couple of grenades. One never knew. I had my dagger in my boot. Donning my sun helmet I left the quarters. I popped my head into the office. "Sergeant Major Hill, I am going into

Kirkuk. If anything untoward happens, then Squadron Leader Thomson is in command."

"Sir. Be careful eh? I am just getting used to you and your ways, sir."

Jack was waiting for me. "This is not the cleverest of moves sir. I mean you could send a radio message."

I shook my head, "I need face to face. If I can't get back then you are in command. The code book is in my quarters, pink file."

"You will be back. Good luck sir."

The lorry was waiting and there were four tough looking Air Force Regiment Erks waiting. "Corporal I'Anson sir. The captain says we are to take you to the residency."

"And back, if possible."

His face did not crack, "We will try sir."

I sat in the cab and I held my German automatic. I liked the Webley but the Mauser had nine bullets. I might need them all. We headed towards the city. As we neared the first building Sergeant Williams rose, like a wraith, "Where are you off to, Corporal?"

I leaned forward, "Taking me for a spin, sergeant."

"Sorry sir, didn't see you there. It is like the wild west from here on in sir."

"Then take the place of one of the men in the back eh, Sergeant?"

He grinned, "Of course sir!"

I felt better with Sergeant Williams in the back. After four hundred yards, he banged on the partition and said, "Watch out from here on in, sir."

"Thank you, Sergeant." I cocked and lifted the Mauser. "Keep your foot down Corporal I'Anson."

"Sir!"

A few moments later two men stepped out with guns and aimed them at us. Corporal I'Anson did exactly as I had asked and he drove right over them. I heard the smack as their bodies hit the solid front of the lorry. I saw a face appear and I fired my Mauser at it. The face disappeared. I heard bullets at the rear and then there was the crack of a grenade. Then there was silence. We had broken through the first roadblock.

Not far from the Residency two men just above me opened fire. Their bullets smashed into the cab. I lifted my gun and fired the rest of the magazine blindly. One must have had a grenade primed for there was a loud explosion. I looked ahead and saw the Residency.

"You had better slow up in case they think we are the villains of the peace!"

"Yes sir. Nice shooting! You would have won a prize at a fair in England with shooting like that."

"I will take that as a compliment."

A lieutenant held up his hand, "Can I help you sir?"

"I hope so. Take me to the Resident. Corporal I'Anson, turn the lorry around and be prepared for a fast getaway."

"Sir!"

I was pleased to see that they had made the building like a fortress. There was wire and there were sandbags. Lee Enfields poked through gaps in the bags. "The Resident is at dinner." I threw him a sideways look and he shrugged. "It is dinner time, sir." In the distance, we heard the sound of firing. It continued as we walked towards the dining room.

The door to the dining room was opened. Lady Isabel was there as was Lord Randolph. Three ladies were amongst the ten guests. There were three officers and the doctor too. Lord Randolph smiled, "Are you here for dinner, Wing Commander?" None of them seemed to notice the sound of firing which came from the east of the town.

"Sir, my men have reported large numbers of Kurds heading towards the town. While it was daylight we were able to stop them but I fear that they will use the night to infiltrate and assault the town's defences.

His lordship looked at the lieutenant colonel who sat to his right, "Pennington-Browne?"

"The Wing Commander may well be right but my chaps are ready for them. I have fought them before when they were Johnny Turk. They soon turn and run when you meet them with cold steel and a Lee Enfield."

Lord Randolph nodded, "So you see, Wing Commander, we have the situation under control."

I was getting nowhere, "Then let me evacuate the ladies and non-essential civilians to the airfield. I can whisk them back to Baghdad if the situation worsens."

Lady Isabel smiled, "As much as I would like to fly in an aeroplane, it sounds most exciting, I fear that we cannot desert the men at a time like this. We may not be able to wield a weapon but our fortitude and support will help them win the day."

My head drooped, "Very well but I must warn you that by morning there will be no way to get from here to the airfield. We had to fight our way here."

The doctor stood, "What you could do for me Wing Commander is take the six wounded men to your airfield. Perhaps they would be safer and besides we don't have room here for more wounded."

"Of course, sir."

We went to the room they used for the wounded. I had been there. There was a corporal and five privates. Two of the privates needed stretchers. As they were carried out to the lorry I tried one more time, "Doctor I am not exaggerating the situation. Mosul and Ebril are both surrounded by a sea of Kurds and Turks. Kirkuk is stuck out here and Sheikh Mahmud is closer than the Resident thinks."

"I am a doctor, Wing Commander. His lordship listens to the military men, not me."

Sergeant Williams met me at the door. "The patients are in the back sir but we better get a move on. The gunfire has been getting closer. I think they are closing in."

The lieutenant who had taken me to the Resident nodded, "I fear the sergeant is correct, sir. The men who were guarding the buildings to the north are pulling back."

I saluted, "Good luck Lieutenant. I will have to pull our men back. If you are overrun try to get to the airfield."

"Thank you, sir but I suspect the colonel will have us stay at our posts until the very end."

I climbed into the cab. "When we reach our men, Corporal, stop to pick them up. Until then drive as though the devil himself was behind us."

"Sir!" Corporal I'Anson roared towards the airfield. We still had to negotiate streets filled with insurgents and rebels. I had my pistol and a grenade ready. I saw the flash of muzzles and heard the reports as the Kurds fired from concealed positions. I fired at the flashes and I heard Sergeant Williams shout, "Open fire!" The Corporal was magnificent. He kept driving even though the windscreen was shattered by bullets. I saw that his face was cut by flying glass but his dour face never changed. With no windscreen, I was able to fire out of the front. I drew my Webley and fired both guns. As we neared the corridor guarded by our men he slowed.

Sergeant Williams shouted, "All aboard lads! Our shift is done!" There was a wan cheer and I felt the lorry rock as they climbed aboard. A hand banged on the side and we drove off. As our gates closed behind us I wondered just how long we could hold out.

Chapter 14

The wounded men we had brought were taken to the sick bay and Sergeant Williams and his men went for some well-deserved food. I had to forego my repast for I needed to speak with Baghdad. This time I did not write my report to be read, I spoke with Baghdad. I wanted Sir John to know just how dire the situation was.

Sergeant Major Hill found me as I had just finished, "Come along, sir. I had the cooks keep you something hot. You have done all that you can. Whatever happens in Kirkuk is out of your hands now. You'll do no-one any good if you fall sick."

I smiled, "Yes mother! I am coming."

I did feel better with food inside me. Jack and some of my officers had stayed in the mess. I had company while I ate. The sounds of firing grew as the Kurds did what I had predicted and launched an attack at night when we were grounded. I finished and pushed the plate away. After lighting his pipe Jack asked, "Well sir, what is the plan for the morrow?"

"That is a tough one. Ebril and Mosul need support too. We have three squadrons. I will have to let Squadron Leader Williams watch out for Mosul. Jack, you will take your buses to Ebril. You know it better than anyone. Paul and I will try to help Kirkuk."

They nodded. Acting Squadron Leader Ritchie said, "We won't have as far to come and rearm sir."

"True but we are running out of munitions. Mosul needs supplies but so do we. It may be we have to do what we did in Baghdad and take out large areas. If we can clear a field of fire for the defenders then, at night when we cannot fly they will have a better chance of keeping them at bay." I stood. "Get some sleep and I want us in the air as soon as dawn breaks. I will go and see Sergeant Major Shaw. I need to know how many kites we can get into the air tomorrow."

The Sergeant Major was in the Sergeant's Mess. They all stood when I entered, "At ease. Just wanted a word with Sergeant Major Shaw." He was seated with Sergeant Major Hill.

"Drink sir?"

"No thanks, Daddy." I turned to face Shaw. "How many kites can we get into the air tomorrow?"

"One of your Snipes needs a major overhaul. A bullet cut an oil pipe. There are gaskets which are shot. That will take a whole day sir. Two of the Number 18 Squadron's Bristols need re-rigging. They were badly shot up. They might be ready for late afternoon. Squadron Leader Thomson's squadron will be lucky to get eight up sir. The interrupter gear has gone on one. A second needs a new undercarriage. A third will need a new fuel tank and a fourth has to have a new engine. We are going to cannibalise what we can. Sorry sir. I know it isn't what you wanted to hear. The lads worked until dark. We tried to work with lights but that attracted snipers who started taking pot shots at us."

I held my hands up, "No criticism. Your lads are doing the best that they can. Tomorrow will be a critical day." I told the two of them what we had planned. "The Snipes will come back to rearm as often as we can. If we can hang on for tomorrow then Sir John might get reinforcements to us."

"We will hold on sir. We can't let the buggers drive us out!"

"You are right, Sergeant Major Hill, but I am not certain that this desert is worth the deaths we have suffered already."

I added more to my letter to Beattie and then retired. I was asleep in an instant. I was woken by gunfire. I looked at my watch. It was 0315. Grabbing my pistol, I ran outside. I saw the flashes of guns outside the perimeter and then heard Captain Daniels shout, "Open fire!" I heard the rattle of Vickers and Lewis guns and the cracks of rifles. Our double ditches would keep them from getting too close to the fences but a stray bullet could hit one of the aeroplanes. They were three hundred yards from the fence but a Lee Enfield could travel much further than that. In a way, I was relieved that they were firing at my men. They, at least, had the protection of sandbags.

I ran to the Captain. "Captain Daniels, we have some grenade rifles, don't we?"

"Yes sir, about half a dozen of them but what good are they going to be? We can just see the muzzle flashes."

"When we have spotted these chaps from the air they tend to bunch up. There might be one muzzle flash but that might conceal eight men. When you kill one of them another takes his place."

"It is worth a try. Sergeant Coates go and fetch the rifle grenades. Have them at ten-yard intervals. Send a barrage over towards the muzzle flashes."

I aimed my pistol at one such flash and fired four shots. I had no idea if I hit anything but even a ricochet could cause damage. Our heavier firepower meant that we had the upper hand but we could not allow the firefight to continue. The longer it did so the more chance we had of losing another aeroplane. As soon as the grenades were used we saw, in the flash of the explosions, that there were large numbers of tribesmen. The grenades broke the back of their attack. After half an hour, there were no flashes. They had withdrawn.

Captain Daniels looked at me, "Off back to bed sir?"

I shook my head, "I am flying at dawn. I will go and have an early breakfast."

"Right sir."

"As soon as it is dawn get your men to make sure that the men outside are all dead. Collect their weapons."

The gunfire had woken most of the pilots and the sergeant cook looked in dismay as we all entered the mess. "Sir, we haven't got it all ready yet!"

"Well give us a cup of tea and get a move on!" As we drank our tea I went over with my pilots, what I intended. After my talk with Sergeant Major Shaw I knew that I would have far less aeroplanes than I needed. There would be just fifteen of us in the air. I nodded to the Bristol pilots, "Have your gunners keep the heads of the rebels down. Use Mills bombs if you have to. Use your bombs judiciously. You have four times the bomb load of the Snipe but don't drop them all at once. There is too great a risk of collateral damage."

The breakfast came and we all ate well. We knew that it would just be corned beef sandwiches for lunch if we were lucky enough to have the time to eat. Jack stood, "I will keep you informed by radio of the situation at Ebril, sir."

"We just need to hold them back, Jack."

As I headed towards my aeroplane Marshall ran from the radio room, "Sir, a message from Baghdad. They are sending the

Vernons with four hundred Sikhs and 11 Squadron is heading up to Mosul. It is escorting a convoy with supplies."

"That is excellent news. Tell Sergeant Major Hill and then radio both Mosul and the residency to let them know that help is on the way."

I felt more confident as I climbed into my Snipe. We had just a few hours to hold and then the 14th Sikhs would arrive. As soon as I was in the air I flew a box pattern to allow the rest of the two depleted squadrons to form up on me. It allowed me to see that the residency was surrounded. I saw Kurdish and Turkish flags all over. That would make it easier for us. I would attack wherever I saw a flag. Once we were all in formation I led my squadrons towards the flags.

They had learned to respect aeroplanes and they had created a gun emplacement on every flat roof. With sandbags in front of them they were protected from machine gun bullets but not from bombs. My Snipes had to endure the worst of the ground fire but our bombs cleared the guns and the Bristols had an easier and less dangerous task as they used their bombs to clear large swathes of the city captured by rebels. While the Bristols used their bombs, we flew closer to the residency and fired our Vickers to clear away the rebels who were getting closer to the defenders.

Without bombs and bullets, we headed back to the airfield. Sergeant Major Shaw and his men raced to rearm the Snipes. As they were doing so I heard the familiar throb of Napier Lion Engines as the Vernons of 70 Squadron brought in the first contingent of Sikhs.

Sergeant Major Hill came over to me. "45 Squadron left Mosul this morning sir. They are going to follow with the rest of the men. There will be four hundred and eighty reinforcements. That will sort the buggers out, eh sir?"

"I hope so, I sincerely hope so."

I decided to delay the next flight. I wanted to coordinate with the Sikhs. I watched the huge aeroplanes land and then taxi. Colonel Pemberton strode over to me with his adjutant, Major Goodall.

"Wing Commander. We have two hundred and eighty men here. Can you give me an assessment of the situation?"

"I can do better sir. If you would come up in a DH 9A with me I can show you."

"Good gracious." He smiled, "Well it will be something to tell the grandchildren."

I turned, "Flight Lieutenant Cartwright, I will take your kite up. Get the Colonel a helmet, goggles and a flying jacket."

"Sir."

"Come with me Colonel." As we walked I told him what we had done, "We have slowed down their advances but they have large numbers. My aeroplanes can go up as soon as your chaps attack. You just need to tell me what you want us to do."

Cartwright arrived with the equipment and he helped the colonel to don them. We managed to get the bemused colonel into the gunner's cockpit and secure him in. "We can talk but you will have to shout. Just ignore the gun. I will fly as steadily as I can. Don't be afraid to hang on. It can be quite scary."

I did not mention that I had been thrown from a Gunbus and had to hang on for dear life. I still remembered my comrades singing the Daring Young Man on the Flying Trapeze in the mess!

I took off and climbed gently. Cartwrights' gunner would not appreciate having to clear vomit from his seat. I flew over the places we had bombed. "This is where we hit this morning!" I flew over the residency. "They are getting closer by the minute."

The colonel shouted, "How accurate are you chaps with these bombs?"

"I can show you. Pick a target!"

He shouted, "Over there about a hundred yards behind us I can see a fellow with a machine gun on a roof!"

He was looking behind us and I looked in the mirror. "I see it. Hold on!"

I turned and attacked at thirty feet above roof top height. Ignoring the bullets flying towards me I dropped one bomb and then pulled up. I heard the colonel shout, "Good gracious!" as the bomb took out the machine gun and the men on the roof of the building.

I headed back to the field and landed. The colonel was flushed but he was also grinning. "Extraordinary. Better than artillery. Look Wing Commander if you can clear us a path to the Residency that would be tickety boo!"

"We can do that."

He looked at his watch, "1400 hours?"

"Yes colonel. I will get the radio operator to warn the garrison in Kirkuk."

I gathered my pilots around me. "We go in this afternoon three abreast. I want to progressively bomb the route into the town. The Sikhs will be following close behind us. When you have dropped your bombs then strafe the streets to the side. You Bristol pilots can have your gunners cover the Sikhs as they go in. When you are out of ammunition then head back and rearm." I paused. I had debated whether to tell them about Barnes. I decided I had to. "One more thing. When I found Squadron Leader Barnes and his men I saw that they had been beheaded. I hope they were dead before that happened but if you are forced down then do not surrender. We are fighting fanatical savages."

Their faces were sombre and I saw that my words had hit home.

Just then I heard the sound of Jack's squadron as they returned from Ebril. I saw that a couple of them had been damaged. He would be lucky to be able to take half a squadron out. I walked over to him. He lit his pipe and nodded towards the Vernons, "That is a sight for sore eyes."

"It is." I told him what we intended. "Ebril, what is the situation there?"

"They are holding. They have solid walls there and we managed to stop the rebels from infiltrating."

"Then have your aeroplanes serviced today. Tomorrow I will give you the remains of 18 squadron and you can get rid of the last of the rebels. Henry is heading to Mosul."

"You are confident that the Sikhs will do the trick here, sir?"

"I am."

We took off at 13.45. That allowed us to get into formation and begin our attack precisely at 1400. The Sikhs were waiting just beyond our gates. They were used to dealing with fighters like the Kurds. The Afghans on the north-west frontier fought the same way. I waited until we were fired at before I dropped my bombs. My wingmen dropped theirs a few moments later. It meant we cleared a large area. The concussion swept down the road. We climbed and banked so that we could take the streets to the east of the main road. I saw, in my mirror, the second three drop their bombs a further one hundred yards along the road.

I dived and looked out for targets. Rifles fired at us but I saw no targets. They were using cover. Simpkins' guns sounded and I saw men fall. He either had better eyes or more luck. I banked to starboard and saw men on a roof with a machine gun. Their attention was on 18 squadron. I opened fire and killed them and demolished the gun. By the time the bombing run had finished the Sikhs were at the residency. As we landed I saw the Vernons of 45 squadron approaching the field from the south as they brought the rest of the Sikhs.

I landed and the mechanics and armourers raced to refuel and rearm my Snipe. By the time we were ready the Sikhs had disembarked and were heading out of the airfield towards Kirkuk. Any doubt that they were going to win, now evaporated. We took off and I heard, on the radio, that the enemy were fleeing and heading to Sulaimaniya. That changed everything. Instead of bombing Kirkuk we chased the survivors east. We didn't waste bombs for they had spread out. Instead we used our guns. When they were empty and we turned to head home we passed over many bodies and dead animals. Sheikh Mahmud had lost. The Turks who attacking Mosul and Ebril were still a threat but we could now turn our whole attention to them. The airfield and Kirkuk were safe.

When we returned to the airfield I saw that Sergeant Major Shaw and his men were busy working on the damaged aeroplanes. I headed for the shower. I did not think that having a somewhat pungent, not to say downright smelly commanding officer, would do anyone any good! I stayed in the shower longer than I had planned. The water was hot! That in itself was a novelty. It was usually lukewarm. When I was dressed I headed for the office.

I was greeted by a serious Sergeant Major Hill. "Sir, we have had a message from Mosul. Those Halberstadt attacked the Ninaks when they were on the way back to the airfield. They were out of ammunition and they lost two of them. Even worse they managed to damage the Vimy Air Ambulance."

"Damn!" I had been too smug. As soon as I had discovered that the Count had not died in the raid I should have expected something like this. Of course, the Halberstadt was too slow to engage any of our buses in combat but an aeroplane which had no ammunition was an easy target.

"Send a message and say that I will bring my Snipes there tomorrow and we will deal with the Turks once and for all."

I summoned Acting Squadron Leader Ritchie and Jack Thomson. I told them of the disaster at Mosul. "Jack, you and I will head up to Mosul tomorrow. I know half of your buses are being repaired. We will use the ones that remain. Paul, I need you with the Snipes tomorrow. How is Cartwright?"

"Better sir."

"Can he command?"

There was a slight hesitation and then he nodded. "He will be fine sir."

"Good then go and fetch him and I will give him his orders."

After he had gone Jack took out his pipe and, after he had it going, he said, "You have a plan, I believe?"

I nodded, "We will try something I learned in France. We will use the Hun in the sun."

"Hun in the sun?"

"You and your Ninaks will be bait. You are going to bomb Faysh Khabur and Kahnik tomorrow. You will use up your ammunition. I will wait in the south east as high as I can get. If you have your gunners take a Lee Enfield with them then you won't be entirely defenceless. We will dive from the sun and, hopefully, end the threat."

"Seems a good idea to me."

Cartwright and Ritchie returned, "Sir?"

"Flight Lieutenant Cartwright I need you to command the Bristols. Can you manage that? Answer me honestly. There is no shame in admitting that you aren't ready."

He gave a thin smile, "No sir, the Squadron Leader's death hit me hard but I can cope sir. Thank you for your patience."

"We have all been there, Flight Lieutenant. Until we get a replacement you will be Acting Squadron Leader. It will look good on your record."

"Thank you, sir."

I was on the radio as soon as they left to inform Sir John of the events. He told me that he would be up to see me in the next day or so. It seemed a little ominous. However, he was able to confirm that Baghdad was now secure. We had broken the back of the revolt. Now we had to end the threat of the Turks.

I had seven Snipes to take to Mosul and five Ninaks. The rest would remain at Kirkuk. They would be repaired and could be used to patrol when they were ready. I had two days to find and destroy the aeroplanes which now posed a threat. A Vernon could be knocked from the sky by a Halberstadt!

We landed at noon. Woollett and Williams were awaiting me when I landed. I had told them that they should not take off before I got there.

"Henry, David, I want you to take your aeroplanes and clear the high ground and land as far as the river. Bomb the bridges if you have to. I don't think the Halberstadt will bother you there but it doesn't matter if they try. I shall be high in the sky waiting for them. It is Jack who is the bait. Five Ninaks will seem like a tasty morsel."

Squadron Leader Williams said, "Sir, make sure you get the bastards. They killed four young men yesterday!"

"I will, don't you worry. They will pay!"

As I led my six Snipes up into the sky I thought back to France. That was the last time we had done this. Then the enemy had been German pilots. They were good. These Turks had never fought in a dog fight. They would be overconfident, having attacked aeroplanes which could not fight back. I knew that the pilots would be itching to get back and repeat their success. I had worked out that they were using a radio in either Faysh Khabur or Kahnik. I suppose we could have gone over the river and bombed their field; it had to be close. However, I was aware of the trap that Squadron Leader Barnes had fallen into. They would have guns waiting. The Count knew the vulnerabilities of aeroplanes.

We climbed to ten thousand feet. It took over twelve minutes. We would descend much faster. Importantly we would be dots to the Halberstadt. They would not have the time to climb. I watched the Ninaks as they bombed first, Faysh Khabur and then Kahnik. Jack did a good job. After they had dropped their bombes he strafed them. I hoped he had hit the radio. I watched as he began to head home and I put the stick forward. I was gambling. I saw the seven Halberstadt as they raced from the north. They were well below us and the sun was behind us. The Turkish pilots would be keen to hit the Ninaks. The Turks were also using the sun. The difference was that Jack knew they were coming. His gunners would take out their Lee Enfields and give them a shock. There was little chance of them bringing one down but it would concentrate the attention of the Turks and they would not see us.

We flew in two lines of three with Acting Squadron Leader Ritchie as a backup in case we missed. I did not think that we would. Jack was leading the Turkish fighters towards Mosul. The Turks would expect that. It bought time for us to be able to attack. I saw the machine gun fire on the leading Halberstadt as he opened fire. He was lucky and one of the Ninaks was hit in the tail. They were a well-made aeroplane. I had told my pilots to hold their fire until they could not miss. I was the only one with dog fight experience. If they fired too soon they might run out of ammunition. We were travelling faster than the Snipe had ever flown. Dropping from ten thousand feet to almost ground level built up speed. The Snipe was very agile and responsive. I began to pull back on the stick and then I cocked both Vickers. I lined up on the rearmost Halberstadt.

The pilot made the error every new pilot made. He did not look in his mirror. Once you had been in combat you developed a tic, constantly flicking your eyes to the mirror. He did not move and I waited until I was a hundred feet from him and then I fired. I used a ten second burst. That was more than enough. My bullets stitched a line along the fuselage and then into the pilot. There was no armour behind his seat. The aeroplane plunged to the ground. The second Halberstadt had not seen the fate of his companion. I fired a longer burst and I shredded his rudder. He turned to see who had hit him as his aeroplane went into a death spiral. This time someone did see and the next two began to climb.

Simpkins took one and Marshall took the other. Their Snipes were much faster. They had seen me and they waited until they were just fifty feet from their target. It was their first kill and they could not have had an easier one. Simpkins' bullets hit the fuel tank and one of them exploded. That left three Turkish aeroplanes. Their pilots had heard the explosion. They gave up all thoughts of taking out the Ninaks and they went in three different directions. I followed the leader. He was the best pilot. I saw the evidence of that as he climbed, banked and twisted at the same time. It was good flying but it was futile. My Snipe was both more manoeuvrable and faster. I had fought and killed better pilots. I closed with him as he headed back to Turkey. He made the mistake of trying to out climb me. I could reach five thousand feet in under five minutes. It would take him thirty-eight minutes to reach the same altitude. I waited until I knew that we were over Turkey and I was just thirty feet behind him. His twists and turns had been in vain. I had one Vickers which I had not fired. I opened fire and kept firing as two hundred and fifty rounds tore through his rudder, fuselage, pilot and engine. The Turkish aeroplane spiralled down. I, lazily, followed it. I saw that the fates had decided to take it home and I watched as it plummeted to crash in the middle of the Turkish airfield. I turned my Snipe and headed home. I saw that only Snipes were in the air. My pilots had destroyed the other two. The Halberstadt threat was over.

My pilots were waiting for me at the border. I pointed south and I led them back to Kirkuk. I got on the radio and spoke to Mosul. I told them that the Halberstadts were all destroyed and that I would be returning to Kirkuk. Jack came on the radio to tell me that all of his pilots and Ninaks were safe. He was heading home too. The Turks had abandoned Faysh Khabur. The invasion was over.

When I landed at Kirkuk word must have got around about our victory for every pilot, mechanic and rigger was there to applaud us. I had claimed another three victories but my men had destroyed the other four. That was the day when they realised they were fighter pilots. There was something different about shooting down an enemy aeroplane rather than dropping bombs on houses and strafing infantry.

Sergeant Major Hill looked more like a proud grandfather than a fearsome N.C.O. "Sir, can I salute you. Three aeroplanes destroyed in one engagement. I have never heard the like! You will be getting a bar for you V.C. I daresay!"

I shook my head, "They were Great War relics flown by fanatics." I nodded towards Ritchie, Simpkins and Marshall who were being lauded by their peers. "But I wouldn't say that in front of those lads. I was proud of them today. They followed orders. They were as good as any of the pilots I led in the big one."

Sergeant Major Hill nodded, "Aye sir. They are the future but you showed them what us veterans can do!"

There was a party atmosphere in the mess that night. With Kirkuk safe, the Turks retreating and seven kills for the squadron, there was every reason for celebration. Jack sat with me after we had finished the meal and had broached the port. "You are still not happy, are you sir?"

"No, Jack. Sheikh Mahmud is still there and Count Yuri Fydorervich is still alive. I won't be able to sleep nights until he is dead and the Sheikh is under lock and key. Until then this land is still not pacified." I smiled, "But I am pleased that today worked out. You didn't mind being bait?"

He laughed, "We were in no danger. My gunners still had a few rounds left and the Ninak is a tough bird sir. Between you and me I think that the men in Squadron Leader Williams' squadron panicked just a little when they were attacked. The Ninak is faster than the Halberstadt. Had they dropped to the deck and headed for the airfield they would have been safe. The squadron leader has more inexperienced men in his squadron than the rest of us. They will learn."

"And we have a visit from the Air Vice Marshall in the next couple of days. I don't think there is anything sinister in it but let's make sure that he can find nothing wrong with the base."

Jack shook his head, "Sir, this is not even your base! It was Squadron Leader Barnes'!"

"For all his faults, he was one of us. We owe it to Sergeant Major Hill, Sergeant Major Shaw, Acting Squadron Leader Cartwright and every man in the squadron to present them in the best light."

"Yes sir."

Chapter 15

To be fair everyone pulled their weight. Every aeroplane was repaired. All evidence of the battles around the airfield were eradicated. It was as though every man wanted to show our leader that we might have been bloodied but we had not been beaten. Sir John arrived three days after our aerial battle and he came in a Vernon. He was accompanied by a second Vernon. He had his staff with him. He beamed when he strode over to me, "Splendid victory. There are many at the Ministry who want to give you another gong!"

I shook my head, "There are others who deserve that sir."

He nodded, "Mr Balfour said that you would say that. Make four or five recommendations and I will see that they are given medals. This could have been a shambles but thanks to you and your squadrons we came up smelling of roses." He waved his hand around the airfield. "I know how hard this was. Lord Palmer was eulogising about you. If he had his way you would be knighted!"

"Sir!"

"I know, Harsker but that is what people are saying about you. Now we need to deal with this Sheikh Mahmud. That is why I am here. The Turks have given up. This was their last throw of the dice. His Majesty's Government wishes to bring Sheikh Mahmud to book. We don't want to lose more British soldiers to take Sulaimaniya and so we have devised a strategy." He pointed to the second Vernon. "There are some delayed fuse bombs on board that and they are part of the plan."

He had me intrigued. I wondered what they had in mind.

He turned, "I will inspect the field, they will expect that and then you and I will go and visit with Lord Palmer. He wishes us to dine with him. Tomorrow will be time enough for our briefing."

That was fortuitous. I had known that Sir John was coming but I had not known when. He would have expected a decent meal. We could now give him one! A day later than might have been expected.

Sergeant Major Hill had accommodations for our guests. As we climbed into the cars the Resident had sent for us Sir John said, "Shame about Squadron Leader Barnes. Many people felt that he had potential. He was well connected you know?"

I nodded and did not voice a reply. He was wrong but he did not know the man. He was going on hearsay and what his friends had said about him. Professionals who knew him had seen his flaws. They had died with him but I wondered, as we headed through the bombed streets, how many more Barnes were out there.

Lord Palmer had had time to clear and clean the area around the Residence. It looked as though it had just had a little minor damage. I had seen it from the air with bullet holes and broken windows. He shook Sir John's hand first. "Sir John, your arrival was timely. Were it not for you and your airmen then I think the League of Nations would have had a serious problem." He turned to me and grasped my hand in his two, "And you, dear fellow! Those medals you wear were truly earned. My sister had no fears when things looked darkest for she knew you and your chaps were out there. Come along. Let us go inside where it is cooler!"

This time it was Sir John who was the guest of honour and he was placed between Lady Isabel and her brother. Colonel Pemberton was on the other side of Sir John. I guessed the three would discuss the strategy for holding on to Kirkuk. The doctor was to my right.

"How is the wound, Wing Commander?"

"It is Bill. You did a good job Doctor. I have picked up a few wounds in my time."

Lady Isabel sipped her sherry, "You wouldn't expect to get such a wound normally, Wing Commander."

"No, Lady Isabel but aeroplanes are not always as reliable as you might think. They often break down. In the Great War that often meant landing behind enemy lines. That is why I always carry a range of weapons in my cockpit."

She laughed, "You are a resilient and surprising man, Bill. Your wife is a lucky woman."

"I don't think she would agree with you there, your ladyship. She has to stay at home and look after two young children. I am missing them growing up. And, missing all the mischief they get up to."

"You wouldn't be able to have them posted here with you. That would be far too dangerous."

"It would indeed, Doctor. How was it here before the Sikhs arrived?"

"You were right about them coming at night. None of us got any sleep. His lordship issued guns to everyone."

Lady Isabel laughed, "I hadn't fired a gun since I was a young woman back in the nineties. I have to say I found it fun. I am not certain I hit anything for we were firing in the dark but I felt I was doing something useful rather than just holding soldiers' hands and saying, *'there, there'*."

"Nothing wrong with that your ladyship. My wife was a nurse and it is how we met, in hospital in London."

The meal, under the circumstances, was excellent. It was enlivened by our conversation. The Doctor was an interesting man and he was coming to the end of a career in which he had served the Empire in its far-flung outposts. He pointed to Colonel Pemberton, the commanding officer of the Sikhs. "I served with the Colonel when he was just a Captain on the North-West frontier." He shook his head and laughed, "In those days he was as mad as a bucket full of frogs! He once dispersed a riot with his sword. Led a dozen chaps with bayonets fixed and charged two hundred Pathans. I don't think they believed what they were seeing. Now he is someone who has dedicated his whole life to the Empire."

Lady Isabel said, "As have you, John."

"No, Lady Isabel. This is my last posting and I go back home next year to Yorkshire. I have a home there close to the Yorkshire Moors overlooking Whitby. The Colonel will go back to India. He won't go back to England."

"Why ever not?"

"He had a wife and children. They were stationed with him. While he was in the hills chasing Afghans, a flu epidemic swept through the fort and his family died. When his two brothers died at Ypres that was the end of any hopes or thoughts he had of returning home. He will die in India."

I looked at the Colonel. When I had taken him up in the Ninak I had wondered at his fearlessness. Now I understood. The Colonel saw death in uniform as a vindication of his life.

In the car going back Sir John said, "You are a surprising man, Wing Commander. It was inspired to take the Colonel up in the Ninak. He is a bit of a dinosaur but you showed him the potential of the aeroplane. I think you breathed a little bit of life into him."

"Nice chap sir."

He nodded, "Now we have a plan to end this Sheikh Mahmud's revolt, once and for all. We are going to give him one more chance to make peace with us. We have sent one of his chaps with an order to come to Baghdad peacefully."

"One of his chaps, sir?"

He nodded, "That is why I was talking to the Colonel. The Sikhs captured forty or fifty Kurds the other day. One of them was the Sheikh's nephew. We are sending him back with the order."

I had a sudden thought, "Did the prisoners say anything about the Count?"

"You seem obsessed with this fellow but yes they did. Apparently, the night you bombed his home and car he was with Sheikh Mahmud at some sort of feast or orgy. I confess I didn't go into too many details. Seemed a little sordid to me."

We had reached the airfield and I said, "Nightcap in the mess sir?"

"Good idea. I still have more to tell you."

It was late and they were clearing the tables. However, the sight of two senior officers who wanted a drink halted that. The sergeant steward poured two large whiskies and his face told me that he hoped it would just be the one. "You can go off duty now Newton. I will turn off the lights."

"Are you certain sir?"

I nodded, "Go on. I insist."

Sir John held up his glass, "Cheers!"

"Cheers."

"Just as well really. What I have to tell you is for your ears only. I personally do not expect Sheikh Mahmud to comply with our orders. I know London and Baghdad think he will but this fellow wants power. We are going to order him to come to Baghdad and account for his actions. He won't turn up. What I want you and your wing to do is this. When he does not show up you will drop an ultimatum from your aeroplane. At the same time, we want your bombers to drop the delayed fuse bombs we brought around the town. They will go off at six hourly intervals. Twenty bombs will make him realise what will happen if he continues to refuse."

I sipped my whisky, "And if that fails, sir?"

"You have even less faith in his word than I do."

I shrugged, "If Count Yuri Fydorervich is still alive then he won't allow the Sheikh to surrender himself. He is his meal ticket. I think we need a backup plan."

"Which is?"

"If he does not respond to the bombing then I go back in and this time destroy his headquarters. I would have done it before but…."

"Orders. I know. Let us take it one step at a time. I will be off to Mosul tomorrow. The Sheikh's nephew will need a couple of days to take his message to Sulaimaniya. I would like to see how things are in Mosul. I want you and your wing to scour the country and eliminate any pockets of Turks and Kurds who are still holding on. The Vernons will extract all the wounded and take them to Baghdad and bring back fresh troops. By then we should know if the Sheikh has agreed."

It was a plan. However, I was not certain it would succeed. "Very well sir. I have the list of men who I think deserve medals. I would also like to promote Flight Lieutenant Ritchie to Squadron Leader. It makes it easier for me to lead the wing."

"Good idea. Is Cartwright ready to take over Barnes' squadron?"

"If I say I am not sure then that tells you all you need to know sir. He will make a good squadron leader I am just uncertain if he is ready yet."

"Well Squadron Leader Woollett has one of his chaps he wants promoting, Flight Lieutenant Davis."

I nodded, "A good chap sir. I served with him in Heliopolis as well as down at Baghdad."

"Then that appears to be settled. I will leave the arrangements for your wing to you. You will have Woollett and Williams' aeroplanes too."

While they prepared the Vernons to take the troops and Sir John to Mosul I gathered my pilots. I had spoken to Henry and David on the radio and they would be operating north of Mosul. "We are going to sweep east and north east. You will be operating in flights. Any one in Turkish uniform is fair game. Any Kurd with a gun is a target."

Squadron Leader Ritchie asked, "What about Sulaimaniya, sir? That is still a Kurdish stronghold."

I nodded, "There are moves afoot. Sir John and I want to solve the Turkish issue first. If we have our northern borders secure then we can deal with Sheikh Mahmud and believe me, we will."

I allowed Squadron Leader Ritchie to organise the flights. He gave me Simpkins and Marshall as my wingmen. They had flown with me before and Ritchie showed that I had made a wise choice.

As we passed Ebril I noticed that they had repaired the damage to the walls already. The convoy which had brought supplies had also brought troops and they had gone directly to Ebril. We spied our first Turks twenty miles from Ebril. It was a convoy of six vehicles. They were skirting the high ground and heading for the Tigris. Sir John was worried that groups of these survivors could band together and be a threat to some of the smaller detachments which were dotted around the border. I dropped my first bomb ahead of the lead lorry while Simpkins dropped his first behind them. They were effectively trapped on the road. Marshall's two bombs exploded in the middle of the convoy. We made two passes with machine guns and left the convoy a smoking charnel house. As we headed north west we saw that the other flights had been ahead of us and there were more bodies on the road. As we were at our limit we returned to Kirkuk. We had lost no aeroplanes and the land had been scoured. I radioed the information back to base.

Sir John sent me a radio message congratulating us. We were stood down until he returned. I sat with Jack and Paul in the mess. "We need these next two days, sir. The buses need a good overhaul."

"I know but I have spoken with Sergeant Major Shaw. He will work on my flight first. The day after tomorrow I intend to fly to Sulaimaniya."

"I thought we were stood down, sir."

"We are Paul, but Sir John has sent an emissary to the Sheikh ordering him to present himself at Baghdad. I want to fly over his residence and encourage him to comply."

"You are looking for Count Yuri Fydorervich aren't you sir?"

"You know me well, Jack. Yes, I suppose I am."

I took off, two days later with Simpkins and Marshall. Sulaimaniya still had no Union Flag flying over it. Sheikh Mahmud was as defiant as ever. We reached the town at noon. We flew in fast and low. Rifles were fired at us but our speed meant that they did not stand a chance of hitting us. I saw what had been the residence of Count Yuri Fydorervich. It was a black hole in the ground. I then led the flight over Sheikh Mahmud's home. It was there I saw Russians. There were three of them. Although they wore turbans they had blond beards. It was enough proof for me that the Count was still alive. I took my flight around the walls. I needed to work out where to drop the delayed fuse bombs. I did not think that the Sheikh would comply. I found twenty places where the explosions would disturb the peace and tranquillity but civilian casualties would be kept to a minimum. They were also well away from the mosques. If we damaged one of those it would be a disaster.

The next two days were the quietest I could remember at Kirkuk. We had no sorties and the buses were all in a perfect state of readiness. As soon as the new squadron leader arrived to take over the Bristols then Jack and I could head back to Baghdad. I might even manage some leave.

Sir John arrived. "Well, Wing Commander, it looks like Sheikh Mahmud has decided to ignore the summons to come to Baghdad. He should have arrived yesterday and he did not. I will have the ultimatum prepared. Will it be the Snipes or the Ninaks you use?"

"There are just twenty bombs. I will use the Snipes. I overflew the town the other day. I know where to drop them."

"The armourer knows how to prime them. It will take twenty-four hours for them all to explode."

"Sir, there is a risk that we might wound or kill civilians."

"I know. This has come from London. We are just obeying orders."

"I realise that sir but it does not sit well with me."

"I can get Squadron Leader Thomson to do it, if you wish."

Shaking my head, I said, "That would be me ducking out of my responsibility. I will take them. I have identified where the Sheikh is hiding sir. We can destroy that without collateral damage."

"Good."

I asked Squadron Leader Ritchie to drop the ultimatum. We had the twenty bombs on just five Snipes. I spent a long time explaining to the pilots where we would drop them. The rest of the squadron would fly with Squadron Leader Ritchie. They would be a show of strength. We avoided bombing when they were at prayer. I knew that they were sensitive about that. We split up before we reached the town. The other Snipes would draw the fire. We heard the machine guns and rifles popping away at them as we flew around in a giant circle dropping bombs. It felt strange to drop a bomb and not hear an explosion. I hoped London knew what it was doing. The first bomb would explode just six hours later. The rest would go off at irregular intervals.

I dropped mine first and that allowed me to climb and be able to watch both my bombers and Ritchie's buses. When I saw him and his men begin to climb I knew that the missive had been delivered. When the last bomb was dropped we climbed and headed west.

After we landed I felt a little let down. We would neither see nor hear the results of our action. We would have to wait. Sir John was convinced that we would see the results in less than two days but I was not certain.

Squadron Leader Davis had arrived from Mosul the same day as Sir John had returned. He was busy rebuilding confidence in the squadron. It was not just the slipshod nature of Barnes' organisation which had caused problems. It was also his lack of adherence to rules. Sergeant Major Hill was delighted with the new broom. "Now we will see some changes sir. We will make this squadron as good as yours. The basic material is sound. It was just… well you know better than anyone, sir."

I sat with the new squadron leader, Jack and Squadron Leader Ritchie. We had a quiet table in the mess and were able to talk freely. We avoided speaking ill of the dead but between us we were able to paint a picture for Davis. He would have been my choice as well as Henry's. He was a quiet and thoughtful man. He was, perhaps, too cautious to be a fighter pilot but the Bristols were more of a bomber than a fighter.

"And when you are gone sir? Not that I am chasing you away but I will be here on my own, so what is my brief?"

"A good question. Keep law and order. You will need to support the local officials. When the Ottomans ran this country, their officials were corrupt. Many of the people think it is the same. When they get a tax demand they think they can negotiate or not even pay. You will have to help them enforce the rules."

"Good God sir, I am a bailiff now!"

We all laughed, "Perhaps. Lord Palmer is a good chap to get to know. He understands the people and he is very fair. When we pull out you will have less men to guard the airfield and you will be reliant on the garrison at Kirkuk. They are good chaps."

Jack tapped out his pipe, "And Sulaimaniya?"

"When the Sheikh is brought to heel we will retake it. That will be our job. We will have to bomb it. Then we will put a Governor in place there. I am afraid that Kirkuk will have a watching brief on Sulaimaniya too."

"Then life will not be dull, eh sir?"

"Anything but!"

Chapter 16

The bombs must have worked. A delegation arrived the two days later and presented themselves at Lord Palmer's residence. One of them was Sheikh Mahmud's nephew. Sir John invited me to sit in on the negotiations. I did so in the hope that I might pick up news about Count Yuri Fydorervich. Colonel Pemberton was there too.

The delegation of ten were mainly young warriors. They had a mullah with them and two grey haired men. The Sheikh's nephew could speak English and he did most of the speaking. "Your bombs caused a great deal of damage to our town!" He sounded indignant as though we had done that without any good justification.

"Had your uncle come here then that would not have been necessary." The Air Vice Marshall kept his voice as calm and neutral as possible.

"My uncle is a great leader. He is King of Kurdistan."

"He is king of nowhere and he is lucky that we gave him the Governorship. When does he arrive?"

I liked Sir John's bluntness. Mohammed al Mahmud adopted an innocent look. "We are here as ordered in the ultimatum. Why does my uncle need to be here?"

"Because he was the one summoned. Are you telling me that he will not be presenting himself to me as ordered?"

"You do not order my uncle around."

Sir John look at Lord Palmer, "Then these discussions are meaningless. You will all be detained here until Sheikh Mahmud arrives."

"You cannot do that!" The young man translated and all ten became agitated.

Lord Palmer stood and said, firmly, "Any more of this nonsense and you will all be put in chains. Do you understand me?"

Sir John nodded his thanks as they calmed down. "The letter quite clearly stated that unless Sheikh Mahmud presented himself here then we would take further action."

"If you try to take my uncle you will find that his people will defend him to the death. He has allies who know how you fight. You will lose many men!"

My ears pricked up. He was referring to the Count. He was still with the Sheikh. Sir John smiled. It was an oddly evil smile for such a pleasant man. "And you will be here. You will only hear of it after we have taken Sulaimaniya!"

Lord Palmer snapped, "Take them away!"

When they had gone Sir John said, "Of course we have no intention of Colonel Pemberton's men bleeding to take what is, essentially, our own town. Wing Commander can our aeroplanes knock out the Sheikh's headquarters and eliminate all of his strong points?"

I nodded.

Colonel Pemberton said, "I can vouch for that personally. If we could coordinate the attack so that my chaps were in lorries just outside the town. That way, when you attack we can follow behind quickly. The last thing we need is for this slippery fellow to slither away and hide beneath one of the many rocks in this land."

"Quite. If we make the date and time for the attack dawn the day after tomorrow. That will give the chance for Colonel Pemberton's Sikhs to get into position during the hours of darkness and hopefully the Wing Commander will catch him with his trousers down!"

That gave me a whole day to make my plans. The four of us sat in the briefing room with a pot of tea and some corned beef and mustard sandwiches. "We have two tasks. The most important is to destroy the Sheikh's headquarters. The second is to destroy all of the strong points. I propose that the Snipes will destroy the headquarters. That way the gunners in the Bristols and the Ninaks can clear the streets around their strong points. The Sikhs will be going in while we attack. I want the opposition to be neutralized."

Jack said, "And if they flee?"

"Then we follow and use our machine guns to destroy them. We use bombs first, then the Lewis machine gun and the twin Vickers are a last resort."

Jack had the bit between his teeth, "No sir, I meant what if they flee over the border. What if they head to Iran? Do we follow?"

I sat back and sipped my tea, "Do you know Jack I had not thought of that. I was so obsessed with ridding the world of this Sheikh and the Count that I had forgotten how close to the border they are. I will have to seek guidance on this. My gut reaction is that we go after them, no matter where they are but I shall speak with Sir John."

Sir John was busy in the radio room sending a message to Baghdad. "Sir, when you are done if I could have a word."

"Of course." Once outside I led him to my office and closed the door. "A problem Wing Commander?"

"Perhaps. When the rats leave their nest how far can we follow them?"

"How far? Why... of course. Iran. A delicate problem eh?"

"The border is close enough for them to slip over. I am certain that Maivan was where Count Yuri Fydorervich was hiding before he went to Sulaimaniya."

"Leave that with me. I shall radio the British Ambassador in Tehran and ask him to speak with Raza Shah, the King of Iran. He will not be happy about having rebellious Kurds in his land. However, if he refuses us permission then we do not cross the border. Is that clear?"

"Sir!"

"And that includes firing across the border!"

Sir John had thought of everything.

That done I could begin to prepare for what might be the last action in this minor revolt and invasion. I took all three of my guns, stripped and cleaned them. I had already managed to acquire more ammunition. When Captain Daniels had brought in the weapons and ammunition from the men who tried to scale our walls he found some for my Mauser. Once that was done I put the Lee Enfield in its scabbard in the Snipe and secured the ammunition and four more grenades in the netting which I used to hold flasks, food and spare tobacco. I then checked my emergency kit. This was a weekly event. I made sure the hip flask was full of whisky. It made a good emergency antiseptic and had been known to put life back into a failing engine! I made certain that my two compasses worked. When I had been an air gunner I had learned that one compass was never enough. I emptied the water from my canteen and refilled it before adding the tablet which would kill anything noxious. I found it made the water taste disgusting but I always had a little whisky to add. The medical kit was there. It was still unused and the mirror I could use for signalling. With my dagger and penknife my equipment was all ready. Most would be stored in the Snipe while the rest I secreted in the pockets of my flying coat.

The day before the raid I made sure that my aeroplanes were all serviced and ready to go. We would be taking off in the dark. Sergeant Major Hill was going to arrange lanterns to light the runway. I planned on getting as high as possible and then making a slow descent, at dawn to Sulaimaniya. I had Squadron Leader Ritchie ensure that all the men were well rested. Then I went to the office to see if Sir John had left a message.

Sergeant Major Hill stood when I entered. "Sir, I was talking to Pilot Officer Barker. He told me that you found Squadron Leader Barnes and the other lads when you were up at Mosul. I want to thank you, sir. You didn't need to take that chance."

"I did. When I was in the Great War I was shot down behind enemy lines. I was even captured once. Of course, the Germans were more civilised than these Turks and Kurds but I know what it feels like. It is terrifying. We are lucky that all of our kites have made it back to the airfields. If they hadn't then I would have moved heaven and earth to find them and I would have ignored any orders about crossing borders."

"It would be even harder here, sir. This is a desolate country. There is nothing here but desert and rock. I am not sure any pilot would survive more than a couple of hours."

"You will be amazed what a man can do when he is faced with death. When you have something to live for you can endure almost anything."

"Fancy a brew sir? I'll put the kettle on. McIlroy is running an errand for the Air Vice Marshall."

"Good idea, Sergeant Major and I will have a pipeful." The tobacco merchant had been so pleased with our action in saving the town that he had sent a humidor with the mix of tobacco. I had the luxury of knowing I had enough to last me until I reach Baghdad. I reamed and cleaned my pipe first and then packed it carefully without tamping down. I struck a match and the aromatic leaves caught. As I drew on it I tamped it down a little with the end of my finger. That was how you could tell a pipe smoker. One finger had hard skin at the end which could endure the fire from a hot pipe. It was drawing nicely when the Sergeant Major returned with the two cups and a plate of biscuits.

"That smells good sir."

"Help yourself Sarn't Major. I have a full humidor in my quarters courtesy of a grateful civilian."

"I don't mind if I do and a grateful civilian in peace time is a rarity sir. In times of war they do anything for a boy in uniform but as soon as there is peace they whinge on about the cost, the numbers and how they don't need them anymore."

"At least it is better now than it used to be, Sergeant Major. Until the end of the last century if you were wounded or lost a limb then you were scrapped and left to beg. But I think it will always be the same."

We talked of home and peace. Both were alien to the two of us. Daddy Hill had been in even longer than I had. He had been a young soldier in the Boer War. He had never married and I realised that the army was his life.

McIlroy came in. He was out of breath, "Sir, the Air Vice Marshall wants to see you. He is at the main gate. He is off to see Lord Palmer but he wants a word with you first."

I stood. "Thanks for the tea and the chat, Sergeant Major."

"And you sir, it is a privilege to serve with you."

Sir John waved me over to him. "The Iranians say that, if you are chasing Sheikh Mahmud you have his permission to cross the border but if any Iranian citizen is hurt by the R.A.F. then it will have dire consequences."

"Understood sir. If I get it wrong then it is the end of my career."

"Exactly but I don't think that it will be. Good luck tomorrow. I am off to meet with Lord Palmer and discuss who will take over in Sulaimaniya."

"You are confident we will succeed?"

"Yes, Wing Commander. I have no doubts about that!"

One advantage of our early departure was the temperature. It was cooler. As the engines were started I spoke with the three squadron leaders. "Flying in the dark is tricky. When we leave stick to the course and height we agreed. We will not be attacking until dawn anyway. Remember the Ninaks and Bristols will have to coordinate with Colonel Pemberton and his men. Good luck chaps. We will celebrate in the mess tonight."

"Good show, sir!"

I climbed into the Snipe. My twelve aeroplanes were in four lines of three. This would be a test of their skills. We were flying at night for the first time. Admittedly dawn would soon break but, as we roared down the runway lit by Sergeant Major Hill's lanterns it felt like jumping off a precipice as we climbed high into black night. We had the lowest altitude. We were flying at two thousand feet. It took just a few minutes to reach that altitude and I throttled back a little to conserve fuel.

Ahead, I saw the sky lightening as dawn approached. Simpkins and Marshall were on station. Both were confident pilots. In the time we had been in Mesopotamia they had developed into much better pilots. They had known how to fly before I arrived but now they were pilots and more than that, they were combat pilots. They seemed able to read my thoughts and react to every movement of my Snipe.

The sun began to rise and it illuminated the town when we were just two miles away. I began my descent. We would be bombing at less than eighty feet. Simpkins, Marshall and myself had scouted out the town and we knew where the residence was. It was hard to miss for it had the Sheikh's own flag flying from its roofs and was ringed with guns. All the houses with a flat roof around the residence had guns on them. That was more evidence the Count was involved. He knew how to counter aeroplanes.

As I glanced down I saw that Colonel Pemberton's men had left their lorries and were moving in a skirmish line towards the walls. Our delayed action bombs had made holes through which they could enter. Behind me I saw the Ninaks and Bristols as they too dropped to ground level to begin their close support of the infantry.

The sun suddenly blazed as we raced across the walls. We were still in darker skies but we were seen and bullets were thrown into the air. We flew through the lead storm. I heard bullets as they tore through the wings. The Snipe was a tough aeroplane. I saw the residence. I fired a very short burst with my right-hand Vickers. It was more to keep the enemy gunners' heads down than anything else. I released all four bombs. Our plan was for the centre Snipe in the four flights to drop their bombs first. Then we would turn and form a line of eight Snipes which had not dropped their bombs. The four which had would act as flank guards.

Roaring over the residence I pulled back on my stick and began to climb and to bank to port. Simpkins and Marshall banked to starboard. I rolled and fell in to the port side of Simpkins. We all began a slow turn to bring us back over the residence. I saw smoke and flames. Squadron Leader Ritchie was to the starboard side of Simpkins and the two of us began to machine gun the gunners on the roof. I used my right-hand Vickers sparingly. I did not know how many passes we would have to make. Flying over the residence I looked down and saw that we had destroyed it. There would be another seven bomb loads to come but they would ensure that Sheikh Mahmud's residence was completely destroyed. When we reached the walls of the town I saw that the infantry had secured the gates and the walls. The Ninaks and Bristols were bombing selectively. They were targeting the strong points.

I led my squadron to the north so that we could sweep around and catch any vehicles leaving the town. They would head east, to Maivan and Iran. We wanted to stop up all the rat holes. I saw that Squadron Leader Ritchie's bus was smoking and I waved for him to return to Kirkuk. He nodded. In my mirror, I saw that five other Snipes had been damaged. The ground fire had been fiercer than we had expected. I knew that I had been hit but all my controls appeared to be functioning and the damage looked, to me, to be superficial. They too headed back to the base. Their work was done and the mopping up could be left to us. They would be back in Kirkuk in less than an hour. If I needed them I could radio Kirkuk.

I climbed so that the remaining six of us could form two flights of three. I saw that Simpkins and Marshall had both emerged intact as had Barker. Smoke was now billowing and blowing across the burning rebel stronghold. We had to climb so that I could see beyond it. As we ascended I saw lorries and cars fleeing from the carnage of Sulaimaniya. I led my six aeroplanes down to attack them. I had not used my left-hand Vickers and so, as we neared the last vehicle in the convoy I opened fire. The Kurds who were aboard opened fire too. As I roared along the column, firing short bursts from my gun I was aware, from my mirror, that two of my Snipes had been damaged by fire from the walls and the fleeing vehicles. We were so low that damage was more likely. They peeled away, smoking from their engines.

Barker still had a couple of bombs left. He had been the last bomber over the residence and, as we neared the head of the column he dropped the two bombs. We banked and climbed so that we could survey the damage we had done. Three vehicles lay wrecked two others were smoking but two were still intact and had left the main road to head into the hills. We had not yet reached the border but we were a good eight miles from Sulaimaniya and if the cars got into the hills then they could escape into Iran.

Pilot Officer Barker tapped his guns to inform me that he was out of ammunition and Simpkins did the same. I waved them back to Kirkuk. I got on the radio and told them that Pilot Officer Marshall and myself were pursuing two vehicles in the direction of Maivan and that I had buses which were returning with damage. Sergeant Major Shaw would have men ready to deal with any emergency.

In the time it had taken to bank and turn to follow the cars they had split up. We would have to drop low to find them. The road they had taken was not a real road. It was mud and stone. In the rainy season only horses could use it. It twisted and turned through defiles. The two cars would not be able to go quickly. What I did not know was that they were not moving at all. They had stopped and were setting up an ambush. We were just fifty feet above the road when the barrage began. They had a Lewis gun. My life was saved by the radio. It was behind my back and the bullets intended for me smashed into it and my fuselage. They had damaged my controls and the Snipe felt sluggish. I tried to climb and, looking in my mirror I saw that Marshall's Snipe had also been hit but this time in the engine. I banked and came around. I emptied my Vickers into the area where the ambushers were hiding. I had no idea if I hit any but there were only a few shots as I passed over.

 I saw that Marshall was in trouble. He was descending. He was trying to crash land. He was heading towards Iran and that was not good. This was not the place for such a crash landing. There was very little land which was flat enough or long enough. I followed and then I noticed that I was almost flying on empty. I should have had enough fuel. One of the bullets must have hit my fuel tank. Not only Pilot Officer Marshall was going to crash land, I was going to join him.

 We were a good three or four miles from the ambush when Marshall finally put his Snipe on the ground. It was not a great landing. The undercarriage broke and the propeller dug into the ground throwing the Snipe upside down. I could not land close by and, as my engine began to splutter, I looked for any flat ground I could. I found a piece, thirty yards long. It sloped uphill. The engine, starved of fuel, stopped and I coasted towards the sloping piece of rock. My undercarriage also broke but my propeller did not bite into the ground. It was a hard landing and the Snipe spun around but it stayed horizontal. It was not a fiery death. I was alive and I had a chance. I might be far from any help but I was intact and I had my emergency supplies and weapons. If Marshall was alive then I would try to get us back to Sulaimaniya.

Chapter 17

As soon as my aeroplane stopped I unstrapped myself and I reached down to grab my rifle and my emergency equipment. I unclipped the net which held it. I would have to improvise it into some sort of haversack. I climbed out and laid the lifesaving equipment thirty feet from the Snipe. Taking my dagger, I climbed back up and cut the safety harness from the seat. I might need that to carry Marshall back, if he was wounded. I put the ammunition into my pockets and then used the straps to make the net into a haversack. I had a drink from my canteen before I put that in the net again. I had three Mills bombs. I would have to use one to destroy the Snipe. The Vickers machine guns were too valuable to leave for Kurds to take and use against us. I knew it would signal my position but I had little choice. I threw the grenade into the cockpit and then ran. I was well away when it went off but, even so, I was knocked to the ground.

When I rose, I had to orientate myself. I had flown almost a mile after Marshall had crashed. In the distance, I saw the tail of his Snipe and I hurried across the uneven ground. The sun was now getting hotter. I wished I had brought the bisht with me. The Arabs knew how to stay cool in the heat. My flying coat was too hot but it contained my spare ammunition and compass. In addition, if we had to spend a night out here I would need it for the cold. I had no idea what sort of condition Marshall was going to be in when I found him. The men we had shot up were still around. I had them placed about two miles or more away. It would be close. I had to keep looking at the rough ground below my feet and then find a way point to lead me to the aeroplane. As I neared the Snipe I saw that he had been lucky where he had stopped. Thirty yards further on there was a gully and then a sheer drop. I saw his left arm hanging down from the cockpit. Was he alive or dead?

When I reached him I said, "Marshall, can you move?"

"Is that you sir? I think I have damaged my right arm. I can't move it. The left arm I can."

I laid down my rifle and improvised haversack and took off my flying helmet. I felt the sun on my head as soon as I did. "Hang on I will try to get under and release your harness." I lay on my back and slithered along the ground. I saw the bones sticking out of his torn tunic and flying jacket. He had broken his lower right arm. The ulna and radius had both fractured. I would have to open my medical kit. I held his body with my left arm as I reached up with my right to release the harness. I did not want him to fall. I did not want to aggravate his wounds. I flicked the buckle and I felt his weight on my left arm. I moved my right arm to try to support his weight.

"Your right arm is broken. Can you try to roll out and take the weight on your left arm?"

"I will try sir."

I felt his body weight shift and he wriggled. There was a sharp intake of breath as he caught his arm and then he suddenly tumbled and landed on the rocks. He gave a sharp cry. It could not be helped but if the rebels were around they would hear it. I remembered Squadron Leader Barnes. They would not take us without a fight. I scrambled out and helped him to sit up. He was pale and he was shaking. Beattie had told me about that. It was shock.

I took out my whisky flask and opened it. "Take a swig."

He did so and I saw the glimmer of a smile, "Cheers, sir!"

"Now support your right arm with your left. I will try to get a splint."

"Sir."

Running back to the wreck I found a pair of the struts on the Snipe. They had broken. I used my dagger to remove them from the wing. I picked up a small broken piece of wood at the same time. I cut the harness from the cockpit and cut two sections from it. Time was passing and we were exposed. I expected the crack of a rifle at any moment. When I returned to the pale Marshall I used my knife to carefully cut away the jacket, tunic and shirt. I exposed the wound. Marshall looked down at it.

"That is a mess, sir."

"Lucky for you it is your forearm." I moved him so that his shoulder was supported by a rock and the damaged arm lay flat on the ground. I began to use some of my precious water to clean the wound. I held the canteen for him. "Drink." He did so. I took out the antiseptic powder and the dressing. "Look, Marshall, I won't lie to you. This is going to hurt like hell. Bite on this piece of wood." He opened his mouth and I put the wood in his mouth. I sprinkled the power on the open wound and I saw him wince. That was nothing compared with what I would have to do next. I gently placed the two pieces of wood alongside his forearm. Even the slightest touch made him start. "I am going to have to join the ends of the bone together and splint it. Take hold of my flying coat with your left hand." He did so. I took the two ends of broken bones and moved them together. I felt his hand jerk my jacket and he bit through the wood then his head fell backwards to rest against the rock. He was unconscious. I worked quickly. I joined the bones as neatly and carefully as I could manage and, after applying the dressing, tied the two pieces of harness tightly around the splint.

Out of the corner of my eye I caught a movement in the distance. Suddenly a rifle rang out. The Kurds had found us. I had seen the muzzle flash and they were a long way away. The rifleman had fired too soon. I ran to the cockpit. Marshall had a grenade. He also had a canteen. I took them both. The Vickers were under the engine but they were intact and would be a temptation. I took the pin from the Mills bomb and I used my feet to rock the Snipe. I jammed the grenade and its handle beneath the Vickers. If someone tried to get the Vickers then they would set off the booby trap.

I could hear voices in the distance but I could see nothing for there were rocks in the way. I ran back to Marshall and, after putting the canteen in the improvised haversack I slipped it over my back with my Lee Enfield. I had seen the gully some two hundred yards away. If I tried to drag Marshall then the Kurds would see my tracks. There was no option. I picked up the unconscious pilot and draped him over my shoulders. He was a ton weight. I staggered to the gully. It was more than six feet deep. I laid Marshall on the top and climbed down. Then I pulled him down with me. I saw that there was an overhang just ten

Wings over Persia

yards further on and I dragged him beneath it. We would be hidden from view. Of course, if there were snakes or scorpions there then we would be dead men and no one would ever find our bodies.

It was as I took off Marshall's flying helmet that I realised I had left mine some way from the aeroplane. It was too late to go back for it. I took out my German automatic and cocked it. I was just glad that Marshall was unconscious. If they found us then I would be able to save him any more pain. They would not take us alive.

I heard voices. Two of them were Russian. I could not make out all of their words but I heard, 'Vickers'. Then I heard Arabic. This time I could understand it for it was spoken by a Russian and was basic. "You, monkey! Go and search the aeroplane. See if you can get those Vickers. If the aeroplanes come back we can shoot them down, too."

"Yes effendi. Come Mohammed."

The Russians spoke to each other and I could not make out anything. I smelled cigarette smoke and knew that they were smoking. Suddenly there was an almighty explosion and screams. Not only did the grenade go off it set off the unused .303 ammo too. When the bullets stopped I could smell burning. The Snipe was on fire. The Russian voices drew close to me. I could hear them clearer.

"Shit! That bastard pilot must still be alive."

"I told you when we found the helmet that he must be around. Do you think he went to the other aeroplane?"

"I doubt it. We heard that aeroplane explode not long after it crashed. The Count will not be happy that we let him escape. He wanted to question him."

Just then Marshall began to wake. He could not help it. He moaned.

I heard the sound of guns being cocked. A Russian voice shouted, urgently, "It came from the cliff!"

I had no time to think. I had to act. I heard their boots as they ran across the stones. I hurried down the gulley to the place I had entered. As I reached it I heard one shout, "I can see him!" There was a narrow crack above Marshall. They would be able to shoot him.

I just reacted. Had I thought it through I would have realised that they would not do him harm. They wanted him for questioning but I clambered out and as one of them raised his gun I fired four shots from a prone position. They both turned and fired at the same time. They fired at body height and their bullets zipped over my head. One of my bullets caught one of them. He stumbled and his foot caught in the crevasse beneath which Marshall sheltered. He screamed as he fell over the cliff. The noise would have been heard from miles around. On top of the exploding Snipe it marked our position for the Count and any who remained to hunt us.

The second man now saw me and he brought his rifle around to aim at me. I squeezed the trigger and sent all five bullets into his body. His gun fired in the air as he tumbled back dead. I ran over to him to make sure and to see if any of the Arabs had survived. The three Kurds lay dead. I grabbed the headdresses from two of them. The Snipe was a wreck but the smoke spiralled in the air. I ran back to the gully. Marshall had managed to crawl along. I dropped back down and cupped my hands. He stepped on to the and that enabled him to pull himself over the side with his good hand. He shouted in pain as he did so. I retrieved my rifle and improvised haversack. I gave him another drink of the whisky. We were now in an even worse position than before. We had to get away from here as quickly as we could.

I helped Marshall to his feet and wrapped one of the turbans around his head. "Just stand there while I see what the Russian has with him." I wound the second turban around my own head. It would keep the worst of the sun from me. My bullets had made a mess of his body. He had a pistol. It was the same as mine and I took it and the ammunition. He had two German style grenades. They were called potato mashers. I put those in my pockets. Lastly, I found a Polish sausage. We had food. I ran back to Marshall. "Lean on me. We are going to walk back to Sulaimaniya."

"Sir, that is more than fifteen miles away."

I smiled and checked my compass. "Nearer twenty actually we can't go in a straight line like a Snipe. The sooner we start then the sooner we get there."

To get to the path to the south we had to go east. We would be heading towards the Count and the rest of his men. I wondered just how many he had. He was like a cat with nine lives. The sun was beating down and I was grateful that we now had something on our heads. We had two canteens of water. It was as we turned a corner of rock to step onto the path that the thought struck me. The Kurds and the Russians had not had canteens with them. That meant that they were not far from the others. I pushed Marshall into the shelter of the rocks and looked around. Ahead of me I saw that the path turned sharply right and went down steeply. I lay on my belly and slithered like a snake to peer around the bend in the path. The car we had followed was five hundred yards from us. It was below us and we had to pass it to get to Sulaimaniya. Worse there were four men with it. I saw a fifth figure emerge from behind it and I recognised, even at that distance, the Count. He wore his leather coat with the Astrakhan collar.

Marshall said, "Sir what is it?" He had been seen. Once again, they fired prematurely. I turned and looked for a defensive position. We had to get back off the path and take shelter behind the rock we had just turned around.

"Marshall, back up the path!"

I turned and aimed the rifle at the four men who were now coming towards us. I had limited ammunition. I did not want to waste it. The Russians seemed to have plenty of ammunition for they fired at me. The bullets missed and I saw that Marshall had made the safety of the rocks. I ran and joined him. I could no longer see the car but I had only seen four men coming towards us. The Count was staying with his vehicle. Four to two were not good odds when one man could not fire a weapon.

I handed Marshall one of my pistols and said. "You can't fire but hand me the next gun when I finish my magazines." I laid the four spare Lee Enfield magazines next to him. You hold those, right?"

"Sir. Will we get out of this?"

"I will be honest, the odds are not good but we keep fighting. One thing, we don't let them take us alive, John? If I am down then shoot me and then... well you know."

"Right sir."

I lay prone and wriggled so that I could see them as they came up the path. The only other route was up the scree like slope. I felt in my pocket and found the German grenade. I had seen them before and knew how they worked but I had never used one. I had two and I decided to take a chance. I smashed the porcelain top to reveal the priming cord. I pulled it and hurled the grenade over towards the scree slope. If they were coming that way it might hurt them or, at the very least, set off a small landslide. I heard the explosion and a scream followed by the thunder of rocks. I had no way of knowing if I had hurt them, I just had to wait.

I looked along the Lee Enfield's sight. I saw a head appear and resisted the urge to fire. It was some time since I had fired it. My lack of aggression seemed to make them feel more confident and two of them sprinted to take cover closer to me. They were a hundred yards away and I fired three bullets. A cry told me that one had been hit. A third popped his head from the side of the path and emptied a magazine at me. I ducked behind the rock. Some of the bullets chipped splinters from the stone and they flew into the air. I raised the rifle and fired two bullets blindly. I held the rifle to the left. Marshall took it from me. I took out my German automatic and I fired, once again, blindly. Bullets cracked off the rocks and I heard feet as they ran up the path. This was no good. They were keeping my head down. I worked out that there were three of them.

Marshall handed me the Lee Enfield. I raised my head and fired. There was a Russian just thirty yards from me. My bullet caught him in the knee and he fell to the floor. I fired a second shot but he had rolled to safety. I suspected that one of them was working his way up the side of the path. I could shoot him but I would have to expose myself to the two men who lay hidden. I took out my last Mills bomb. I knew the fuses on my own grenades. I pulled the pin and released the handle. I counted to two and then threw it down the path. It went off four seconds later. This time when there was a cry I rose and stood looking down the path. One Russian had been hit by shrapnel. He was dying. The other two had been struck by bits of stone. I emptied the rifle and then dropped it. I drew my Webley and I emptied it at them. I ran to the side. They were dead.

Wings over Persia

I looked down the slope towards the car. The Count was there. He was sheltering behind the large vehicle. I saw that my landslide had sent rocks down. One had smashed into the bonnet. The Count was going nowhere. He raised his pistol to fire at me. It was pathetic. He was so far away that he had more chance of throwing a stone and hitting me.

"John, fetch the Lee Enfield magazines." Where was the Sheikh and where were the Kurds? I picked up the Lee Enfield and loaded another magazine. I had one left. I took aim.

"Are you going to kill him, sir?"

I shook my head. "It would be a waste of bullets. Now the car, that is a different matter." I knelt and took aim just above the left rear tyre. The petrol tank was there. I fired all five bullets to no effect. I reloaded the last magazine. The Count must have realised what I was trying to do for his head disappeared. I caught a movement to the left. It was my third last bullet which ignited the tank. I saw the Count thrown to the ground and the pall of black smoke rose in the sky. The smoke hid him from me.

"Come on, John. Let's finish this." He leaned on me as we started down the path. Just then I heard the sound of a Rolls Royce engine, so did Marshall. We both looked into the air. I saw that there was a Bristol. I reached into my pocket and found the mirror. I began to flash a message to the Bristol. The exploding car had drawn him here. Now I had to bring him closer. I kept flashing until I saw him descending. Marshall began waving his good arm and I kept signalling. I saw that it was Flight Lieutenant Cartwright. He made one pass and then, on the second something was thrown from the gunner's cockpit.

I ran down the path to retrieve it. There was a note inside a flying helmet. I unrolled it. "Vimy on the way. We will cover you. Nasties all around you."

I wondered who the *'we'* was. His Bristol looked to be alone in the sky. I looked around. The nearest landing site was a good half a mile away down the path. The Count lay between me and it. I turned to Marshall. "I am going after the Russian. You make your way down the slope. Take it steady." I handed him the improvised haversack. "There is water and food in here. If anything happens to me…"

"It won't sir!"

I was not certain. I made sure the two German automatics were loaded and with them in each hand I headed down the path. Marshall shouted, encouragingly, "You look like Tom Mix sir!"

I had one grenade left and if the Count chose to hide then I would use it to flush him out. Above me I heard the Bristol as Cartwright made lazy circles just above my head. He was looking for Kurds and not western looking men. The Count would know to stay hidden. If Marshall was going to live I had to use myself as live bait.

I reached the car. The fire was just smouldering. The Count had disappeared down the path. As I cleared the car a gun cracked. It hit the ground just four feet from my foot. The gun fired again. The second shot hit me in the leg. I was not certain how seriously I was hurt. I rolled to the ground and levelled my two guns. I could not see him. I decided to talk to him. I wanted to find out roughly where he was. I spoke to him in Russian, "Count Yuri Fydorervich, we meet again. You are a hard man to kill!"

"Harsker? Ah it is you. I should have realised. You are a dead man. When my Kurdish allies find you, they will give you a slow death. They hate airmen!"

I knew roughly where he was, from the sound of his voice. I holstered one gun and took out the German grenade. I began to crawl. I was aware that I was bleeding from the bullet wound. "Your Sheikh soon abandoned you!"

I heard him laugh. "I was not abandoned and besides my heroic service will bring me even more money when I reach his Persian heartland. There he will be surrounded by his tribal chiefs and you will never catch him. You, on the other hand, will lie in pieces here in this God forsaken country."

I had continued to crawl while he spoke. I smashed the porcelain cap and pulled the lanyard. I hurled it high into the air and rolled to my right. It must have had a short fuse for it exploded above the rocks. I heard a scream. I was on my feet in an instant and limped as fast as I could towards him with a gun at the ready. I had no need to worry. The grenade had taken most of his head.

"Marshall, you can keep coming. It is safe."

As if to prove me wrong the Bristol suddenly dived and I heard the twin Vickers. Marshall sheltered behind the car. I squatted next to the Count. I saw that his pockets were packed with gold coins. He had been right. He had been well paid. I took them. The widows of the men who had died would benefit. The Bristol zoomed overhead and Cartwright waggled his wings.

"Come on John. We had better get a move on. Put your arm around me. If I have to I will carry you."

He shook his head as he joined me. "I don't think so sir. Where is the dignity in that!"

The path twisted and turned. As we rounded one corner I saw the dead Kurds the Bristol had hit. In the distance, I heard the sound of a Vimy and as I peered south I saw it was escorted by two Snipes. Just then the Bristol dived. I could not see the target. It was hidden by a large rock but I heard the explosion as its bombs went off. We were just two hundred yards from the flat piece of ground. I recognised the Snipes, it was Simpkins and Barker. They zoomed overhead and I heard their guns open fire. I could not run. I felt blood sloshing around inside my flying boot. We could not afford to stop. I saw the Vimy preparing to land.

"Let us wait here. It is bad enough landing one of those at the best of times without two cripples getting in the way."

"Cripples?" He looked down and saw my bloody leg, "Sir, you are wounded."

I smiled, "So it would appear."

I heard the six Vickers as they chased away the Kurds who were anxious to get to two airmen and a large aeroplane. The Vimy rolled to a halt and we began to make our way the last two hundred yards to it. I saw Pilot Officer Grundy climb out and open the hatch. He smiled when he saw me, "Good to see you again, sir."

Marshall said, "The Wing Commander is wounded, in the leg!"

Grundy became all serious. "Lie on the bunk sir and let me look at it for you."

As I did so I said, "Marshall here has a broken arm too."

"Don't you worry, sir. We will get you to Baghdad. There are a lot of people who are relieved that you are alive. When you were reported missing there was all hell on."

He took my boot off and paroxysms of pain raced up my leg. Remembering how well Marshall had borne the pain I gritted my teeth.

"You have lost a great deal of blood sir. I will staunch the bleeding and then you had better have some sugar." He looked up at Pilot Officer Marshall. "If you would pop up on the other bunk I will strap you in and we can get off straightaway."

I knew that they would be worried. They had kept the engines running and that was never a good thing.

"That's the best I can do, sir." He strapped me in and handed me a bar of mint cake. I knew that it was pure sugar. He did the same to Marshall and then he shut the hatch and climbed up into the cockpit. I began to eat the sugary confection.

He leaned down once he was in the co-pilot's seat, "You two just enjoy the ride. Next stop, Baghdad."

I had my eyes closed when I heard Marshall say, "Well I didn't expect to get out that alive sir."

"We aren't back yet. Pilot Officer Carruthers will not have an easy task taking off from here." He had done well to land on the tiny piece of flat rock. He was a good pilot and I had to trust in him.

The engines made an incredibly loud noise as he raced along the short flat area he had found on which to land. As he lifted the nose I breathed a sigh of relief. I ate some more of the mint cake although it was far too sweet for me. As he banked I saw some of the dead Kurds my three aeroplanes had killed. The three would escort us back. We had left no dead this time. There were two dead Snipes but an aeroplane could be replaced. Men were harder! The throbbing of the engines sent me to sleep and I dreamed. I dreamed of Beattie and the children and I dreamed of England. I would put in for a home posting. I had done my bit for King and Country.

Epilogue

The sleep I had almost became a coma. I was unconscious for two days while the doctors in Baghdad worked on my leg. When I awoke I found myself in a room with Pilot Officer Marshall. He was grinning when I finally opened my eyes. "You had us worried sir. They only brought you back this afternoon."

"How long since they picked us up, John?"

"Two days sir."

"How is your arm?"

"Thanks to you, sir I won't lose it. The doctor said you managed to join the broken ends. He said I owe my arm and my life to you."

"Nonsense. Anyone else would have done the same."

We had tea brought and the nurse said, as she helped me to sit up "You have a visitor Wing Commander. I have told him he can only stay for half an hour but he is most insistent."

"Thank you, nurse."

It was Sergeant Major Davis. "I am relieved to see you alive, sir. Everyone at the airfield, not to mention Mosul and Kirkuk have been asking after you. I had to see with my own eyes."

I smiled, "It was just a scratch."

"Scratch my… anyroad up you are well and that is all that counts, Wing Commander."

I nodded, "Are my things here, John?"

"Yes sir, they are hanging in that cupboard."

Sergeant Major, "If you look through my pockets you will find some coins."

He went to the cupboard and searched my coat, "Bloody hell sir did you rob a bank?"

"No, Sergeant Major. I took them from a dead Russian Count. It is blood money. The Vikings called it weregeld. Would you see that they are sent to the next of kin of those fourteen pilots and gunners who died up at Mosul. Just say it is from the squadron."

He nodded, "Aye sir. And Sir John is back in Baghdad. He wants to see you. Now that you are able to have visitors I will tell him."

He spent twenty minutes filling me in on the details of how Sulaimaniya had been pacified and what had happened to the pilots and crews whose aeroplanes had been damaged. He was finally chased away by the nurse. Later that afternoon Pilot Officer Marshall was allowed to leave the hospital and return to the airfield to await transport home.

"I daresay I will see you before I leave sir but thanks again. I owe you a great deal."

"We are brothers in arms, Marshall. The R.A.F. is like a family. We look after our own."

The next day a sister and nurse came in to make sure the room was neat and tidy. I knew the reason. The Air Vice Marshall and Sir Percy Cunliffe appeared in the doorway. "I am pleased to see that you survived, Wing Commander." Sir John gestured to the diplomat. Sir Percy has some questions for you."

"Now then Wing Commander what do you think happened to Sheikh Mahmud?"

I said, "I know exactly what happened to him. He fled to his Persian heartland. He is with his tribal chiefs in Persia. I was told by his adviser, Count Yuri Fydorervich."

"He was not killed with the other Kurds who tried to get to you?"

I shook my head. "Two cars escaped our bomb run. One was the Count's and I destroyed that. Sergeant Major Davis told me that they found no sign of the other one. He escaped sir."

He shook my hand, "I just wanted you to know from the horse's mouth. You are a brave man Wing Commander and His Majesty's Government is indebted to you." He nodded and left.

Sir John gave me a wan smile, "That and tuppence will get you a cup of tea. The R.A.F. can offer you something more substantial. You have been awarded a bar to your Military Cross and Pilot Officer Marshall the D.F.C. I wanted the V.C for you but it is not wartime and…"

I held up my hand, "Sir, don't worry about it. I am just pleased that Marshall's courage was recognised. As far as I am concerned all of my pilots deserve a medal."

"They probably do. Now anything else I can do for you?"

I sat up, "Yes sir. I would like a home posting. I have been away from my family for a long time and you don't need me here any longer. The other squadron leaders are all sound chaps."

"You are right about the squadron leaders but I am not sure you are right about us not needing you. However, I think it is right that you be sent home. You will need time to recover in any case." He shook my hand, "Thanks for all you have done, Bill."

"And thank you sir, you have given me something more important than a medal; you have given me back my family."

I left on the same flight as Pilot Officer Marshall. It was a longer flight than the one I had coming out but I didn't mind that. I found that I was in less pain than Marshall. With me it had just been blood loss which had caused the problem. Marshall had bones knitting together.

When I, eventually, landed, at Rochford Beattie, Tom and Mary were there, waiting for me. They ran to meet me as I limped towards them. I had tried to resist the cane but I needed it. Poor Beattie was in tears and she threw her arms around me, sobbing.

Tom just said, "When we get home, Daddy, will you show me your wound?"

Beattie said, "Thomas Harsker!"

I smiled, "I don't mind. I am home now and home to stay. This is the last wound I will have to suffer so why not show it to him? Come on you two. I want to hear all about the new house in France! We will plan a holiday for the summer eh?

Beattie linked my arm, "Home?"

"A home posting. We will be together. We will be a family."

"Then my prayers have been answered!"

The End

Glossary

Beer Boys-inexperienced fliers (slang)
Bevvy- drink (beverage) (slang)
Blighty- Britain (slang)
Boche- German (slang)
Bowser- refuelling vehicle
Bus- aeroplane (slang)
Butchers- look (slang)- butcher's hook- look
Corned dog/Bully Beef- corned beef (slang)
Dewar Flask- an early Thermos invented in 1890
Donkey Walloper- Horseman (slang)
Erks- Slang for Other Ranks in R.A.F.
Fizzer- a charge (slang)
Foot Slogger- Infantry (slang)
Fuzzy Wuzzy- Dervish (slang) named because of their hair style.
Gaspers- Cigarettes (slang)
Google eyed booger with the tit- gas mask (slang)
Griffin (Griff) - confidential information (slang)
Hairies- locals (slang)
Hun- German (slang)
Jasta- a German Squadron
Jippo- the shout that food was ready from the cooks (slang)
Killick- Leading seaman (slang-Royal Navy)
Kite- aeroplane (slang)
Lanchester- a prestigious British car with the same status as a Rolls Royce
Loot- a second lieutenant (slang)
M.C. - Military Cross (for officers only)
M.M. - Military Medal (for other ranks introduced in 1915)
Ninak- Nickname for Airco DH 9A
Nelson's Blood- rum (slang- Royal Navy)
Nicked- stolen (slang)
Number ones- Best uniform (slang)
Oppo- workmate/friend (slang)
Outdoor- the place they sold beer in a pub to take away (slang)
Pop your clogs- die (slang)

Pukka- Very good/efficient (slang)
Reval- Tallinn (Estonia)
Rosy – Tea (slang- Rosy Lee- tea)
Rugger- Rugby (slang)
Scousers- Liverpudlians (slang)
Shufti- a quick look (slang)
The smoke- London (slang)
Toff- aristocrat (slang)
V.C. - Victoria Cross, the highest honour in the British Army

Maps

Mosul
Kirkuk Sulaimaniya Maidan
IRAQ IRAN
Baghdad
30 miles

Griff Hosker
September 2017

Wings over Persia

Other books by Griff Hosker

If you enjoyed reading this book, then why not read another one by the author?

Ancient History

The Sword of Cartimandua Series
(Germania and Britannia 50 A.D. – 128 A.D.)
Ulpius Felix- Roman Warrior (prequel)
The Sword of Cartimandua
The Horse Warriors
Invasion Caledonia
Roman Retreat
Revolt of the Red Witch
Druid's Gold
Trajan's Hunters
The Last Frontier
Hero of Rome
Roman Hawk
Roman Treachery
Roman Wall
Roman Courage

The Wolf Warrior series
(Britain in the late 6th Century)
Saxon Dawn
Saxon Revenge
Saxon England
Saxon Blood
Saxon Slayer
Saxon Slaughter
Saxon Bane
Saxon Fall: Rise of the Warlord
Saxon Throne
Saxon Sword

Medieval History

The Dragon Heart Series
Viking Slave *
Viking Warrior *
Viking Jarl *
Viking Kingdom *
Viking Wolf *

Wings over Persia

Viking War
Viking Sword
Viking Wrath
Viking Raid
Viking Legend
Viking Vengeance
Viking Dragon
Viking Treasure
Viking Enemy
Viking Witch
Viking Blood
Viking Weregeld
Viking Storm
Viking Warband
Viking Shadow
Viking Legacy
Viking Clan
Viking Bravery

The Norman Genesis Series
Hrolf the Viking *
Horseman *
The Battle for a Home *
Revenge of the Franks *
The Land of the Northmen
Ragnvald Hrolfsson
Brothers in Blood
Lord of Rouen
Drekar in the Seine
Duke of Normandy
The Duke and the King

Danelaw
(England and Denmark in the 11th Century)
Dragon Sword *
Oathsword *
Bloodsword *
Danish Sword
The Sword of Cnut

New World Series
Blood on the Blade *
Across the Seas *
The Savage Wilderness *
The Bear and the Wolf *
Erik The Navigator *
Erik's Clan *
The Last Viking

Wings over Persia

The Vengeance Trail *

The Conquest Series
(Normandy and England 1050-1100)
Hastings
Conquest

The Aelfraed Series
(Britain and Byzantium 1050 A.D. - 1085 A.D.)
Housecarl *
Outlaw *
Varangian *

The Reconquista Chronicles
Castilian Knight *
El Campeador *
The Lord of Valencia *

**The Anarchy Series England
1120-1180**
English Knight *
Knight of the Empress *
Northern Knight *
Baron of the North *
Earl *
King Henry's Champion *
The King is Dead *
Warlord of the North
Enemy at the Gate
The Fallen Crown
Warlord's War
Kingmaker
Henry II
Crusader
The Welsh Marches
Irish War
Poisonous Plots
The Princes' Revolt
Earl Marshal
The Perfect Knight

**Border Knight
1182-1300**
Sword for Hire *
Return of the Knight *
Baron's War *
Magna Carta *

Wings over Persia

Welsh Wars *
Henry III *
The Bloody Border *
Baron's Crusade
Sentinel of the North
War in the West
Debt of Honour
The Blood of the Warlord
The Fettered King
de Montfort's Crown

Sir John Hawkwood Series
France and Italy 1339- 1387
Crécy: The Age of the Archer *
Man At Arms *
The White Company *
Leader of Men *
Tuscan Warlord *
Condottiere

Lord Edward's Archer
Lord Edward's Archer *
King in Waiting *
An Archer's Crusade *
Targets of Treachery *
The Great Cause *
Wallace's War *
The Hunt

Struggle for a Crown
1360- 1485
Blood on the Crown *
To Murder a King *
The Throne *
King Henry IV *
The Road to Agincourt *
St Crispin's Day *
The Battle for France *
The Last Knight *
Queen's Knight *
The Knight's Tale

Tales from the Sword I
(Short stories from the Medieval period)

Tudor Warrior series
England and Scotland in the late 15th and early 16th century
Tudor Warrior *

Wings over Persia

Tudor Spy *
Flodden*

Conquistador
England and America in the 16th Century
Conquistador *
The English Adventurer *

English Mercenary
The 30 Years War and the English Civil War
Horse and Pistol

Modern History

The Napoleonic Horseman Series
Chasseur à Cheval
Napoleon's Guard
British Light Dragoon
Soldier Spy
1808: The Road to Coruña
Talavera
The Lines of Torres Vedras
Bloody Badajoz
The Road to France
Waterloo

The Lucky Jack American Civil War series
Rebel Raiders
Confederate Rangers
The Road to Gettysburg

Soldier of the Queen series
Soldier of the Queen*
Redcoat's Rifle*
Omdurman

The British Ace Series
1914
1915 Fokker Scourge
1916 Angels over the Somme
1917 Eagles Fall
1918 We will remember them
From Arctic Snow to Desert Sand
Wings over Persia

Combined Operations series
1940-1945
Commando *

Wings over Persia

Raider *
Behind Enemy Lines
Dieppe
Toehold in Europe
Sword Beach
Breakout
The Battle for Antwerp
King Tiger
Beyond the Rhine
Korea
Korean Winter

Tales from the Sword II
(Short stories from the Modern period)

Books marked thus *, are also available in the audio format.
For more information on all of the books then please visit the author's website at www.griffhosker.com where there is a link to contact him or visit his Facebook page: GriffHosker at Sword Books or follow him on Twitter: @HoskerGriff or Sword (@swordbooksltd)
If you wish to be on the mailing list then contact the author through his website.

Printed in Great Britain
by Amazon